TOMORROW

c. k. kelly martin

ISBN: 1492250872
ISBN-13: 978-1492250876

For those who wanted to know what
came after *Yesterday*

Rage on

also by C. K. Kelly Martin:

ACKNOWLEDGMENTS

I'm extremely grateful to the generous, insightful people who offered their feedback and encouragement on *Tomorrow* before it was released into the wild: Gina Linko (your enthusiasm for and comments on this project meant the world to me); Kelly Jensen (your astute notes helped me chisel this into the book I wanted it to be); my husband, Paddy, who is the best alpha reader that anyone could hope for; and my brother, Casey, who shaped *Yesterday's* outcome when he advised, 'when in doubt, kill someone' and also cast a helpful eye here. I couldn't have done this without any of you lovely folks! Thanks, also, to Leah Wohl-Pollack at Invisible Ink Editing for her marvelous blue-pencil skills, and Shana Corey for getting the ball rolling when she asked if I'd consider writing more about the *Yesterday* universe.

Because things are the way they are,
things will not stay the way they are.
—Bertolt Brecht

We made a promise we swore we'd always remember
No retreat, baby, no surrender.
—Bruce Springsteen, "No Surrender"

PROLOGUE

2063, United North America: Climate change has rendered great swathes of the country uninhabitable, the rise of robot workers has created mass unemployment, eco-terrorism is a constant threat, and a 2059 nuclear exchange between Pakistan and India has torn large holes in the world's ozone layer and pushed humanity's existence towards a cliff.

While unwanted eco-refugees roam the globe, an army of robots defend the U.N.A.'s closed borders and a network of nanites (the Bio-net), operating inside the bodies of U.N.A. citizens, has eradicated many of humanity's old illnesses. The majority of citizens prefer gushi—the nation's full-immersion virtual reality system—to real life, relying on it for information, entertainment, simulated travel, and sex.

This is the background sixteen-year-old Freya Kallas and eighteen-year-old Garren Lowe live their lives against until two biological weapons converge to form a new threat. With no cure on the horizon, the highly infectious Toxo plague threatens to overcome the population of the U.N.A., turning the infected blind and aggressively rabid until they perish of dehydration.

When Freya's brother and Garren's sister are among the first wave of infected, their parents' privileged positions make them privy to a secret that saves Freya and Garren's lives—the existence of a naturally occurring phenomenon located deep within a remote Ontario lake. The time phenomenon hurtles anything that comes into contact with it seventy-eight years, seven months, and eleven days into the past, with its physical end point being a salt lake in Western Australia.

The U.N.A. government has been covertly sending people back in time via the 'chute' for years. A shadowy network of support workers led by 'directors' carry out the U.N.A.'s twin aims of preventing the catastrophic global warming of the future via political means and evacuating influential citizens' loved ones to the 1980s. Fearing that the truth about the time chute and the dystopian future could destabilize 1980s society, the U.N.A. government staunchly protects both secrets, installing memory wipe sequences within its own personnel that prevent them from breaking their code of silence. Meanwhile, civilian time refugees' memories and identities are erased and replaced with counterfeit ones in a process called 'wipe and cover.'

Unfortunately for Freya, once in 1985, she swiftly begins to remember snatches of her real identity and recover her gift of second sight. When Freya spots fellow time refugee Garren on a Toronto street, she can't shake the feeling that she knows him. Soon they're both uncovering who they truly are and must run for their lives or risk having their minds butchered by U.N.A. security forces in a second memory wipe. In the dead of winter, Freya and Garren leave Toronto behind them and head west, determined to evade the U.N.A. and lose themselves in 1985.

ONE: 2063

'm not gifted like Freya. I never saw what was coming back then and if it wasn't for her I wouldn't remember my true past now, either: what happened to me in the summer of 2063, before they sent me through the chute and my life started over.

Back then things were very different. Every morning began with the Dailies, and in late July they were full of the usual propaganda—stories stressing the U.N.A.'s continuing strength in the struggle against terrorism, items highlighting environmental recovery projects, those glorying in the nation's past and ones showing its citizens what a disastrous mess most other counties had made of themselves. In France riots had been raging for weeks, great expanses of Paris, Marseilles, and Lyon burnt to ashes by French defence forces intent on killing the rebels. French citizens were laying down their lives for freedom in a struggle against an authoritarian government, yet the Dailies portrayed the protesters as lawless and France as being rife with corrupt sentiments, unlike the superior U.N.A. and its civilized, patriotic population.

But not all of the U.N.A. equated patriotism with unquestioning allegiance. The U.N.A. grounded movement was seventy million strong. It supported truth over propaganda; employment for people over reliance on robots; real-life experiences over immersion in gushi; and the idea that eco-refugees should be given sanctuary rather than be turned away from our borders or enslaved by the U.N.A. government.

My mothers, Rosine and Bening, were members of the

grounded movement. So were my sister, Kinnari, and I. The official movement was popular and non-confrontational enough that it held on to its legitimacy, but it had to tread carefully. The state came down heavy on anyone who broke its laws or opposed its government in anything but the gentlest, most optimistic tones. Take too tough a stand against them and you were liable to wake up in some forsaken part of the country that was flooded with carcinogen and toxin-laden soil and water, your memory scraped clean, and your soul humming with an obsessive dedication to doing the state's bidding until you keeled over dead, your Bio-net unable to keep up with the extreme contamination your body had suffered.

My mothers never let me or Kinnari forget the thin line we had to walk as members of the movement. They took us to official meetings, signed petitions, assembled for peaceful demonstrations, and encouraged our participation in the youth group, but stayed away from the hard-core fringe faction. Bening always stressed that we had to change the system from within, unlike the grounded devotees who bombed the Ro factories, periodically hacked their way into gushi to distribute anti-government messages, and sheltered refugees.

The future sounds bleak, I know. But I was used to it. Feeling rebellious on the inside, but playing it safe outwardly, for the most part. My mothers used to say that when there were enough of us, things would change. There'd be a tipping point not even the government would be able to deny and they'd be forced to bend to the will of the people, like in the past when there was authentic democracy.

Until that day arrived, I intended to do what I could. Learn things that would help me protect the illegals and the unemployed, who had few rights. I'd already been accepted into a pre-law program and was set to start in the fall. Columbia in New York City. Most of the coastline had been abandoned, but not New York. The U.N.A. had built flood barriers to protect the city from sea level rises and storm surges over forty years ago. Because of its uniquely exposed position after the coastal evacuation of the thirties, New York was always swarming with DefRos, and even so, there were more attempted terrorist attacks there than anywhere else in the country. People hated the West for what it had done to the planet; they wanted to make it pay.

Rosine wished I would go to law school somewhere more inland so she could worry about me less. She'd say that in the same breath that she'd declare how proud she was of me. Few students were being offered law as one of their three approved career options anymore.

But I wasn't thinking about things like law school or the grounded movement on the morning of July 29; I was panicking that it was the day of Kinnari's sixteenth birthday party and I had yet to buy her a present. Rosine had already reminded me twice that week but I'd kept putting it off.

On the twenty-ninth I'd run out of procrastination time and after breakfast I jumped into my trans and instructed it to take me to Moss, the shopping district on the far side of Billings. Kinnari and Rosine loved the rundown old shopping quarter and our house was crammed with antiques they'd discovered there. When you were strolling Moss streets you'd notice that the brick buildings looked like ones from a history book, as though you'd stepped back into the twentieth century.

Normally, the affluent residential neighbourhoods and the D.C. district (where they'd relocated the White House, Lincoln Memorial, and other significant Washington monuments after Billings became the new capital city) were the areas crawling with SecRo patrols because they were the places influential people deemed worthiest of protection. But when Billings Criminal Control was desperate to find a fugitive they'd inevitably send the SecRos to sweep Moss.

I don't know who they were looking for that morning in July, but the streets were thick with Ros; I was scanned by several of them before drifting into an art shop. The dusty store was crowded with paintings—pastorals, portraits, surrealist offerings, and works that my untrained eye interpreted as brand new. Thin strips of yellowing walls peeked through the spaces between the paintings and I suddenly felt very thirsty and very young.

Two women about my mothers' age were chatting to each other behind the counter at the far end of the room, each of them wearing clothing made of antique fabrics that you had to wash yourself rather than the self-cleaning materials that were popular in 2063. Both women looked up as I stepped in their direction. "It's a shame they have to spoil an all-clear day tromping around Moss like that," the woman in the wool blazer said to me.

An all-clear day meant the forecast showed next to a zero chance of storms and that it wouldn't be dangerously hot either. There were few all-clear days in Billings and my mothers had chosen the date of Kinnari's party with the good weather in mind. Her actual birthday was still a week away.

The other woman clucked at the one who'd complained about the SecRos, as though in disapproval of her colleague's frankness. "What brings you this way?" the clucking woman asked me, her face sour.

I didn't know what to tell the woman. Kinnari had everything she needed. So did I. But I had to get something for her birthday. It was tradition. "I'm looking for a gift for my sister," I said. "She's turning sixteen."

"Well, what is she like?" the first woman asked cheerfully.

Open-minded and a good judge of character, for a start. She'd sensed things in her boyfriend, Latham Kallas, that I'd never have guessed were there. He wasn't a carbon copy of his power-hungry father and he wasn't just a troublemaker. He was someone who didn't want to travel the route that had been laid out for him, someone who wanted to go his own way. As for Kinnari, she probably would've been a poet if she'd been born in another time. Or an occultist. Someone who stared into a crystal ball and pretended to see other worlds there. She had what Bening liked to call 'an active imagination.'

"She likes old-time movies," I replied. "And mythical things, like unicorns and dragons."

"Aha!" The woman beckoned me forwards. "In that case, I have the perfect thing for your sister."

I followed the woman in the wool blazer over to a corner of the shop populated with Buddha statues, shaking my head in protest.

Her thin lips formed a knowing smile. "Not the Buddhas, the painting." She pointed up at a ninety-degree angle, and my eyes snapped towards the image of a unicorn, majestic and out of place. It seemed to bow to the observer while a crowd of people in ragged clothing and grimy faces gathered around it, their expressions somehow forlorn and awed at the same time. Normally you see unicorns surrounded by woodland in paintings, but this one was in the midst of a dilapidated urban centre that made the white of its coat look that much more dazzling in comparison. Many U.N.A. cities were in a similar state of rot before the government built the social welfare camps. In the 2030s and early 2040s, U.N.A. crime and death by starvation rates were through the roof.

I didn't know what it meant to have included the unicorn in a scene like that. Hope? Or its opposite—was the painting declaring that hope was only a myth?

"I don't think so," I told the woman. "Maybe something artistic but less depressing."

I watched the woman stifle a smirk. Behind the counter her colleague was still frowning like she wished I'd never walked through the door. I frowned back to let her know I wasn't exactly impressed with her either. She must've read me wrong from the beginning. Taken me for a politician's or wealthy industrialist's kid. Billings was full of them. Young people who were stubbornly sure they'd inherit the earth, never mind that the Pakistan-India War meant crops were failing like never before and countless women were losing their unborn babies to damaged DNA. Nobody knew how long the human race could go on like this. One thing for sure, another nuclear exchange would smother us, even a limited one like the Pakistan-India conflict. There was too much radiation in the air, too many holes in the ozone layer.

"A cloisonné bracelet came in a few days ago," the frowning woman said, her eyes on me but her words directed at her co-worker. "If I recall correctly it might have had a unicorn on it. Why don't you show it to him and see if he likes that any better?"

"Please." Despite my irritation I said it with extra kindness to prove I wasn't the sort of person she suspected I was.

The woman who'd been assisting me disappeared behind a heavy purple curtain and emerged, seconds later, with the bracelet in her hand. "It's a vintage 1970s cloisonné enamel bracelet," she said, passing it to me.

As promised, there was a unicorn on the front. Unlike the one in the painting, this animal was vibrantly coloured—swirling with pink, red, purple, and blue. The floral design and twisted rope detailing in the background were something I could imagine Kinnari appreciating too. The bracelet felt nearly magical in my hand.

"It closes with the metal clasp there," the clerk said, lifting the bracelet from my palm and flipping it over to demonstrate. "It's really quite a unique piece."

Most old jewellery and other collectables were what people called 'salvaged.' Millions of citizens had to leave their homes behind when the government ordered the evacuation of the coasts and arid lands. Others could no longer afford their properties when their jobs were taken by Ros. People desperate or fearless enough to enter evacuated or abandoned areas made a living by collecting and reselling things others had left behind.

It was on the tip of my tongue to ask where the bracelet had come from, but what difference did its origins make? The bracelet's previous owner would probably never be reunited with it.

"I'll take it," I said, waiting for one of the women to scan me for payment.

When I ambled outside with the bracelet I could see the SecRos in the distance. They must have finished investigating this block and gone on to the next. The trans sensed my proximity and opened for me at the exact moment my ears picked up a clattering noise to my left. It could've been anything, but the SecRos' presence had set me on edge. I turned to see a man with dishevelled hair, dark stubble, and clothing that hung askew on his thin frame barrelling up the nearest alley with a stack of ornate dinner plates in his arms. My hunch was that he was homeless. I'd seen enough people that looked like him being returned to the camps to recognize the type and I waved him away, instinctively wanting to warn him about the SecRos.

The man squinted at me as though he didn't understand and I veered back towards the trans to avoid raising any unnecessary suspicion from the Ros. But it was too late. A lone SecRo zeroed in on me and the man in a flash, its monotone voice demanding that the man stop. "What's this about?" I shouted after it, the SecRo hurtling by me and towards the man who was nervously dropping his fancy plates, one by one by one. All but two of them crashed to the ground in smithereens.

"Thank you for your concern," the SecRo said to me, its attention never leaving the unkempt man. "The situation is under control."

"What is the situation?" I asked, jogging towards the man. The SecRos were programmed to respond to human queries when doing so didn't actively interfere with their duties, but sometimes I couldn't help myself and pushed them a little too far. A programmed piece of machinery shouldn't have any power over people.

"This citizen is breaking the law," the SecRo declared as a

second Ro charged up behind it. "This citizen is AWOL from a social welfare camp." Meaning technically homeless, as I'd suspected. And it was illegal to be homeless in the U.N.A. The government said it caused unnecessary discord and that there was no reason anyone should be homeless when they had a government willing to provide for them.

"But it's morning," I argued. Surely anyone had the right to be outdoors during the day. "He was just helping me out with some shopping, carrying my things to the car."

The second SecRo must've been having some kind of vocal malfunction. When he spoke I heard more static than words. The first SecRo repeated his reply for me. "He did not report in to his assigned camp last night. He is already AWOL."

If it was his first offence they'd probably file a report and return the man to the camp with a warning. So far the homeless man had been motionless and mute during my exchange with the SecRos, clasping his two remaining unbroken plates with tired resignation, but at that point his downcast eyes shifted upwards. "I wanted to buy these for my wife," he said. "They'd belonged to her parents. I arrived here too late last night and couldn't get back before curfew fell."

"Your second such AWOL offence," the SecRo declared ominously.

"Look, you heard him," I protested. "He couldn't have reached the camp in time. So what was he supposed to do? If he'd tried and been picked up out on the road somewhere, you would've charged him with breaking curfew." It was stupid, sticking my neck out like that for someone I'd never seen before in my life, and the second SecRo hissed something unintelligible at me.

"Citizen Garren Lowe, your record is currently clean," the fully functioning Ro translated. "Please continue on your way unless you want a charge of aiding an AWOL or an interference notation to be added to your record."

The homeless man spoke a second time, his voice tinged with frustration. "No one aided me. I slept in the alley until the stores here opened." He stared me in the eye, blinking slowly. "But I thank you for trying to help. Do you think…" He peered down at his plates. They were as white as the unicorn's hair in the picture I hadn't bought, except for the edging, which was decorated with a delicate blue floral pattern. "Could you possibly get these to my wife in the camp in Fairfield?" He glanced questioningly at the SecRos. "Is it all right if I hand these to him?"

Clearly the man didn't think the Ros would be bringing him back to the camp. Not right away. Maybe they'd transfer him to a hard labour facility for a detention period, something they were in the habit of doing with people who didn't toe the line. Conditions in the labour facility would be worse than in the Fairfield welfare camp but markedly better than being sent to a toxic environmental site.

I couldn't tear my eyes from the man's hands. Curved around the clean white plates, his fingers were shaking.

If the SecRos were people instead of machines they might have allowed the man to give me the plates. After all, what harm could some fine china do? But the Ros refused. Each of them promptly locked a metal hand around the man's arms. He ground his teeth together and grimaced as they zoomed away with him, leaving me staring at the freshly shattered china at my feet—the remnants of the final two plates that the man had dropped when whisked off.

Some of the new pieces were sizeable (one of the dishes had broken straight down the middle) and I closed Kinnari's unicorn bracelet around my own wrist to give me two free hands. Then I bent down and started gathering up the best pieces. At the time I wasn't sure what made me do it, except that the plates had meant something to the man, who was as human as I was.

I loaded the fragments into my trans and headed home, not in the mood for a birthday party and definitely not in the mood to meet Latham's parents, who I'd heard him complain about on several occasions by then. At least three-quarters of what was wrong with the world was down to people like Mr. and Mrs. Kallas throwing their weight around, but I'd have to smile at them and nod politely.

When I arrived back at the house my mothers were already busy helping the people they'd hired from the camps for the day to set up party tables in our backyard. Because of Bening, who was a scientist and always working on important projects, we were well off compared to most people. Enough so that Kinnari and I went to the most prestigious school in Billings along with the children of politicians and industrialists, and our mothers could throw a lavish birthday party. While the majority of the U.N.A.'s employed population lived in claustrophobic apartment towers, my family owned a five-bedroom house on a large, fully landscaped lot. And while the diet of the lower classes was composed mainly of algae, green super rice, insects, and lab-created meat, my family often ate real meat and costly rare vegetables and fruits.

No wonder the shop clerk had mistaken me for one of the elite. People who didn't know me often made the same mistake. If they were strangers of an influential class they'd more or less act like I was one of them. If not, they'd either be deferential or treat me with thinly veiled disdain, like the woman in Moss had.

I stored the china fragments at the bottom of an old chest in my room and avoided the backyard for as long as was humanly possible, pulling out my bike and cycling as far as the main road. The sky was a perfect shade of blue and the sun—warm but not blistering hot on my skin—felt like a friend rather than the enemy it so often was.

For a few minutes I even forgot about the shattered pieces, and when I remembered it felt like I'd already made up mind to bring the fragments to the Fairfield camp. I'd finished my volunteer hours with Michael Neal, the lawyer who offered free legal advice to the camp residents, in the spring, but I was sure he'd let me put in additional time. Visitors couldn't just show up at the camps whenever they wanted; you needed clearance.

Without the names of the AWOL man or his wife, Michael Neal was my best route in, and I was more relaxed by the time I returned to the house. I helped the live band—a cellist, several violinists, and a flute player—set up outside, unfolding chairs for them on the lawn and bringing them refreshments. Then I hunted down Kinnari to give her the unicorn bracelet before her guests showed up.

"It's beautiful," she said, instantly locking it around her wrist. "Thanks, Garren." She leaned affectionately into my arm. "I love it. Did you get it in Moss?"

"Just this morning," I admitted.

"This morning!" She punched me lightly on the shoulder. "You're hopeless."

I rubbed my upper arm, pretending her tap had wounded me. "The place was buzzing with SecRos," I told her, keeping the part about the homeless man to myself. Kinnari would have felt sympathetic towards him but would've lectured me for challenging the Ros. She would've been right, too; there was no use in arguing with machines. "There was a painting in the same shop you might have found interesting," I added. Kinnari's eyes lit up as I described it, her curiosity piqued.

"Maybe I'll go in and have look," she said. "From what you've said it sounds like the unicorn is a messianic figure."

"How old are you turning next week?" I asked with a chuckle. "Ninety-one?" Half the time Kinnari could be as immature as any other sixteen-year-old and the other half she was coming out with things that made her sound like the voice of ancient wisdom.

"That would mean I was born in what?" She stared up at the ceiling as she did the math. "1972? Isn't that more your era than mine?"

Judging by my record collection—which included piles of Springsteen, Pink Floyd, Led Zeppelin, Queen, Neil Young, Bob Marley, and David Bowie—she had a point. "I have old tastes but I'm a young soul," I teased, because that was something Kinnari had been talking about a lot lately—reincarnation. She and Latham had been getting into spiritual exploration stuff together. Karma. Meditation. Numerology.

At the time I thought most of it was for fun, but now I think Kinnari genuinely wanted to believe in something more and was searching for it. I remember how happy she was at her party later and how everyone fussed over her. Latham held her hand for at least an hour without letting go, and I remember thinking that it must have driven his mother crazy because everyone knew Mr. and Mrs. Kallas were no fans of the grounded movement and therefore not fans of love matches. No doubt Mrs. Kallas expected the Service to create a suitable match for Latham when he was ready to have children. Her husband's disapproval was probably his reason for not making an appearance at Kinnari's party after all.

Having been left alone to deal with my sister's birthday, Mrs. Kallas tried to put a brave face on things, chatting good-naturedly with my mothers. Latham was focused on Kinnari, oblivious to the way his sister, Freya, busied herself with leaping on everything their mother said, relentlessly mocking her. If Mrs. Kallas weren't married to the vice president of Coppedge-Hale Corp., the government's largest supplier of DefRos and SecRos, I might have even felt sorry for her. As it was, it amused me to watch Latham's sister try to get the better of her.

At first, anyway. Then I began to think back to the scandal four years earlier, when an illegal had been discovered working as a nanny and domestic servant for the Kallases. The Dailies had broadcast an image of the desolate woman in SecRo custody. Obviously Coppedge-Hale Corp. hadn't wanted it to look as though any exceptions were made for their VP.

For days afterwards, everyone at school stared at Latham and his sister in the halls. Freya seemed sad and angry and one day I saw her take those feelings out on another student. The Ros witnessed it too and filed a discipline report. I didn't personally know Freya back then but everyone knew who she was. Feeling sorry for her, I walked up to her and said something that I've long since forgotten.

For years after that we barely exchanged a word. Sometime later I began to notice her watching me. Initially I suspected she had something against me because of my grounded beliefs, but sometimes...sometimes the look seemed to say something else.

People still looked in 2063. There were still attractions. Between young people especially. Mostly they just didn't add up to much. People searching for permanent attachments invariably allowed the Service to match them up and 'grounded sex' had fallen out of favour, even with many grounded members. The majority of society had developed a pathological distaste for the exchange of bodily fluids, which made things difficult for people like me. Most of the girlfriends I'd had would cuddle and closed-mouth kiss but loathed being more physical than that. They saved the rest for gushi. Admittedly, sometimes I did too. Sometimes it didn't feel like there was much of a choice.

So I didn't think of Freya in that way. Not in 2063. Not when her mother started to fight back and I made an excuse to pull Freya away from the scene. At the time I would never have guessed the daughter of Coppedge-Hale's VP could be someone I'd be interested in; I was only being nice. Didn't like to see her looking embarrassed. There wasn't anything more to it. Freya was beautiful, yeah. So was everyone I went to school with. It doesn't mean anything to be beautiful and it meant still less in 2063.

But Freya did get to me. We were standing close to the band, listening to them play Bach, when she said, "I wish I had your mothers for parents. They're so cool."

That was something I hadn't expected, even after hearing her argue with her mom—that someone like Freya Kallas would respect Bening and Rosine, whose beliefs were contrary to almost everything she'd grown up with.

"A lot of people think they're kooks," I said, my shoulders stuck in a half shrug.

"Only stupid people. And who cares what stupid people

think?"

I felt my lips dart into a smile. "Exactly."

Freya wanted to escape her mother for a while so we went up to my room to listen to music. When I showed her how to use my old turntable, she held the records with a reverence that made me trust her a little more. For someone who wasn't grounded, she had decent taste in music. She liked everything I played for her—Neil Young, Patti Smith, and The Band—and said her favourite musician was Hendris, the Jimi Hendrix/Janis Joplin hybrid who was the only genetically spliced rock star Chinese scientists had created that had any genuine talent.

Freya and I didn't talk much, mainly just listened to sounds from the past spin around at a rate of thirty-three revolutions per minute. That was another good thing about Freya I discovered on July 29, 2063. She knew how to listen, and for a few seconds during "Heart of Gold," Freya had a wistful expression in her eyes that I thought meant she was about to tear up.

I think if she had, I might've changed my mind about her completely, not just halfway like how it happened on July 29. Maybe I'm wrong, but now that I'm with Freya it's tricky to remember the past exactly the way it was instead of how I'm tempted to see it in the present. My head wants to insert feelings where there might not have been any, because I know what came later.

Love isn't linear. It moves backwards too. Like time, as it turns out. I didn't think I loved Freya Kallas in 2063 but now there's a part of me that feels as if I always have. Not the part that went to the Cursed camp with jagged pieces of china and became ensnared in things that alternately frightened and compelled me, but some essence that can't be pinned down in hours, days, and years.

In a way, there can't be a before I fell in love with Freya anymore. And yet, the things that happened to me in the summer of 2063—things that had very little to do with her— changed everything.

TWO: 1986

S he's dancing when I get to Rachel's party—spinning around in a tight circle with her fists folded up close to her chin, red ringlets bouncing on her shoulders to the rhythm of Pet Shop Boys' "West End Girls." My smile sticks to my teeth as I edge closer to her. Freya looks funny when she's drunk. It's like she gets so damn intent on whatever she's doing that she just might implode. The room's dark and crowded and my shift ran late, so an ordinary person wouldn't know to expect me at this exact moment, but Freya does. Her eyes catch on me and hold. *Hold, hold, hold.*

The moment stretches into forever. Just Freya and I staring each other down and wondering how we're supposed to act after this morning's fight. Am I still angry? Is she? Since I've already smiled I guess I've forfeited my chance to be mad. My stomach clenches for a second as I wait for her to react.

And then I see it. Her grin begins to bloom. At the corners of her lips first and then spreading to her cheekbones and her glimmering eyes. She opens her fist and beckons me slowly forwards with outstretched fingers. I don't think anyone would be able to resist that motion. She's so sexy, even when she's drunk enough to make me want to laugh at her.

I squeeze by birthday girl Rachel Chung—a waitress with a Pat Benatar shag haircut who Freya works with at Il Baccaro— and stand close to Freya, sweeping my left hand through her hair. No matter what Freya does to her hair it's always as soft as silk. The dye jobs and perm haven't changed that.

"Hi," Freya mouths, leaning forwards to open her lips and

kiss me. I taste the vodka and orange juice she's been drinking. I'm sure she can taste the cigarette I smoked outside before coming up too, but she doesn't complain about it.

I turn to plant a birthday kiss on Rachel's cheek, and two seconds later Rachel's tilting her body away from me so she can fake-fall into my arms. This is just what Rachel's like when she's plastered, Freya's told me, a compulsive flirt who doesn't mean anything by it.

Since Rachel's celebrating I don't even shoot her a disapproving look, just catch her in my arms and plant her solidly back on her feet. "I'm sorry!" she slurs, grabbing for Freya's wrist as she pitches forwards. This has also happened before, Rachel abruptly remembering that as Freya's boyfriend I should be off limits and then swiftly apologizing.

Freya's fingers re-form a fist and she raps lightly on her friend's forehead, like a physical wakeup call. Then the two of them begin dancing again like nothing happened, and I weave back through the crowd and into the kitchen to get myself something to drink. There's only warm beer left so I take a bottle for myself and then pour water into a paper cup for Freya. By the time we leave the party, hours later, she's almost sober again and I'm halfway to drunk.

Crisscrossing drizzly Vancouver streets together on the way back to our apartment, the uneasy feeling that creeps under my skin when I'm lying awake at night begins to steal in. It's like...like maybe I'm only dreaming and none of this is real. It's like, for a second or two, if I'm not careful, I could forget where or *when* I am and fade away.

This is one of the reasons I don't like to drink too much. Why chance having that feeling at times when you don't have to? The other reason is I want to keep my brain in prime condition. As Freya has pointed out more times than I can count, it makes no logical sense to worry about my mind while voluntarily poisoning my lungs with tobacco. I know she's right; I've seen pictures of lungs that look like charred meat. And that's why I'm trying to quit. Because I want to live to one hundred without needing an oxygen tank.

In the beginning I thought I had the habit under control. But a cigarette is an easy hit of calm, and I can't see what the tobacco is doing to my lungs. The damage doesn't feel real.

"Are you going to throw up?" Freya asks, her hand squeezing mine. She's so solid, so *there* with me as we turn onto East Fourteenth Avenue that the uneasy dead-of-night feeling doesn't have a chance to take hold. But I'm still fucking craving a cigarette like nobody's business.

"I look like I'm going to throw up?" I say.

"Or pass out or something." It's no secret that I have trouble sleeping and we both have bad dreams sometimes, but not as often as before, and in the future they're bound to be rarer still. If I could shake that uneasy dead-of-night feeling and give up smoking, things would be almost perfect.

By December we should have enough money saved to get out of British Columbia and travel. Europe, definitely, but Africa's at the top of the list. The plan is to see all the amazing animals we'd lost to extinction and the places we were never free to travel, and then settle in somewhere breathtakingly beautiful by the sea or the mountains, somewhere your eyes can get lost in the view on a daily basis. We're thinking about this Spanish town called Ronda that's perched on a cliff. You'd only have to look up a photograph of the Puente Nuevo to figure out why anyone would want to live there. Freya's been checking Spanish tapes out of the library to learn the language.

In Vancouver we have both mountains and ocean, and overall life's been good—lots of hard work to keep a decent roof over our heads while squirreling money away—but we've also seen the killer whales swimming off the Pacific Coast. Porpoises, sea lions, bald eagles, and seals too. And we've been skiing, hang-gliding, board-sailing, and white water rafting.

In the beginning we had a shitty apartment and equally shitty jobs and could barely save a dime. Now the job and money situations aren't bad, but we're working so many hours that we don't have much time together. We both picked up second jobs over at Expo, the World's Fair being held in Vancouver this year. Freya also waits tables at a restaurant on West Broadway while I tend bar at a place in Gastown called Greasy Ryan's.

There are lots of things we'll miss about Vancouver when we go, but neither of us wants to share a country with the director's security team forever and relocating south of the border sounds like it would be worse—crawling with U.N.A. forces dedicated to changing the path of human history. I hope they succeed, but knowing what their methods are like, we need to stay out of their way. They didn't trust anyone to keep their secret, not even most of their own security personnel. They'd have butchered our minds or killed us rather than risk the truth about the future coming to light.

"I didn't think I even drank much," I tell her, squeezing her hand back. "I guess I was just tired to start out with." Neither of us usually overdoes it with alcohol. I've only seen Freya out of her mind drunk once since we got here and the other three times were more like tonight.

"We've both been working hard," Freya says. "And you never sleep."

"I sleep," I counter, because I don't feel like getting into this again. "Lately I sleep almost as much as you do. Or I did—until I started trying to give up smoking." I've mentioned the eerie middle-of-the-night feeling once or twice, but there's nothing Freya can do about it so what's the point? Jumping back seventy-eight years in time screws with your head. That's just how it is. And we'll never see the people we left behind, never even know what happened to them. These aren't easy things.

Freya's eyebrows pop up to form sharp slants. "You're blaming your sleep issues on giving up cigarettes? C'mon, you had problems before you ever started smoking. And it's not like you've even quit yet."

No, I haven't quit yet. I want to, but there's a nearly full package of smokes crammed in my jean jacket pocket that's calling my name. "Look, what do you expect me to do? If I can't sleep, I can't sleep, okay? Harping on it doesn't help."

Freya inclines her head up to meet the rain. "Saying the word 'harping' doesn't help either."

This is how our arguments usually start. Swinging in from nowhere. I say something that she doesn't like and then she says something that I take the wrong way and before you know it we're on opposite sides of an issue that didn't need to be an issue.

This morning it was the laundry. Freya was supposed to have done it two nights ago but didn't get around to it. I tried to do a load or two before heading over to Greasy Ryan's yesterday afternoon, but one of the machines downstairs was broken and someone else's clothes were spinning around in the other two. I left Freya a note asking if she'd throw our stuff in the washing machine, but she forgot. So this morning I had to pull a dirty shirt out of the hamper and put it on, which shouldn't matter except the little things seem to add up, even when you think you're not keeping track.

Things like me oversleeping too often and slowly poisoning my lungs, and her wanting to talk certain things to death and leaving wet towels on the floor, her clothes in a heap in the bedroom, and piles of dirty dishes in the sink. But none of these issues are the real problem. It's just that I'm only nineteen and Freya's only seventeen. Our paperwork lends us a couple of extra years but essentially we're what people in 1986 would call 'playing house.' We're not used to being half of something bigger and it's tricky. Before this neither of us had a job or had to keep on top of cleaning, cooking, and hitting the supermarket. Where we're from, the laundry did itself. And on top of that, we're the only two people who know what each other's been through. The pressure builds quickly.

"Bad choice of words," I apologize. "I didn't mean it." I look Freya square in the eye so she can see I'm sincere. Her hair and skin are damp. So are mine. Vancouver Mays are drier than winter but that's not saying much. "And I'm too tired to fight again tonight." I run my fingers along her wet cheek.

"Yeah, me too." Freya leans her head against my shoulder as we walk. She's only about five inches shorter than I am, less in the heels she's wearing, and she has to tilt over a little to do it. "But we're so good at it."

I let go of her hand so I can wrap my arm around her waist and pull her closer. "We're good at a lot of things."

Whether we're fighting or not.

We're almost home now. Only steps from the apartment. Freya stops on the sidewalk and turns to face me. Her eyes are definite; she knows what she wants. I do too, and I reach for her. Freya presses her wet lips against mine, sinks her hands into my back pockets and clutches my ass. The rest of her begins to melt into me in slow motion. Her thighs, her hips, her breasts. It happens by degrees but takes no time at all. She quiets my head and does the opposite to the rest of me. It's amazing how that works. Almost as simple as flicking a switch. I kiss her back, my hands on her waist and my tongue on fire.

It was never like this with anyone else. Not that there were many other girls back then, but I don't think it would've made any difference. I can't imagine feeling this way about anybody but Freya.

We make each other spark.

Like this moment, in the rain, when we're getting so heated out on the sidewalk together, drops running off my face onto hers and our bodies already not our own, that it's hard to stop and walk away, even for a minute, even just to get inside. But when I feel Freya shiver in my arms it wakes me up. I tear my mouth from her skin and tell her I'm taking her upstairs.

She doesn't answer. She just walks into the building alongside me, starting things up again in the elevator. When the door pops open I make a beeline for our apartment, fumbling for the keys in my jacket pocket. We stumble inside, heading for the bedroom, hurling ourselves at each other on the unmade bed.

Shortly after coming out west we went to a clinic that gave Freya a prescription for birth control pills. Waiting for them to take effect was rough, but the last thing we wanted was to drag a third person into the equation, so we managed it.

In the beginning I thought it might be harder for her to get used to being together like that, never having been in the grounded movement. But it seemed like second nature to her. When I whispered that to Freya during our second time together, she folded her hands across her bare chest and said, "It's because it's you."

I grinned so hard that she covered her face with one arm, embarrassed. I pried it gently away and leaned over her to say, "It's the same for me. It's *you*."

Now neither of us says anything. We peel off each other's clothes, tonight the same as so many other nights we've spent together in the past fifteen months, our hands sliding frantically in and out of curves and my mind nowhere but on the girl laid out next to me on the rumpled bedspread.

THREE: 2063

Michael Neal told me it was difficult to find volunteers of my calibre and level of commitment and that he'd be happy for me to assist him in the Fairfield camp again that coming Saturday. On August fourth I caught a commuter train to Great Falls, where the camp had sent a trans to bring me the rest of the way to Fairfield. The U.N.A.'s high-speed rail network, the Zephyr, didn't have stops in Fairfield or Great Falls, so the journey was always slow. It'd been blistering hot the day before, impossible to stay outside for more than a few minutes without enhanced protective clothing and the help of a porto-cool that interfaced with your clothes to act like an air conditioner. Today there was a storm warning in place, and the winds buffeted the trans around like it was a toy as I stared out the window at the dark clouds closing in on me.

Most people didn't think Fairfield was much to look at, malt barley fields almost as far as the eye could see, dissolving into the mountains in the distance. A mammoth hurricane/flood/earthquake-proof domed structure rose up out of the farmland like a mutant mushroom. But it was unusual to see crops growing out in open ground rather than in the vertical farms that were common in the day, and every time I went to the camp I found myself mesmerized by the golden fields. There were some traditions the U.N.A. didn't like to give up, and one of them was the illusion that Americans had a sacred relationship with the land, which meant maintaining farmlands like those in Fairfield long after they'd let the environment in other states bake to the point where life had become too expensive to continue to support it.

You couldn't call the Fairfield camp itself ugly but it wasn't pretty either. Bening liked to describe it as "a Greek village on steroids." A village where ninety-eight thousand people lived in the same immense white stone building. While the child residents were sent to a school in Great Falls during the day, the adult Cursed toiled for their food and keep, either working in the barley fields (weather-permitting), performing menial jobs in a Ro plant in Helena, a filtration facility in Denton, or various tree and vegetation planting sites throughout the state.

Because Billings was the U.N.A. capital and a big manufacturing centre, Montana's unemployment rate was the lowest in the country and the Fairfield camp was one of only three social welfare camps in the state. Whenever anyone from the grounded movement campaigned in favour of more rights for the unemployed, others would inevitably counter that the Cursed had everything they could ever need and were already too pampered.

It was true that there was no sickness, hunger, or physical abuse in U.N.A. social welfare camps. Like so many other industries in the U.N.A., the camps were operated mostly by Ros, and robots had no interest in actively abusing people. All they did was follow orders.

But as I got out of the trans and was scanned by a waiting SecRo, my stomach began to sink the way it usually did when I entered the camp. The china in my bag clattered with every step but the SecRo clearly hadn't considered the contents a threat and said nothing. I'd paid a specialist in Moss to successfully restore the plate that had broken neatly into two halves. The other dish was still in pieces.

Inside, a domestic Ro led me through an airy long white corridor to the usual consultation room I shared with Michael Neal. He must've caught an earlier train, before the weather began to turn, because unlike me he was on time and already conferring with a client. That was what Michal Neal insisted on calling them, 'clients,' although no one in the camps had any way to pay him.

"This is Garren Lowe, my assistant," Michael said to the woman seated in front of him. "Garren, this is Lucy Garcia. She's been telling me about a property issue she and her husband have been having."

"His father willed us the place," Lucy explained, reaching out to shake my extended hand. "He said it was fully paid for but the government had papers saying otherwise. They evicted our family."

I'd heard similar stories a dozen times; people's property usurped because the government felt they had a better use for it. They knew people like Lucy didn't have the means to fight them very hard. If it weren't for lawyers like Michael, the Cursed wouldn't have any legal assistance whatsoever, and as it was he was continually stonewalled by the governments and its allies, facing an uphill battle on nearly every occasion. Lucy would be lucky if she and her family were offered even a small settlement sum.

Michael repeated the details the woman had already told him and I wrote them out by hand in a paper notebook. In practical terms the action was unnecessary, as everything we said was being recorded. But people liked to see the activity—it made them feel as though something was being done.

During Michael's questioning it came to light that Lucy was a descendent of a woman named Marian Anderson, a delegate to the U.N and the first African American to sing a leading role with the Metropolitan Opera. She'd sung at President Dwight Eisenhower's inauguration. John F. Kennedy's too.

I watched Michael begin to get excited as he probed further and then disappeared behind his eyes to confirm Lucy's information on gushi. "Now, this will help your case immeasurably," he said, swiftly returning his attention to us. "The government won't want to be seen mistreating the descendent of such an esteemed American historical figure. If we threaten to pass that info on to the grounded movement we'll certainly be able to get a healthy settlement out of them."

"But my relationship to Marian Anderson has nothing to do with the facts surrounding the property," Lucy countered, an anger line slashing her forehead. "That shouldn't have any bearing on the outcome of the case."

"It shouldn't," Michael agreed. "But it will. If you want me to leave the fact of your relationship to Ms. Anderson out of the case, I can, but it would be to your detriment. One has to use whatever leverage they have these days and this is your best chance."

Lucy looked at me and slowly shook her head, disappointment settling on her features. "What a world we're giving you," she murmured. "What happened to this country?"

"Ros and fascists," I mumbled, before I had a chance to stop myself. I wasn't in Fairfield to spout my personal beliefs; I was supposed to be helping Michael.

"Ain't that the truth," Lucy said, sounding like someone from an old-time movie.

I suddenly remembered the Abraham Lincoln quote grounded hackers had splashed over the Dailies one morning in April. "America will never be destroyed from the outside. If we falter and lose our freedoms, it will be because we destroyed ourselves." But I'd said too much already and bit my tongue, the quote repeating in my head.

"Do whatever you have to," Lucy advised Michael. "We'll worry about the rest later."

Michael smiled as if she were joking, but there was a quiet steeliness about Lucy that told me otherwise, and when she was leaving the consultation room later I excused myself, pretending that I'd missed breakfast earlier and wanted something from the dining hall level. I followed Lucy stealthily down one corridor and then another, trying to formulate a question about the dishes in my bag that wouldn't sound suspicious.

"Have you lost your way?" she asked, turning to look at me.

"Not exactly. I... Do you know many of the people who live here?" I patted my bag, the fragments clanking in response. "I met a man from here who wanted me to give these things to his wife but I never got his name. Or hers."

"Names would've been useful," Lucy said, arching an eyebrow. "You won't get far without names. Thousands of people live here. You know that."

I lowered my voice. "This one was an AWOL. It was his second offence. I ran into him in Moss last Sunday, trying to buy back some china that had belonged to his wife's family. The Ros took him. I wasn't sure if he'd be back here yet or—"

"Or serving a detention period," Lucy finished. "That narrows things down. You're looking for the wife of a man who's been missing from the camp since last Sunday."

"Saturday," I corrected. "He was out in Moss all night on Saturday. That was the reason they picked him up."

We'd paused in the hallway and a lanky, bearded man who was probably Michael Neal's next client marched by us. Lucy reached out and gripped my wrist, urging me forwards. "Look, this man isn't wanting for anything serious, is he? Because I can't be involving myself in any—"

"No, no." I matched her stride, not knowing where I was going. People in the camps were skittish—they'd already lost so much—but most people would've acted the same way as Lucy under the circumstances. You had to be fierce, insane, or desperate to risk aligning yourself with a future wipe and cover case. "I don't have any reason to think there were any serious charges. He was only skipping curfew. I just thought that his wife should have these because he'd been buying them for her when he was taken." Aside from the single repaired dish, they were only pieces that used to be something. But he'd gotten arrested for them. That made them important.

"I can show you the way to one of the dormitory levels," Lucy said. "Since you have clearance that shouldn't be a problem. But I don't know anybody like you described. You'll have to make inquiries yourself."

I thanked Lucy and followed her into the nearest elevator where she requested level nine. Personally, I'd only been inside the dorms once, on my first visit. One of the few human administrative staff had directed a domestic Ro to give me a full tour. The Ro had started at the second sub-basement level and guided me through a lengthy expedition of the camp—from the medical floor to the swimming pools and sporting/games level up to the general auditorium, then to the administrative floor, running track, cleaning and sanitation level, the shopping concourse (stocked with minor items that had to be worked additional hours for), dining hall/food prep section, and finally the dormitories. If you were Oliver Twist, most of the camp would have looked like paradise, but when you reached the dorms it was a slightly different story.

As we arrived at level nine Lucy wished me luck, her hand on my back giving me a gentle push out into the dormitory. I stumbled away from the elevator and directly into the overcrowded space where a portion of residents slept. It was several times the size of a football field and arranged in endless alternating rows of bunk beds, stacked three high, and seating areas for people to socialize or lounge in. On my first visit to the camp I'd been surprised to find many of the recreational levels empty. But I should've suspected it would be that way—the unemployed weren't any different than anyone else—they spent the majority of their leisure hours on gushi.

Nine was a family dormitory level. I could tell by the presence of children and the mixture of men and women. Other than that, this dorm looked identical to the one I'd seen previously. It was like an ant farm. A perfectly clean, perfectly ordered, and perfectly inactive ant farm. Only these were no ants, they were people. Thousands of them. Many stretched out in their beds while others curled up in the lounge areas. Either way, ninety-five percent of them were hiding behind their eyes, living out spare hours of their lives in some other place. *Gushi*.

Anyone who put in a full day's work was rewarded with the U.N.A.'s drug of choice, and these people were taking their reward. I couldn't blame them; if I were sleeping on a bunk bed stacked three high with no personal space of my own, nothing to my name, and no future ahead of me, I'd want to escape somewhere too.

I began shuffling down the rows, the noise from my bag announcing my presence to anyone who was in the moment with me rather than drifting in fantasy. A guy roughly my age, with close-cropped hair and skin so pale it was nearly translucent, was watching me from his middle bunk. When I waved at him he looked away, pretending I was invisible. "Hey," I called, bolting over to him regardless. "I'm looking for someone. A woman whose husband is probably in detention for being AWOL and has been away from the camp since Saturday."

The guy's irritated eyes bore into mine, but he said nothing. It was like being watched by a hungry vulture from above.

"I have some of his stuff," I continued. "I thought I'd get it to his wife, if I could." I turned to gaze at the long line of beds awaiting me. How would I ever find her in this crowd?

"What do you have that's so important?" the guy asked with a cock of his head. "Something valuable?"

A number of motionless SecRos were interspersed throughout the dorm, silently maintaining order. They'd be on us in an instant if this guy tried something, but that didn't necessarily mean he wouldn't. "Only to him," I said, laying a protective hand across my bag.

"Relax." The guy jumped down from his bunk. He was exactly my height. Our eyes lined up evenly as he stepped towards me. "There's someone I can ask for you. Take a seat. Make yourself comfortable." He peppered those final words with sarcasm and disappeared into the crowd.

I lowered myself onto a section of the long, grey couch to

my left. Next to me, a woman in her thirties sat with her legs crossed at the ankles, staring into her own private gushi world. If I touched her or addressed her directly she'd land back in the dormitory with the blink of an eye. Undisturbed, she could remain like that for hours, until she needed to eat or drink something or relieve herself. That was how people were in 2063. Chronically distracted by illusion.

Already I was getting restless waiting. Did the guy who'd spoken to me have any intention of returning? Michael Neal would be wondering where I was. He must have started without me by now.

I waited another three minutes and then began wandering the aisles again, at first only speaking to the handful of aware people I spotted, and then beginning to touch the shoulders or hands of people on gushi, pulling their consciousness back into the dormitory to answer my questions about the AWOL man. I'd just begun speaking to a dark-skinned girl no older than Kinnari when the guy who'd offered to help me materialized at my side.

"Someone wants to speak with you," he said. "Come with me."

We careened past countless beds, making so many sharp turns that I wondered if I'd be able to find my way back to the elevators. Suddenly the air smelled liked cloves. We neared a crowd of fifteen to twenty people gathered around a lounge area that had been pushed flush against the nearest beds, giving the man in the centre of the circle room to demonstrate. He was standing in front of an easel, creating a pencil portrait of the older woman standing next to him. A bag of cloves hung from the back of the easel, which solved the mystery of where the aroma was coming from, and he must have only just begun the drawing, as the sole marking on the paper was a rough oval representing the woman's head.

"While proportions vary from person to person and alter with age, there are some general guidelines you can use," he declared. "Viewed from the front, a head's width is approximately two thirds of its height. The first quarter measures from the crown of the head down to a person's hairline. The second quarter…"

Beside me, the pale-skinned guy was nudging my arm and pointing me to the right, towards someone I'd—at a glance from the corner of my eye—judged to be a child. As I swivelled to take the figure in it was obvious he was a full-grown man, maybe seven or eight years older than me, yet no taller than five foot three. Virtually no adult males in the U.N.A. were that short anymore. Genetic engineering didn't allow for things that would be considered faults. Shyness. Allergies. Colour blindness. None of these things happened anymore. Not inside or outside of the camps. Not to anyone under the age of thirty.

The short man saw my eyes on him and stepped towards us. "I'll take it from here," he said, giving my chaperon a meaningful look. The younger guy nodded abruptly and spun on his heel, beginning to retrace his steps through the maze of bunk beds.

Meanwhile the man was pulling me over to the nearest unoccupied bunk. "Just sit," he whispered. "It's better not to get too far from the group. They'd take more notice."

"Who?" I sat down next to him, less than twenty feet from the crowd gathered around the drawing instructor. "The Ros?"

"Or one of the human administration. Anything unusual attracts them so you better show me whatever's in your bag. We'll pretend we're concentrating on that." The man scratched at his hairline, inclining his head to indicate the instructor. "Supposedly the smell helps boost his creativity. In the past they used cloves for things like bad breath and toothaches but I'm not fond of the stink. I'm Isaac by the way. Isaac Monroe."

I opened my bag for him and pulled out the intact dish. He'd already lost me. What were we doing if not trying to uncover the identity of the AWOL man so that I could hand over my pieces?

"I'm looking for the woman these belong to," I said,

explaining the situation that had gone down in Moss the previous weekend.

"Unfortunately, I have no idea who she is." Isaac stared into the distance where the instructor was pencilling in his subject's deep-set eyes. "Sorry to mislead you. I just had to take this opportunity. I've seen you around a few times, heard from various people that you've been helping out Michael Neal."

"And so?" My heart had begun speeding. We'd only been talking and I already felt as though I was breaking the rules.

Isaac rubbed a hand under his chin. "So you want to be a lawyer, huh? Want to help these people?" He turned his head away as he added, "You must be grounded, am I right?"

Obviously someone had been talking about me. One of Michael Neal's clients, most likely.

"What's it to you?" I said, gravel in my voice like a tough guy.

Isaac smiled like my defensive attitude didn't faze him. "Maybe nothing. I thought I might know something that would mean something to *you*, if you're serious about wanting to help."

"The only thing I'm serious about at the moment is trying to get this man's stuff back to his wife." My tough guy voice was gone. I was just like Lucy on the elevator, afraid to bring down any real trouble on myself. The corners of Isaac's lips dipped but there was still levity in his eyes. "Wait, what do you mean by 'these people'? Aren't you one of them?"

"At heart I am. You can see it just by looking at me, can't you?" Isaac didn't wait for me to answer. "But I don't live here. I'm only visiting." He took the plate from my hands and ran his fingers gently around the rim. "I can try to find the owner of this, if you want to leave it with me. You'll never manage it on your own."

"How do I know you'll give it to her?" The instructor must have made a joke we'd missed. The people around him were laughing lightly.

"What would I want with a lone piece of china? This isn't

worth anything on its own. You'd need a set." Isaac winked at me, laid the dish down between us, and hopped up from the bunk.

"*Wait.*" I said it loudly enough that the woman posed in front of the instructor glanced sharply over at me on the bed.

Isaac Monroe kept walking and didn't look back. When he'd reached the spot where I'd first caught sight of him, he folded his arms and directed his attention to the art lesson. I slid the dish back into my bag and crossed over to him, my voice a whisper. "What exactly did you mean about helping?" As anxious as I was, the thought that I could do something tangible to change things was irresistible. Staying off gushi as much as was humanly possible, paying lip service to the cause, and listening to speeches by small-time grounded politicians who would likely never get into office wasn't enough. Neither was helping Michael Neal, and maybe law school wouldn't be, either. There had to be something more.

"You're moving to New York." He tilted his head and continued to peer fixedly at the instructor's likeness of the woman. "Did I hear that right?"

"In September."

"It's important to have solid grounded allies in New York. That's a point of entry for a lot of people." Illegals. Refugees who came by sea and eluded the DefRos. "But this isn't a good place to go into details. You really need to check out one of our art courses, if you're interested. There's a lesson coming up next Friday."

"Art courses?" Was that all this was—he was trying to recruit more people into an art class?

"Authentic approaches to life through art." Isaac tightened his grip on his arms. "You probably already know something about the importance of art in connecting people to a healthy, grounded life. But I think there could be some things you don't know too."

"What does any of that have to do with me moving to New

York?"

"That depends on you. But if you want to check out the course it's over at the main library in Billings. It might take you a couple of lessons to get something out of it. And maybe you *won't*, but if you come, be sure to bring a pencil and sketchbook."

My heart was thrumming hard again. "Are these classes dangerous? I don't want to walk into something that..." That I couldn't walk away from. I didn't want to be wiped and covered and sent off somewhere to die, my body riddled with toxins. That fear was what held the grounded movement in check and kept it from becoming a revolution. People were so damn scared all the time that it paralyzed them.

"Trust me, you won't be in any danger there," Isaac said. "It's just a place where things get decided."

I didn't ask which things. I could tell by the way Isaac's eyes had clouded over that he wasn't going to unload any more useful information.

"Maybe I'll see you there, then," I said, non-committal. "Did you mean it about the dishes? About trying to track down the man's wife for me?" Because I wasn't used to looking down at adult men, I had to put extra effort into maintaining eye contact. My eyes were getting dry from the effort of not blinking.

"I'll do what I can."

That was all I could ask. I had to get back to Michael, and Isaac was right, I'd never manage to find the AWOL man's wife on my own. "Thanks," I told him. "I appreciate it." I stuck out my hand and Isaac snorted but shook it. Then I dug into my bag for the collection of fragments and repaired plate and presented them to him.

As I backed away from the crowd and began threading back through the bunks, I felt a rush of wind at my side. "Malyck Dixon," a voice said. I turned to find Isaac half a step behind me. "He's the one who didn't come back on Saturday and hasn't been around since. His wife's Cleo. I've never met them but their dorm is level twelve. Lots of worse things happen out there than some smashed china and a few weeks in detention, you know?"

I exhaled stiffly. "I know that."

Isaac veered away from me before I could say anything more, and several minutes later I still hadn't found the elevator and had to ask a little boy to lead me out of the dorm. Back with Michael Neal in the consultation room after the next client had left, I came clean about my search for Malyck Dixon and our accidental crossing of paths in Moss.

"You have to be more careful with the SecRos," Michael warned. "You don't want too many interference instances added to your record."

They didn't wipe and cover people for running their mouths off to the SecRos like I had, or normally assign detention periods for it either, but when they scanned you and saw your record, any programmed patience the SecRos ordinarily had with humans would no longer apply. They could hold you for hours at a time and would thoroughly question and investigate you whenever you crossed their path, increasing your likelihood of accruing additional charges if you happened to be involved in any illegal activities.

I nodded and pushed my hair out of my eyes. "You're right. I need to watch my step."

I didn't mention Isaac Monroe, the art lessons he was pushing, or anything else. I sat extremely still in my seat and asked Michael if he had any background info on the next scheduled client, my pen paused at the top of the blank sheet of paper in front of me and my mind temporarily pushing the nagging curiosity about next Friday's library meeting into the shadows.

FOUR: 1986

In the morning there's a bird singing out on the balcony. We don't have a feeder, but lately the same brown-and-grey bird keeps returning to hang out on the railing. At least, I think it's the same one; I don't know anything about birds and I only wake up for long enough to register the sound before falling back to sleep, my body still spooned around Freya's. I don't have to be at work until noon today and the light leaking in through the curtains is an early morning blue.

The second time I wake up, Freya's shaking my shoulder and peering down at me with serious eyes. For a couple of seconds I think I must have overslept. I've already been late for two shifts since Expo opened at the start of the month; I can't afford to screw up again.

"Garren," Freya says urgently, "get up. Reagan's been shot." The two of us have gotten into the habit of not saying each other's names out loud much, except when we're alone and can be our real selves instead of the Holly and Robbie aliases that have helped keep us hidden.

That makes something as simple as my name sound intimate on Freya's lips, but what I hear now is alarm. In my newly conscious state I don't understand what she's telling me. Ronald Reagan was shot back in 1981. The shooter, John Hinckley, Jr. was found not guilty by reason of insanity and locked up in a psych ward somewhere.

"What?" I murmur. "*Again?*"

"It's on the TV right now. He was doing a Memorial Day

address at Arlington National Cemetery." Freya's changed into jeans and a maroon button-down shirt, and she folds her arms at her waist and stares impatiently through the open doorway into the hall. A newscaster's voice is saying something about clearing the area, his tone controlled but laced with urgency.

I throw my legs over the side of the bed, grab for my jeans on the floor and tug them on. Freya and I sit on the living room couch with our shoulders pressed together, the TV tuned in to ABC news. The correspondent on the scene in Virginia stares penetratingly into the camera as he declares, "At this time no one can confirm the president's condition, but as we saw, the shooter has been apprehended."

"The secret service rushed into the crowd and took him down right away," Freya explains.

"Did you see him?" I ask. The Arlington crowd is chaos. A swarming mess of soldiers in formal military uniforms, politicians in sedate suits, and smartly dressed civilians, almost everyone but the soldiers either panicking or freezing in place.

We both must be thinking the same thing. Is the U.N.A. responsible for this? Last time, Reagan was only shot *once* during his lifetime. The occasion back in 1981 everyone knows about. This second shooting wasn't part of American history as we knew it. Neither was Mitchell Nelson, a congressman from Texas and America's current Vice President. Freya and I have talked about him before, theorizing that Mitchell Nelson must have something to do with U.N.A. plans. Otherwise, wouldn't George Bush, Sr. be the current Vice President like he was the first time around?

"Only from behind when one of the security guys tackled him to the ground," Freya replies. "I couldn't even see that clearly. It happened so fast." On screen, sirens wail, and back at the studio the anchorman is narrating over footage of the anxious crowd dispersing. Ten minutes later the network begins to replay Reagan's Memorial Day speech. "They loved America very much," he says solemnly. "There was nothing they wouldn't do for her. And they loved with the sureness of the young."

That's when it happens. A bullet to the neck brings Reagan to his knees. A burly bodyguard throws himself in front of the president and takes one to the chest. In the crowd, security men rocket in the direction the shot was fired from. As ABC slows the footage, I think I spy the shooter holding his gun aloft, not trying to hide his guilt.

"I can't believe they got to the president," Freya says, lifting her feet up on the couch with her and wrapping her arms around her knees. "He's not going to make it." But Freya only sees things about people close to her or events that will directly affect her; she's only guessing about Reagan the same as anyone else would.

The bullet to the neck reminds me of a woman I knew and something that shouldn't have happened to her. For a moment my mind races down a different track. "Maybe he will," I say. "Maybe they didn't get an artery."

"Maybe." Freya smooths her lips together. "I don't even know what to hope for. If this is the U.N.A.'s doing, they have their reasons, but it seems wrong to wish for anyone's death."

Freya and I have been having versions of this conversation for over a year, questioning how much wrong a person, organization, or country can commit in the name of a greater good and still consider itself on the side of right. I don't know how to quantify the answer, but every time I think of the U.N.A. lurking in the shadows something inside me revolts. The fate of the entire world is at stake and the U.N.A.'s influence is great, but that doesn't make them the voice of reason. They've been wrong about so many things.

And still, that doesn't mean I want them to fail either. If global warming could be stopped in time there'd be no eco-refugees, no Pakistan-India nuclear exchange. The world would have a chance.

Freya and I hover in front of the TV for over an hour before the newscaster announces, "President Reagan has succumbed to the grievous injury he sustained while addressing the crowd gathered at Arlington National Cemetery. We have also learned the shooter is thirty-six-year-old Stephen Hewko, a motorcycle mechanic from Delaware." The newscaster is the picture of solemnity as he adds that a statement about Vice President Nelson taking the oath of office is expected shortly.

First, the Space Shuttle Challenger disaster four months ago, and now this. The Americans will be in a tailspin.

Freya looks dazed as she gets up from the couch and drifts towards the kitchen to open a can of Coke. "They're really doing it," she says. "They're changing things."

My brain begins to race and then, just as abruptly, crashes to a halt. This is too much to process. Everything changed for us when we were sent back and now it's time for the change to hit everyone else, only they can't see the ripples the U.N.A. have set in motion. Aside from the directors and their teams, Freya and I are the only ones to realize what they've done.

Damn, I need a cigarette. What did I do with my jean jacket last night? I pad into the bedroom and throw my shirt on, scouring the bed and floor for any sign of my jacket. "I hung it in the hall closet," Freya shouts in after me. "If you're quitting, how come there's a package of cigarettes stuffed into your pocket?"

"Last pack," I swear. "When I finish them, it's over."

I trek back into the living room and along the hall, where I reach into the closet and tug my cigarettes and lighter from my jacket pocket. Then I bound back across the room and pull the sliding door open. The brown-and-grey bird has flown off somewhere, leaving the balcony to me. Out there with my feet bare and my shirt hanging open I feel like someone who desperately needs to quit smoking. As the first cigarette of the day fills my lungs, my shoulders unknot and my brain begins to relax.

"Hi, Robbie," a voice greets. It's my neighbour's kid, Dawn, out on the next door balcony, and I stare at my wrist to check the watch I'm not wearing. Shouldn't she be at school now?

"Hey, Dawn," I say. "What time is it?"

Dawn shrugs, her straw-coloured hair rippling in the breeze as she leans over the railing. She's about thirteen years old and wearing the same purple corduroy overalls that I see her in roughly every third day. Sometimes Freya and I hear Dawn's mother shouting through the wall, her words thick like someone trying to speak with their mouth full, and a couple of times when I passed her in the hallway I would've sworn I'd smelled alcohol on her breath. But mostly when I see Dawn, her mom's either out somewhere or asleep.

"Around eight-thirty," Dawn adds, chewing on her hair. "Time to do up your shirt, maybe." Her sarcasm makes me laugh and I jab the cigarette between my lips so I can get down to buttoning. Dawn has more tolerance for Freya, who let her hang out at our apartment and fed her mint ice cream with chocolate sauce the time she got locked out, than she does for me. I think Dawn just accepts me as part of the package deal.

"Better?" I ask, turning to give Dawn a look at my buttoned shirt.

"If you could line the buttons up properly," she says dryly.

I glance down at my wrinkled shirt and hear her snicker. The buttons are perfect; Dawn's just entertaining herself.

"You're way too easy," she says, pulling away from the railing to reach for the sliding door behind her. A second before she disappears into her apartment, she cranes her neck back and adds, "See ya, Robbie."

"See you," I tell her.

Alone on the balcony I finish my cigarette before stubbing it out against the railing. When I move back inside Freya hands me a bowl of Count Chocula mixed with Wheaties, my cereal combo of choice. We settle back onto the couch together, a worry line between Freya's eyes as she methodically chews her Cheerios. "I'm going to be thinking about this all day," she says, "wondering what they're planning next."

"Me too. They must've already made a lot of changes that weren't high-profile enough for us to pick up on." The talking heads on the TV are long-faced and craven, and I squeeze Freya's knee reassuringly. "They've probably given up on us. They have bigger things to worry about."

I don't entirely believe that, but maybe it's true. They were relentless in their pursuit last year. If Freya hadn't seen them coming, we wouldn't have stood a chance. But with the future's fate resting on their shoulders, how much could two young people like us matter to U.N.A. forces anymore?

Our hands wind together as Freya and I watch Reagan take a bullet to the neck again. People will be seeing that image repeated all day long. The entire nation must be in a state of shock.

One of the newscasters says Mitchell Nelson is scheduled to take the oath of office in approximately an hour. Freya reluctantly stands, leaving her cereal bowl orphaned on the couch. "Let me know if anything else happens," she says. "I have to hop into the shower." I'd forgotten that Freya has to be over at Expo soon and automatically frown. I wish there were more time before she had to leave, that we could spend the day together adjusting to the implications of the shooting.

Freya's lips smack against mine just before she disappears, and when she pads into the room minutes later she's wearing one towel and has swept her hair up in a second. I tell her she didn't miss a thing, and Freya unwraps her hair and begins towel-drying it. Her legs are perfectly smooth under the bath towel. I can't resist reaching out to wrap my hand around the back of her knee and running it up her thigh a little.

Freya's fingers play with my hair. I lean my head against her belly and listen to her say, "Hey, did I mention Dennis and Scott invited us to a barbecue they're having on June fourteenth?"

"I don't think so. I'll try to book the day off." Dennis and Scott, a gay couple who helped us get this apartment, are two of

Freya's best customers at Il Baccaro. Dennis and Scott know the super because they used to live in a larger unit here, before Scott inherited a pile of money from an old aunt and bought them a house over in Kitsilano, just a few blocks up from the beach.

Freya's really fond of them both and has referred to Scott and Dennis as the uncles she never had. In 2063 no one would bat an eyelash at their relationship, but in 1986 there are people who hate them on sight. Those people would hate my mothers too. I think about Rosine over in Toronto all the time and wonder how she's getting by. They stole her memories of Bening when they wiped and covered her and sent her back into the past with me, but other than that, she's still the same person.

In some ways, the 1980s is the time before people ruined the planet, and in other ways, it's a nearly barbaric era. So much hate and judgment based on race, gender, and sexual orientation, things we paid little attention to in 2063.

"Okay," Freya says lightly as she pulls away to continue getting ready. "Have fun watching the new future unfold."

I smirk at the phrase 'the new future.' There was a fork in the road we weren't sure was coming, but now it has, and after Freya leaves for work I watch Mitchell Nelson officially become the forty-first president of the United States. He's about six feet tall, pale, clean-shaven, and unremarkable looking, except for his eyes, which appear steely yet sincere. I keep staring at him, looking for signs of U.N.A. allegiance in his face.

Finally I have to cycle over to Expo to put in a four-hour shift. A pall hangs over the crowd as I load people on and off the skyride gondolas that give you a bird's-eye view of the fair. Snatches of conversation about Reagan and Nelson flit by my ears as I take people's arms to help them. Only the kids seem unaffected by the news. The children are usually the ones who get most excited about the gondola, but normally it seems as if most people who pass through the fair's entrance gates are ready to believe the future is full of promise. Today, when that might be closer to true than it's been in a long time, people probably believe it less.

The gap between the crowd's sadness and anger and my own feelings of confusion and endless possibility makes me edgy. Because I have three hours between the end of my Expo shift and the seven o'clock start at Greasy Ryan's, I head back to the apartment, hoping to catch up with Freya, who has the night off.

Despite the weird atmosphere at Expo, I've gotten through half the day on a single cigarette and I'm fighting the idea of smoking a second when the phone rings.

"Hello," the female voice says. "Is this Robert Clark?" No one calls me Robert. To everyone aside from Freya I'm always 'Rob' or 'Robbie,' but I tell the voice yes. "Holly Allen's suffered a concussion and we're currently examining her at Vancouver General Hospital," the voice explains in a perfunctory tone.

My brain stutters over the information. At first hearing some stranger say 'Holly' tricks me into thinking she must have called the wrong phone number and be talking about someone else.

But I'm Robert Clark, just like she said, and Freya's Holly Allen. *The* Holly Allen who is lying injured in a hospital bed.

"A concussion?" I repeat breathlessly. "What happened? Is she okay?"

"She took a fall and lost consciousness briefly," the woman explains. "But she's awake now. I'm not yet sure whether they plan to release her tonight or keep her overnight for observation."

"I'll be right there," I tell her.

Head pounding, I tear into the elevator with my bike, fly up Main Street, and shoot along West Twelfth Avenue. This is one of the times I wish we still had the money-pit car old Freya bought us—a thought that flings my mind back to the moment old Freya was murdered. It was both a miracle and a nightmare, and almost as incredible to me now as the day it happened. That older version of Freya coming to help us because I'd *died*. I would've done the same thing if I'd lost Freya that day, thrown myself back into the chute another seventy-eight years so I could try to rescue a newer Freya and Garren. But I didn't have to. Freya was the one left to face another journey through time, and then decades of waiting for the right moment to save me, giving us both another chance.

The memory deepens my anxiety. Timelines tangle in my brain, fraying, unknotting, and snapping before slithering back together. *Freya has to be okay.*

It's a primal, paranoid fear. Losing her. There's every reason to think this Freya—my Freya—will be fine. Otherwise the woman at the hospital wouldn't have said they'd release her tonight or tomorrow.

Within fifteen minutes I'm tearing into the E.R. and giving them Holly's name. It's another thirty-five minutes of staring anxiously at my hands and feeling sweat gather around my hairline until they call for me. A male nurse takes me in to see her, and Freya smiles tiredly up at me. "I'm okay," she says. "Just stuck with a headache."

I rub her arm, so relieved to see her in one piece that I exhale like someone blowing out a match. "What happened? My mind was running wild."

"Didn't they tell you I was all right?" Freya's forehead crinkles in sympathy.

"They did." I shrug, suddenly feeling ridiculous.

The nurse hands me an information packet. "Sorry to interrupt. She can explain when you get home, but there are some things I need you to look out for. We can't release her unless there's someone to watch over her for the next twenty-four hours."

"I'll do that," I say quickly.

"Good," he says. "You need to keep an eye on her. If her speech becomes slurred or if she gets confused or the headache worsens, or there are any other strange symptoms, bring her back right away. She should be woken up every two hours during the night so that you can check that her condition hasn't changed. And her family doctor should check her out again in a day or two."

"When can I go back to work?" Freya asks, her fingers bunching up in her lap.

"Not until you see your regular doctor and he tells you it's okay. For the next few days we don't want you doing anything except taking it easy, all right, honey?" Freya nods obediently and we both listen to the nurse explain that it could be a week or two before she's back to her old self.

But at least she can come home with me now, and Freya and I slowly make our way out of the hospital together. I hail a passing cab, thinking that I'll have to come back for my bike tomorrow night when it's safe to let Freya out of my sight again. In the backseat of the taxi, she begins to tell me about the accident. "I was almost home when I saw an old man running after his dog on the sidewalk, shouting after it. I was closer than he was and I thought I could catch up with the dog. But the thing was so strong—it looked like some kind of Rottweiler mix, all muscle—that even when I'd hooked my fingers around its collar, I couldn't make it stop. It kept yanking me along. We were coming up to the corner and I slammed right into a person who'd just rounded it from the opposite direction. I fell over and conked my head on the sidewalk."

I wince. "That must've hurt like hell."

"I don't know. I don't remember my head hitting. Just the stuff that happened before. And when I woke up there were a bunch of people leaning over me and I heard the ambulance siren. One of the women told me I'd been knocked unconscious and said not to get up. It was weird; it felt more like a dream than real life. The doctor says I could be foggy for a little bit. Light-headed and dizzy, that kind of thing." Freya squints like the sun glinting through the car window is burning her retinas. "Mostly it's the headache that's bugging me, though."

I remember the nurse saying Freya could have a pain killer, and when we get back to the apartment and she's settled herself on the couch, I bring her two aspirin. Then I call Greasy Ryan's and talk to my boss about needing tonight and tomorrow off. He's not happy about it but grudgingly says he'll call around to find someone to pick up my shifts. Luckily Freya's bosses at the restaurant are more understanding and tell her not to even think about coming back until Friday.

Freya and I spend the next twenty-four hours living in slow motion, me bringing her fluids and food and periodically quizzing her about how she feels. A couple of times, while she's sleeping, I sneak out to the balcony for a smoke. The rest of the time we're camped out in front of the TV watching a weird combination of music videos, American political news coverage, and soap operas. Freya isn't used to being under the weather—in the future no one really gets sick anymore and injuries heal fast—and after the first night she starts pushing herself harder than she should, listening to the Spanish tapes and rearranging stuff in the hall closet.

When I lecture her about needing to rest, she says we've both been so busy for so long that she doesn't know how to take it easy anymore. "I get that," I tell her. "But your brain needs a break."

"Like your lungs," she counters. "So how about this? If you stop trying to ration that last pack to make it last forever and quit right now, I'll go sit down again."

I root my hands to my hips and resist the urge to roll my eyes. "What's the point of that? I told you I was quitting anyway. Just this final pack and that's it."

"I know." Freya's gaze is so level you could stack a set of encyclopaedias on it. "I just want to make sure."

Sometimes a person wanting the best for you doesn't feel the way it should. If I want to taper off cigarettes rather than quit cold turkey, I shouldn't need anyone else's approval to do it, even hers.

"I'm nineteen, you know. It's not like I'm going to get hit with lung cancer next year, Freya." So maybe the package on the coffee table won't be my final one, so what? The thought feels like a stupid little rebellion even as it's sprinting through my head.

"I don't want to be having this conversation with you for the next twenty years," she says. "You were supposed to quit months ago."

It's true. I started talking about quitting in February. But I'm not going to let Freya pressure me into doing it today just because I wish she'd go lie down. "And you've left this place a mess a thousand times," I tell her. "So I don't see you changing in a hurry either. On any other day your dirty dishes would probably be clogging up the sink right now, but as soon as you're supposed to rest, you can't leave the closet alone. You're just using me as an excuse."

It's not the worst fight we've ever had, not even technically a fight, but not a conversation I want to continue either. "I have to go get my bike at the hospital," I grumble. It's been exactly twenty-five hours and five minutes since I met Freya there. She doesn't need watching anymore and anyway, she won't listen to me about taking it easy.

Freya's nostrils flare as she looks away. I lurch towards the coffee table to scoop up my cigarettes and say, "Just try not to hit your head again, all right?"

She smiles like I'm being an idiot. "Don't get lung cancer on the way to the hospital," she quips, her eyes flashing with mischief.

I can't help it; a tight grin cascades across my face and next thing you know we're both chuckling at ourselves. Give us another couple of years and maybe we'll be smart enough to skip the majority of our arguments and zip straight to seeing the funny side of things.

I bend down by Freya's spot in front of the hall closet and kiss the crown of her head. "Back soon," I tell her.

Outside the air feels cool but dry. Here and now there's no such thing as an all-clear day and, with a few exceptions, no reason to fear what the weather will bring.

I walk idly in the direction of the hospital, not in any hurry to arrive, my right hand digging into my pocket for a cigarette that I don't *want* to want. I have it lit for roughly six seconds before I toss it to the ground and crush the ember under my shoe, fighting myself now. Impulsively, I yank the entire package free, scrunch it in my hand, and toss it into the nearest garbage where it falls on top of an oily napkin and a can of Tab.

I want to pick the cigarettes up and shove them back into my pocket so badly I can taste it. Ash and desperation. I fight that too. If I can survive the trip seventy-eight years back in time, recover my memory despite the scientists' wipe, and successfully evade the director and his men, breaking a ten-month-old habit should be no sweat.

Once I reach my bike and climb on, the ride distracts me from the craving a little, but I resolve not to tell Freya that I tossed the cigarettes yet. I need to quit for myself first. If I make it through the next couple of days without a smoke, I can share the news with her.

Inside our building I squish into the elevator with my bike. The enclosed space smells like meaty pizza and my stomach begins to rumble. Thirty seconds later I'm sliding my key into our door. I was sure I locked it when I left, but it's open. I turn the knob and wheel my bike into the hallway.

The apartment entranceway reeks of pizza too, so maybe Freya ordered from Domino's. I hope so. We ate a couple of hours ago but I'm already hungry again.

I lean my bike against the wall and venture into the living room, expecting to find Freya on the couch with a fat slice of pepperoni and sausage pizza in her hands. Instead, I almost trip over the overturned chair that's been pulled away from our dining table. Did she fall again? I shouldn't have left her. I should've waited until she'd gone to the doctor and been given a thumbs-up.

No. It's not that. It's worse. My gaze leaps around the living room, landing first on the coffee table. The magazines, cactus, and other plants it was littered with when I left are scattered across the floor as though someone swept the table clean with a stroke of their arm. The lamp shade's crooked too. The record player hangs open and the handful of vinyl albums I own have been emptied onto the ground, their hollowed-out sleeves lying haphazardly among them.

I run into the kitchen and step into the middle of an identical scene, all the cupboards ajar, the handful of towels we normally keep in the bottom drawer lying scattered along the counter with the stove manual and record player warranty. We bought the record player second-hand, but the old hippie who sold it to us still had the warranty. I don't know why we kept the paperwork. Nothing we have is worth much.

Now I'm running. Into the bathroom and then the bedroom. Searching for Freya and making a silent wish that this is only a robbery. The pair of ten-dollar bills that was on top of our bedroom dresser earlier today is gone. Someone has rifled through everything we own, torn our clothes off the closet hangers, and tossed our underwear, socks, and shirts onto the floor so I have to wade through them to reach the other side of the bed and peer into the nightstand. We never had anything important in it—just a stack of bills and receipts. On top of the nightstand there's a photo of a blond boy in a small oval frame, a model from a department store ad who Freya thought looked like her brother when he was younger. Of everyone from home, he's the one she misses most.

"Freya! *Freya!*" Shock's kept me quiet until now, when her name explodes from my larynx as I lumber back through the apartment, looking for missed clues. She wouldn't have left without leaving a note. Not when she knew I'd be back before long. That means she must've been here when the place was hit.

Who else would take her but *them*? An invisible hand reaches inside my chest and twists my organs sideways. When Freya and I first started running I thought I'd lost everything but didn't understand why. She's been miles ahead of me all along, and in her absence I feel as if I'm being forced to play her part. Only I don't have her ability, just instinct.

I imagine her being hurled into a car trunk, her head smacking against the interior. The mental picture sends me cringing worse than a brutal punch to the gut. The simplest thing could hurt her now and what they'll do to her is anything but simple. The bastards want to make her forget all over again and they don't care what it will cost her. Or maybe this time they mean to skip the procedure and just kill her instead. They see us as a threat that we aren't—a tremor that would send their house of cards crashing and ruin the world's second chance.

My thoughts are dark and horrible, every last one of them. But I can't let it end like this. There has to still be a chance. We can't have come all this way for nothing.

I don't know where to start looking, but nothing matters now except finding Freya.

I have to go.

FIVE: 2063

Thursday, August ninth was Du Monde Day and as usual, Bening, Rosine, Kinnari, and I went to the National Mall for the annual celebration. Angry clouds were spitting down on the mass gathering and the day had a weather rating of three, indicating the rain would probably soon be worse and there was some possibility of tornadoes in the area. The Montana Emergency Management Agency's tornado tracking technology was fairly accurate—and should've been capable of warning us if we needed to evacuate the immediate area before anything hit—but Mother Nature was still capable of surprising us and the crowd of over a million and a half that stretched from the Capitol building to the Lincoln Memorial seemed antsy as President Ortega took the stage to the strains of the national anthem. There'd been a bombing in Kansas City two months earlier that had destroyed miles of Zephyr track and killed five civilians, and lately the Dailies had been ramping up our fears that there were larger terrorist attacks to come. It didn't matter how many SecRos were among us keeping guard on the National Mall; people felt like sitting ducks. If a tornado didn't get you, maybe a terrorist-designed virus would. Our scientists were constantly updating the Bio-nets that protected us but no one could forget the hemorrhagic fever that had killed one hundred and thirteen people in Denver five years earlier.

As President Ortega waved, we all raised our voices to join in the singing of the national anthem. To remain silent would've been as unpatriotic as staying home.

"Oh brave nation, born of two mothers.
Oh brave nation, ever brighter, ever stronger, ever free.
From far and wide, united, we stand on guard for thee.
Our sanctuary, our glory, lie within your hills and valleys.
Your waters run clear, your skies remain sacred.
Forever, brave nation, we exult you.
Hands on our soaring hearts, feet grounded in your soil.
And this be our motto: there is nothing too great you can
ask of us
Nothing we will not cede
May the star-spangled banner long wave
over our brave nation, the land of the free."

Du Monde Day—a tradition the French had started two decades earlier and that had rapidly spread to most of the countries across the globe that were still functioning as civilized—was full of contradictions. Morning Dailies aside, it was intended to be a twenty-four-hour period where U.N.A. citizens stayed off gushi and joined their countrymen and other nations in celebration of *vraie vie*. The irony was that while in theory, United North America professed to love authentic life, it had little fondness for it in practice. The country ran on the toil of robots and the hope that the majority of its citizens would remain asleep or silent to its abuses of power.

For the U.N.A., Du Monde Day was mainly a PR exercise. The feed sent out from Billings, D.C. to other countries would reveal a mass of citizens so dedicated to their nation and to the value of real life that they had braved the wet weather, storm warnings, and the looming threat of terrorism to gather at the National Mall. Meanwhile, many of us wouldn't have been standing in the eerily damp bluster if the SecRos didn't keep track of attendance. We'd all heard rumours about the government making inquiries about area residents who stayed home.

Next to me, Kinnari was shivering, and I watched her reach

into her collar to inch up the warmth setting on her clothing to better protect her from the elements. As was tradition, the crowd joined hands as the president began her address. She praised our courage in coming to the National Mall to celebrate with her despite the weather and said she would require more of that courage from us in the days ahead to continue the battle against terrorism and the fight to restore our country's natural environment.

"We are marching towards ultimate success," President Ortega declared. "I know you can feel this and that we are a proud, strong people dedicated to each other and to this fine, brave dream realized in the flesh as United North America. John F. Kennedy, one of the United States' finest presidents, once said, 'As we express our gratitude, we must never forget that the highest appreciation is not to utter words, but to live by them.' And so on this day, and every other, I ask you to live by the ideals of the U.N.A. and the authentic life it reveres. If you do so, it will reward you by continuing to offer back to you everything you need."

One and a half million people roared and clapped in appreciation, the wind biting at our skin and the clouds malevolent. The sporting and acrobatic demonstrations held in the airspace above the National Mall were still to come. So was the yearly skystory display—overhead hyperrealistic recreations of great moments in U.S. history played out against a backdrop of clouds—and the live musical performance by opera singer Arlette Courtemanche. Unlike most pop music sensations, Arlette was a genetic original, not a spliced star, a darling of the official grounded movement.

Physical segments of the Du Monde celebration were cancelled because of the weather almost every year, and a low boo echoed throughout the crowd as it was announced that the high winds had made the acrobatic and sporting performances too dangerous. Arlette glided out onto the stage with an acoustic guitar around her neck to the sound of that disapproval. She looked exceptionally small in the distance, which reminded me of Isaac and made me wonder, like I had on and off all week, what would happen at the library art lessons the next night.

Because opera wasn't my thing, I wasn't paying much attention to Arlette initially. But it only took a few seconds to realize that she wasn't actually singing opera. Her fingers were strumming the chords of what sounded like an old folk song. Bening and Rosine swapped knowing looks and before I could ask them what was going on, the song had captivated me.

It was about us. The U.N.A. when it had been the U.S.A.

"From California, to the New York Island
From the Redwood Forest, to the Gulf Stream waters…"

Nearby, someone began to sob. Only one person at first and then pockets of desolation began to spread throughout the National Mall, an inner sadness made audible. I heard someone behind me declare, in a pained voice, "Why is she doing this? Today's supposed to be a celebration, not a lament."

"A lament's more honest," a contrary voice said back.

I glanced over my shoulder, my eyes landing on the face of a man several years older than my mothers. Tears had burnt his eyes a brilliant watery blue, a colour and emotion so arresting that it took me longer to look away from him than it should have.

Sandwiched between descriptions of the national beauty of the old America, the song kept returning to the simple refrain, "This land is your land, this land is my land." With every word, the song stung. The Redwood Forest, suffocated. California, deserted. That was U.N.A. reality. Chills inched up my arms as I straightened my back and squinted at Arlette in the distance, remembering she'd been born in San Jose, before Canada had been unified with the United States and before the evacuation of California. Either Bening or Rosine had said so when they'd seen the Du Monde Day program.

Arlette's longing for the country of her birth, a place that didn't exist in the same way anymore, put a lump in my throat I didn't know how to get rid of. What did it feel like to love your nation that much? I'd been raised to believe the U.N.A. was a colossal compromise of principles. There were so many worse places in the world that eco-refugees attempted daily to reach our shores in hope of obtaining what we had. Food, water, some semblance of security.

And with all that, it still wasn't enough. The U.N.A. had to stand for something greater. That was what the grounded movement had drilled into me since I could speak.

I believed it there and then—standing motionless on the lawn of the National Mall, listening to the cries of people who had lost something dear to them—more than I ever had. This land should be ours. Not the Ros' and not the government's. And our lives, for better or worse, should've been our own too. Lived in the real world, in real time, not wasted on a virtual universe. A mob near the stage had begun to shout at Arlette, either not realizing they were dismissing their own past or not caring. I laughed soundlessly; we couldn't even agree on the matter of the land being ours. As wholeheartedly as I believed in a grounded life and true freedom, millions of others preferred force and illusion. There was no true unity in the U.N.A. We were like a random group of people shipwrecked on an island together.

I'd known that already, but not the way I came to realize it on that afternoon. I probably would have gone to the Billings Library the day after even if I'd never heard Arlette Courtemanche bring people to tears, but she stirred something inside me out on the National Mall during that rainy Du Monde gathering. I didn't want to wait years, maybe decades, for the U.N.A. to change. If we waited, maybe it would never become the better place we dreamed of. If we waited we would likely only run out of time, run out of oxygen, run out of undamaged DNA to continue the species with.

It felt as if I was probably already too late when I strode into the Billings Library on the evening of August tenth with a pad of paper under my arm and a sharpened pencil tucked behind my ear. It felt more like an act of stubbornness than one of rebellion. You can't give up when you and the people you love are still living and breathing, even if logically you know your days are numbered. I was overflowing with the need to do something. Scared as I was, I was ready.

The smell of cloves reached me in the hall before I stepped into the brightly lit room one of the librarians had directed me to. The old U.S.A. had closed most of its public libraries thirty-five years earlier, but when the grounded movement succeeded in having grounded education restored in 2050, many of the libraries were reopened. I loved the aroma of old paper and the heaviness of a book in my hand. But the cloves reeked, countering my warm feelings for the library, even as the stench revealed that the same instructor I'd encountered in one of the Fairfield camp dormitory levels was teaching "Authentic approaches to life through art."

Seats were arranged in a semicircle around him, an easel in front of each one, and I dropped into one of the few remaining empty chairs, glancing slyly at the other people in the classroom. They all had their own pencils and sketching pads, but aside from that there was no visible common denominator between the students—my classmates were of various ages, races, and genders, and Isaac was not among them. Nobody paid me the slightest attention and soon the instructor was guiding us through a shading exercise.

There was a reason I hadn't done any drawing since I was eight years old and my egg, as I followed along with our instructor, looked morosely saggy on the otherwise unblemished paper. I did a little better at the line drawing exercise and listened to the instructor wax on about the relationship between art and the love for physical life. "You can't devote yourself to capturing the life force in the crook of someone's little finger, for example, and not realize the perfect uniqueness of that individual," he said. "That appreciation for the unique unites us, when we let it. Real perfection is flawed, not sterile like what one encounters on gushi."

"Lots of people don't like imperfection," the brown-skinned, dark-eyed woman seated next to me interjected. "And the more time they spend on gushi the less tolerance they have for it. How do we combat that in other people?"

"Does anyone have any ideas?" The instructor whirled around, his eyes scanning the room in search of someone ready to volunteer a nugget of wisdom. "You." He pointed at a middle-aged man with a beard, who spluttered and shook his head. "You, then." The instructor's finger aimed my way.

"By stealth," I joked. "So they don't know we're doing it."

The instructor smiled but we both knew I hadn't really answered his question. If I knew how to make people appreciate the merits of being grounded, I wouldn't be sitting in his class. That was the problem; I didn't know how to help.

No one had a sound answer for the woman, and by the time we'd completed another exercise and the session was beginning to break up, I was asking myself why I was hanging out in the Billings Library pretending to be an artist. Did Isaac get some kind of kickback from referring people to the course? Had he been stringing me along with that talk of doing something to help? It seemed I'd wasted most of my night. Before long it would be curfew.

A few of the other students were talking amongst themselves as the instructor began to pack his things away. My chair screeched as I impatiently pushed it back along the floor and got to my feet. The woman next to me—the one who'd posed the question about tolerance—stood up quickly alongside me. I guessed she was in her early twenties, older than me but not by more than five years.

"Will you be back?" she said. "Things get more interesting as we progress."

"Someone else promised the same thing about the class, but I don't know, I think it might have been a misunderstanding." I stifled a yawn. "I don't have much artistic ability and I'm leaving Montana soon, anyway."

"I bet that's not true about your artistic ability." Her mouth slipped into an easy smile. "Your egg shading showed potential." She was teasing and I felt my cheeks begin to blush in response, chiefly because she was older than me and may have been flirting. Or maybe I was misreading her and she was just friendly. "Can I ask who recommended the class to you?"

"Just a guy named Isaac. I hardly knew him." I didn't bother with Isaac's last name; I didn't expect her to know who I was talking about.

"If you care about things you really should stick it out," the woman advised, her eyes gleaming. "Minnow would know if you were right for this, believe me. You must show promise."

"What does that mean? Do you people always speak in code?" I drummed my pencil restlessly against my leg. "Look, I need someone to be straight with me and spell out what I'm doing here. I came because I thought I could do something. Not learn how to draw a straight line. And who the hell is Minnow?"

"*Isaac* is Minnow. I just thought"—the woman shook her head—"everyone who knows him calls him Minnow. Sometimes I forget that."

A trio of people squeezed by me on their way out of the class. I hopped back to make room for them. "It's a nickname," the woman continued from her side of the divide. "Because of his size and because the word sounds a bit like 'Monroe.' Some of his old school friends started it years ago and the name stuck."

"So you do know him."

"I know him, yes. He's done a lot for a lot of people, me included." The woman reached out as if to brush my forearm with her hand, her fingers pulling away before they could reach me. "Come back and you'll see. Sometimes it just takes a while to—"

"I don't have long. I have to be in New York in a few weeks." My arm tingled where she'd almost touched me. It wasn't only that she was pretty; I already explained that didn't mean much in 2063. She had an aura about her that I wasn't used to—a heady mixture of mystery, self-discipline, intellectual curiosity, and compassion. Our brief conversation on the tenth wasn't enough for me to glean all those things, but I saw enough to convince me to come back, and when I returned to the Billings Library on the seventeenth and then the twenty-fourth, I found myself increasingly drawn to her.

The woman's name was Seneval—I learned that and other things about her during my subsequent classes—but mostly people wanted to know about me, my beliefs and dedication, what I thought I could do for the movement. At the same time they were judging Silas, the middle-aged bearded man the instructor had singled out on my first night. It wouldn't have been obvious to anyone who dropped into the class looking for a drawing lesson but, as Seneval explained it to me on the seventeenth, these were gateway meetings, a vetting process. If enough members of the class voted that they could trust Silas and me, we'd be moved up the chain where someone more important would deal with us.

Aside from the awkward first class, Silas spoke passionately about the changes he wanted to see in the U.N.A. One night he seemed especially angry as he said, "I've seen too many bad things in my time. The Ros, the government, gushi—all of it has a tighter grip on people with each year that passes. We're a country of sleepwalkers now. We've given our freedom away for the sake of leading quiet lives dreamt out in a fantasy world. Meanwhile flesh-and-blood people waste away in the camps. If we don't put a stop to it soon, every last one of us will be in there eventually, prisoners without any need for bars because we've stupidly embraced this fate." He slapped his thigh, his cheeks ruddy. "Well, I've had enough of it, at last. I'm tired of being afraid to act. Tired enough to risk whatever I have to in order to change things."

I wished I were as brave as Silas, and I was sure the class would approve him. My own fate, I was less certain of. I answered my classmates' questions as truthfully as I could, telling them I had no objection to passing information on for the movement when needed, but not weaponry. I didn't want to be responsible for hurting anyone. I would help illegals if they were looking for sanctuary, but not terrorists. I could recruit for the underground movement, if they wanted me to, sending people to classes like this one, but I wanted to remain at a distance from the hard-core movement. I didn't want to do anything that would get me wiped. I wasn't ready for that kind of sacrifice.

The fear seems ironic now, because not long after that I was wiped and covered anyway, but not because of anything I did. Only to save me. The people I was ready to act against rescued me. Because of Bening and because they didn't want the entire U.N.A. population of 2063 to perish. They thought they were doing the right thing and I can't entirely fault them. The truth is, I might be dead if not for them. Me and Freya both.

But I can't forgive the way the scientists played with our minds and how the director's security forces tried to chase us down like animals. U.N.A. motives and methods are as complex now, in 1986, as they were in 2063. Not simply evil but misguided.

Things seemed more clear-cut before I was sent back. I thought, as the minutes of art class slid by, that I could just tick boxes in my head and live by them. Help but don't hurt. Rebel but don't stick out your neck so far that the government steals your sense of self as punishment.

I was frustrated by the pace of the screening process, but I understood the need for it. As well as the standard amount of caution the group proceeded with, there were concerns about my age. Some people thought I was too young to be serious about the cause while others believed my youth was an advantage because the young had more to lose than anyone. I heard those things from Seneval, who sat nearest me. She was the one who questioned me most deeply, often whispering to me during class. Whoever was in charge had probably assigned her to me because she was closer to me in age than any of the other people in the art course.

Seneval didn't just grill me; she shared things about herself too. Every U.N.A. citizen had to perform eighteen months of compulsory government-assigned work starting when they turned twenty-one. Hers had been at Yellowstone National Park, helping out at the visitor centre and sometimes assisting in doing food drops to the grizzly bears. She said the grizzlies had been in trouble for over half a century because of the destruction of the whitebark trees. The seeds found in whitebark cones were an important part of their diet.

"What a lot of people don't realize," she explained, "is that the only reason there are any grizzlies still left in Yellowstone is that the biologists began genetically engineering them to be born with something more like a dog's digestive system. But they still need a massive amount of food and it's easier to maintain the numbers of other dwindling animal populations, like moose, if the rangers keep the bears' bellies full. The mutation wasn't intended to change them in other ways, but it has."

"What ways?" I asked. "And how come no one knows about this—the bears not being real bears anymore?"

Seneval shrugged. "It's not a secret. But you know how it is, that isn't the kind of thing the government likes to put on the Dailies. Besides, most people just wanted to pretend certain things are like they've always been. The important thing to them is that bears are still in the park. They don't want to look below the surface and hear that grizzlies like to live in packs now, which isn't normal bear behaviour aside from mothers and their cubs, and that they no longer hibernate."

It was my second week of class when Seneval told me about

the grizzlies, the two of us talking under our breath while the bearded man quietly conferred with the woman seated next to him. One of the funnier aspects of the vetting process was that my artistic skills were progressing. Probably his were too.

During the third class I learned Seneval's parents had been salvagers. They'd gone down to southern Nevada with a crew six years earlier and never returned.

My pencil had been skating across the page, sketching 'negative space,' and I pulled away from the page and froze with my pencil in the air. "None of them?" I asked. "The entire crew disappeared?" The bottom half of Nevada was abandoned, only patrolled by DefRos for defence purposes. The second you crossed into abandoned land you had no one to rely on but the people you'd come with. While the Ros would approach to scan you, if you read as a U.N.A. citizen, they would leave you alone, for better or worse. DefRos didn't rescue. Their mission was only to expel and destroy illegals.

"All twelve of them," Seneval confirmed. "Last anyone heard they were salvaging in Hawthorne."

"I'm sorry. How old were you when they went missing?"

"Seventeen." Seneval focused on her paper, concentration lines criss-crossing her forehead. "My younger sister and I went to live at the camp in Fairfield."

"That must've been hard, having to take care of your sister on your own and adjusting to life at the camp." I shuddered to think of Kinnari growing up in such a soulless place, sleeping in a bed sandwiched between seas of others.

Seneval nibbled her lip, her eyes never leaving the paper. One of our fellow students was posing as a subject that day, a man with a long, straight nose and eyes that appeared perpetually startled. I glanced down at the space between the man's nose and the curve of his upper lip that Seneval had captured faithfully on her page. How many lessons had she sat through? I bet she could've taught the course herself.

"Most of the people there keep to themselves a lot, like you must've seen while you were visiting," she said. "But my sister and I learned to swim in the camp. An older woman who used to live right by the water in North Carolina taught us. So it wasn't all bad. We'd never been swimming before. And that's where I met Minnow. After my comp work was finished he got me my job too."

"Where do you work?" I'd only be able to make one more art class. After that I might never see Seneval again. She was so different from everyone else I knew; I wanted to find out more about her while I had the chance.

"Wyldewood." She glanced up at me with a guarded expression, her spine straightening against her chair.

Wyldewood was a shopping centre right off the I-90 near Laurel. It catered to people over the age of sixty who had fond memories of the suburban shopping mall experience. Essentially the centre was the equivalent of a dozen super-sized Walmarts but with superior interior decorating. Wyldewood had waterfalls, copious amounts of greenery, and an indoor beach with a blue sky as convincing as any you'd find on gushi.

I'd gone with my grandparents a few times, to help them pick out furniture and various decorative items. Not that they really needed me for that; at Wyldewood you were assigned a personal shopper as you walked through the door. I'd heard that some grounded folks just went for the social interaction. Oddly enough, a few people even went with their domestic Ros in tow.

Tranquil as it was to look at, I couldn't understand Wyldewood's appeal. What was the point of spending hours ogling mundane objects you probably didn't really need in the first place? At least in Moss you could discover forgotten treasure.

"I have a tough time picturing you in Wyldewood," I confessed. "It doesn't seem like your scene."

"Yeah, well, we're not all lucky enough to be able to choose law school," Seneval said coolly. "I was fortunate to get into Wyldewood. That's how I see it."

My jaw dropped an inch before I snapped it shut again. "There's nothing wrong with Wyldewood. I didn't mean it like that." I'd been saying all the wrong things. Seneval was a proud person and didn't want me feeling sorry for her; I should've been able to see that.

I watched Seneval's pencil poke through her paper. "Damn." She tore the page from her easel and crumpled it up. As it fell towards the floor, I reached for it, grasping it in my left fist. "It doesn't matter," she said. "I botched it. Just toss it and I'll start over." She was already making a stroke on a fresh page.

But I didn't throw away her drawing. I smoothed the paper down and slid it between the pages of my notebook. "To remember you by." I smiled flippantly to undercut the implications of my actions. It didn't escape me that I'd been rescuing a lot of damaged or abandoned things lately. The unicorn bracelet. Cleo's plate. Seneval's unfinished sketch.

"You're still coming next week, aren't you?" The worry in her voice changed my demeanour to serious.

I almost lost my grip on my pencil, regaining it just before it had a chance to slip. "Is that when things will finally be decided for me—next week?" My life was on a knife's edge of changing. What would the movement ask of me in New York?

Seneval's lips set in a somber line. "Minnow wants to meet with you Tuesday night. Do you think you could make it out to Wyldewood to speak to him?"

"Why Wyldewood?" I'd been back to the Fairfield camp every Saturday to help Michael Neal with his clients but hadn't seen Isaac again. The time I tried to search him out on level nine I'd only gotten lost in the dorms again. Anyone I'd asked him about either didn't know who Isaac was or pretended to be clueless.

"He lives there," Seneval explained. "We work together."

"Wait. You *live* at Wyldewood?"

Seneval stared at our subject, her hand beginning to recreate the curve of his top lip on her page. "Almost everyone who works at Wyldewood lives there too. We don't earn enough in wages to live any other decent place."

Guilt for my privileged upbringing kept me silent. I'd already put my foot in my mouth enough times that night.

"So will you be there Tuesday?" she asked.

"I'll be there."

I didn't loiter around when class was done; I took off as fast as I could. At home I flipped through my notebook and opened to Seneval's crumpled drawing. The hole in the paper was tiny. She hadn't needed to throw it away. She could've finished the picture.

Sometimes, during those weeks we shared a class, I'd find myself thinking about Seneval while I was at school. No one else knew about her or the art class and that made the secret feel like something more than it was. Rosine and Bening thought I was at a friend's house. I'd never breathed a word about Malyck or anything else and it was as if Seneval and I were on the verge of something together, like soldiers about to go into battle. Only there was no *together*. She'd just happened to be in the same room as me for a time. I was her job. Part of her cause. None of our conversations meant anything more than that.

If you've ever felt like you could be friends with someone but knew you didn't have the time or the opportunity—that was how it was with me and Seneval. I didn't know how she felt about me or even what I meant by 'friends.' I only knew, when I fell asleep that night after class, that I was feeling the seeds of something that would never grow.

SIX: 1986

T he few tools we own—a hammer, screwdriver, and wrench—are bundled in a plastic bag we keep in the hall closet. I grab the screwdriver and drag the overturned dining room chair into the bedroom with me to open the vent that's spaced four inches from the ceiling.

I'd honestly started to think they'd stopped looking for us. Now I know we stayed too long, got too comfortable.

I yank the grill off the vent and toss it onto the bed. Reaching inside, I close my fingers around the gun and box of bullets we bought when we first reached Vancouver, a tight roll of twenty-dollar bills totalling eight hundred dollars, and two sets of fake IDs for Freya and me under the names Chris Henderson and Amy Lewandowski. We have more money at the bank, but I don't have time for that. I load the gun, then shove everything into my duffle bag along with a fistful of underwear, socks, and T-shirts that I swipe off the floor. I throw a single pair of jeans into the bag along with them and hoist the strap over my shoulder.

Too late it occurs to me that I'm already letting their trail go cold; I should've run out to the street to catch sight of anything suspicious when I first saw that the apartment had been ransacked. My legs whirl me out to the balcony anyway. I stare up and down Fourteenth Avenue hoping my eyes will snag on something—anything—that will help lead the way. When that doesn't happen I turn and step back inside, freezing as I hear someone burst through the front door. I jump back onto the balcony, easing the sliding door shut as quietly as I can. Whoever it is won't have seen me yet—the balcony isn't visible from the entranceway.

But what if it's Freya and she wasn't taken after all? I stare through the glass, hope dying inside me as a balding man with severe sideburns glares back. He breaks into a run when he spies me, jerks the sliding door open and grabs at the front of my jacket, wrenching me inside with him. The duffle strap slides down my arm as I stumble into the apartment.

For all I know, this man's only one of many the director's sent, and if the others reach me I won't stand a chance. I draw back my fist and hit his Adam's apple dead-on, just like I saw old Freya do on the day she saved us. The man instinctively bends at the waist, both his hands releasing me. I stomp on his left foot with all my weight and watch him buckle in pain, skirting to his side to push him back out onto the balcony and lock the door behind him. Flustered, my fingers trip over the locking mechanism. The man's tanned hand closes around the exterior handle just as I successfully lock the door. Momentarily proud of myself, an involuntary smile begins to burn into my cheeks.

The feeling doesn't last a second before the man reaches into his blazer for a holstered gun. I twist to run, hearing the glass shatter behind me.

Out in the apartment corridor, I launch myself in the direction of the stairwell, wondering how much of a lead I have, whether they've had a chance to mess with Freya's head yet, and what I can do about any of it.

I don't look back. My ears tell me that my tail hasn't reached the stairway yet, and instead of running down to street level I ease the third-floor doorway open, squeeze through it, and close it gently behind me. What now? *Think, Garren. You got away from them in Toronto. You can do it again.*

I duck down beside the doorway so the man won't see me and hunch, poised to jump him if he comes through the door.

Seconds later I hear shouting from the stairs.

"We have to find him," a choked voice barks, allowing me to hear the damage I've inflicted on his windpipe. "I almost had him. He can't have gotten far."

"He didn't pass me," the second voice responds.

Damn, there are at least two of them after all. Maybe more.

With no way out, there's only one thing left for me to take a chance on. *The elevator.* I scuttle along the hallway towards it and jab at the 'down' button. The ordinarily sloth-paced elevator opens for me within three seconds. Like fate, the bald man who grabbed me upstairs hurtles breathlessly into the corridor behind me.

Leaping onto the elevator, I poke repeatedly at the 'close' button. "You only need to push it once you know," the girl next to me quips. Dawn, in skin-tight white jeans and a red turtleneck. *Shit.* She must have missed them upstairs by seconds.

Finally the door responds, sliding shut and leaving the man panting in the hallway. "Listen, Dawn, I'm in trouble here," I spit out. We've both been lucky so far but I can't put a thirteen-year-old kid at risk, even if it might help me. "You don't want to be next to me when we reach the ground floor." I hit 'two' for her. "Get off there and stay as long as you can. See if Mr. Deering's home to let you into his apartment for a while." Stew Deering, a World War II hero who's hard of hearing but loves to talk all the same, is like the building's mascot, the kind of person who would do anyone a favour.

"What's going on?" Dawn asks, her face sharpening to an unhappy point. "What do you mean you're in trouble?"

"People are after me." I bite down hard on my lip. "They're in the building. I need to get out of here, if I can. But right now you need to stay away from me." The bell chimes as the door opens on the second floor. Dawn stares at the doorway gap as if internally debating what I've told her.

"Do it," I urge, grabbing her arm and pulling her towards the door.

"Ouch!" Dawn jumps out, her eyes shooting daggers at me. Her annoyance barely registers. The look's already fading, morphing into something I don't expect. Dawn reaches into her pocket, her fingers emerging with a long key hanging from a pink rabbit's foot chain. "My mom's Sunbird is parked out front," she says, tossing the keychain into the elevator with me. "It's the red one. She's out cold. She won't notice it's missing for a while."

I'm speechless. Only when the door begins to close do I reach down for the keys and shout after her, "Thanks!"

Tonight, the elevator's usual snail pace feels like the speed of light. I hit the ground floor in no time, dart out of the elevator with my duffle bag still slung over my shoulder, and run full out for the street. Scanning left and right, for the Sunbird and the men who are after me, I careen onto the lawn and then the pavement. *Got it.* Dawn's mom is parked behind a Toyota about forty feet to my left.

I thrust the key roughly into the lock and turn, venturing a glance over my shoulder as I drop into the driver's seat and start the engine. A thin man in acid wash jeans is spurting after me. He must be the other one from the stairwell and I peel away from the curb so fast that the right side of the car scrapes the Toyota's bumper. I don't hazard another look back; I keep my eyes on the road ahead of me, flooring it onto Main Street, where I weave in and out of traffic like a maniac.

If they catch me, I won't be able to help Freya. We'll both have our brains turned inside-out. On the other hand, if I lose the director's men, how will I find her?

I don't know what to do. I need help.

I hang a right onto Broadway, zigzagging northwest on some kind of autopilot as I try to chase the director's logic in my head. Would he risk dragging Freya all the way back across the country, to where Canadian operations are based, before performing the procedure? Or could he have it done somewhere closer? And why now? Does it have something to do with the

Reagan shooting? The director told Freya that news of future environmental instability and the Toxo plague could destabilize current society. But we were never going to tell anyone about the U.N.A. and its plans. We would have kept quiet forever.

So many questions. And none of them are bringing me any closer to Freya. Should I head for the airport and hop on a plane to Toronto? Should I stop the car now and let them take me, just for the chance to get close to her?

I can't think. Can't work this out on my own. There's a guy at work I trust as much as I can trust anyone, aside from Freya. He ran away from his asshole parents in Lethbridge, Alberta when he was sixteen and has been working at Greasy Ryan's for the last couple of years. But Sheldon Ostil's only a year and a half older than I am. He wouldn't know how to deal with this. And he and his girlfriend had a baby girl just a couple of months ago. The last thing I want to do is bring trouble down on him and his family.

Wait. Suddenly I know who Freya would want me to go to. Dennis and Scott. I've only met them a handful of times, but I know where they live. They gave us their old couch when we moved in. Dennis has a bad back and can't lift anything heavier than a case of soda, so Scott and I hauled the couch out to his van, drove it over here, and then crammed it into the elevator.

I feel better having a plan of action and I continue in roughly the same direction, heading for Kitsilano while intermittently checking the rear-view mirror for any sign of a tail. Considering I don't know what kind of car the director's men are driving, it's not surprising that I don't notice anything strange. And then I lose the chance to notice much of anything because the car's crawling to a halt, the steering wheel turning heavy and unresponsive in my hands, and multiple dashboard warning lights flashing. I fight with the wheel, guiding the car sluggishly towards the curb.

It won't move another inch. The Sunbird's as dead as anything you'd find rusting in a junkyard. Stalled next to a white

Honda, I jump out of the Sunbird with my duffle bag and begin jogging towards Dennis and Scott's place, cursing out loud in frustration. I'm easier to spot on foot, but it's only about four blocks now and I don't have a choice.

I imagine what Freya would say, seeing me pant. Something about lung capacity and cigarettes. It's not the cigarettes making me breathless, though. It's the thought of never seeing her again.

When we arrived in Vancouver last March we were in the weirdest mental state imaginable, wanting to celebrate our survival but still in shock over the things we'd remembered. We rented the first apartment we stumbled on that didn't require references. It was a hellhole but the price was right and we knew it was just a stepping stone.

We found Christmas lights on sale at a bargain store and taped them up on the ceiling so the place wouldn't look as creepy in the dark. We didn't have a TV then. Just a portable radio with a built-in tape player. At night we'd turn off the lamps and ceiling lights, plug in the Christmas bulbs, and dance in the dark to the radio. Fast or slow songs, it didn't matter. Art of Noise, Elvis Costello, Madonna, the Ramones, Thin Lizzy, Alison Moyet, Billy Joel, Billy Idol, Billy Ocean, whatever. We danced to anything, including music it was nearly impossible to dance to. And when we were too tired to move but still couldn't sleep because our minds were running wild, we'd read to each other from a stack of books we'd bought at a second-hand store. It was always the scary stuff we wanted in those early days. Things like *Carrie*, *The Picture of Dorian Gray*, and *Dracula* made us feel more normal, like we weren't the only two people in the world who'd gone through something crazy.

Sometimes we read each other to sleep, one of us pushing the paperback at the other to take over when we couldn't force our own mouths to form words anymore. One time Freya even sang me to sleep with a medley of new wave tunes. The last thing I remembered hearing that night was her voice in my ear crooning, "So many adventures couldn't happen today. So many songs we forgot to play…"

I'd know that voice anywhere. Soft and strong and one-hundred-percent herself. In my head I hear Freya sliding over Alphaville's imagined synthesizer notes like it did that night and…

No, I can't. I need to concentrate on running. If I don't stop thinking about her I'll lose power in my legs, just like what happened with the car, and come crashing to the ground.

I push myself to go faster, my head swivelling on my neck, watching out for anyone taking extra notice of me. The daylight's fast disappearing and with it I feel Freya drift farther away. Rounding the corner onto Dennis and Scott's street undetected is a minor victory but I don't slow down. I hurl myself up their front steps and lean on the doorbell until Scott, sweaty and out of breath in shorts and a sleeveless T-shirt, opens the door for me.

"Jesus H. Christ, Robbie," he says, pushing his mop of blond hair off his face. "Where's the fire?"

I barge into the house with Scott, throwing my bag on their terracotta tile floor. "They took her," I croak, my hands on my knees as I lean over to fill my lungs. "Freya's gone."

SEVEN: 2063

When Kinnari told me Latham had scored tickets to the freshly announced Hendris concert in Chicago, my mind jumped to Freya. She'd be bouncing off the walls at the thought of seeing her idol. "She's leaving the music business and becoming a painter," Kinnari explained "She's been talking about it for the last two years and now she's finally doing it. This is going to be her farewell show—one-hundred-percent grounded—and we're going to be there live in the flesh, can you believe it!"

I don't think I'd seen Kinnari that excited since she was six, when Bening and Rosine got permission to buy our beagle, June. You could only qualify for a pet license if you were well-off. There'd been so many animals set loose in the thirties and forties, when people couldn't afford them any longer, that a massive culling had taken place across the U.N.A. and a stringent new law been passed. We'd had June— who was always wagging her tail and ready to play—for five years before she slipped out of the house one evening while Rosine was walking through the front door with her hands full.

With her implanted microchip, June should've been simple to locate. The SecRos took off behind her only minutes after she'd gone missing. They found the chip on a scrap of lawn near the main road. Someone must've carved it out from the skin between June's shoulder blades and nabbed her to sell on the black market. Kinnari cried every night for a week. I almost cried the night the SecRos told us myself.

"There's a ticket for you too," Kinnari said, grinning at me like her six-year-old self. "Latham has the transit documents and everything."

"When's the show?" I was all set to go. I'd feel better about Kinnari heading out to Chicago if I were with her. It wasn't like I could protect her from a bomb or virus, but that's one of those crazy things you think to yourself—that your presence has the power to keep someone safe.

"Tuesday. Completely last minute. But so many people want to go, the concert's already sold out."

Tuesday the twenty-eighth. The same night I'd promised Seneval I'd meet Minnow at Wyldewood. "This coming Tuesday. Are you sure?"

"This Tuesday," Kinnari repeated.

I leaned one of my shoulders against the wall. "You know Bening and Rosine will never say yes." If I couldn't go I didn't really want Kinnari there, either. She'd be on the Zeph for ages. What if terrorists targeted it again?

Kinnari rolled her eyes. "I know they won't. But they don't need to know about it. And you know as well as I do this concert is exactly the kind of thing they would've been into when they were our age." She pressed her palms together and gave me a pleading look, not unlike the way June used to stare at me when I was eating. "Don't guilt me, okay? It's not going to change my mind."

"It's a bad idea. Things are so scary out there lately."

"You didn't think it was a bad idea a minute ago. And things are always scary."

Where was the ninety-one-year-old side of my sister when I needed it?

"Come on, Garren," she prodded. "I can't believe you're not jumping at the chance to do this. It's Hendris. She's a legend in her own time. In the future people will feel about her how you feel about Springsteen and David Bowie."

I laughed. "She's not *that* good."

"Yes, she is. You just won't let yourself see it because you think all the best stuff is in the past." I only thought that because most of the best stuff *was* in the past. Besides, Kinnari was nearly as big a fan of old music and movies as I was. My sister charged ahead, not allowing me a chance to object. "And we're asking Freya too. You're starting to like her, right? We'll have a great time, the four of us."

"I never disliked Freya."

"I know. I only meant that it seemed like you two were starting to connect on my birthday. She's not how we thought." We'd never really talked about Freya before but I understood what Kinnari was saying. Our grounded friends and the ideas we were raised with aligned us with a certain point of view, one that didn't usually think highly of politicians or the corporations that had created the SecRos and DefRos. I'd despised the idea of Luca Kallas without ever having met him.

"Yeah, I know." That wistful expression of Freya's I'd spied during "Heart of Gold" flashed behind my eyes. "And maybe the four of us can hang out some other time, but I can't go on Tuesday. There's this thing I have to do."

"What thing?" Kinnari demanded.

"It's private. I can't say."

"Private." My sister's face turned impish. "Anyone I know?"

I shook my head and glanced at the floor. It was easier just to let her think this was about a girl. "I'm not giving you a name so you can forget it."

"I must know her if you're being so secretive."

"Still not telling." I smirked as I looked Kinnari in the eye. "The important thing is that it's better if you don't go to the show. It's so far away. And a lie like that will come out sometime. You know how you are about telling Bening and Rosine the truth." Kinnari's dedication to it was almost compulsive. She'd spilled the news about her and Latham seeing each other within twenty-four hours of the onset of their relationship, despite suspecting our mothers might disapprove because of his reputation. "You'll crack and tell them."

"I won't *crack*, Garren. And it's only five hours on the Zephyr. It's not like I'm going up to Hudson Bay or something." In reality a trip to Hudson Bay would probably be safer. Millions of people had moved up over the former Canadian border since the evacuation, but the U.N.A.'s far north was still sparsely populated and therefore attracted less terrorist attacks. "So you just go do your private thing on Tuesday and I'll do mine, okay?"

My foot scuffed against the floor. "Fine." I sighed noisily.

After that I didn't waste my breath trying to talk Kinnari out of the Hendris concert. She was going and that was it.

The next day I found out Freya couldn't make it out to Chicago for the show, either. She was being punished for fighting with her mother and was only permitted to leave for school, so it would just be Kinnari and Latham heading out East for the concert. Now I wish I'd done things differently—done anything to stop Kinnari from going with him. But at the time I left things alone. Ultimately I thought she had the right to do what she wanted.

On the morning of August twenty-eighth, Kinnari left early. In 2063 the U.N.A. had school throughout the year, but the summer months were full of optional days students could use to complete their required volunteer hours. With Latham's connections he'd arranged to make it look like he and Kinnari were doing a twelve-hour stint at the Fairfield social welfare camp that day. I told my sister to be careful and stick close to Latham, and in return she told me she hoped whoever I was spending the evening with was worth missing the concert for.

When Kinnari said that I pictured Seneval's dark eyes. So close I could see my own reflection in them. I felt a dull ache under my ribs.

"She's worth it," I said.

At school later I was distracted, and my friend Mara kept poking me to get my attention. Mara was always physical when we were near each other in public but the few times we'd gotten close in private had seemed strained. It'd been simpler to put the other side of our relationship aside and just stay friends. "What is with you today?" she asked, leaning into me in the school hallway between classes. "You're like someone in gushi withdrawal."

The generation before us was full of gushi burnouts. It was the reason the government had caved to the grounded movement and reintroduced the old school system. So many of the kids educated solely on gushi had breakdowns, even the politicians had to admit gushi use needed to be restricted. It was part of the reason they made the Cursed work.

"I'm just bored," I lied. "It seems pointless to be here when we're so close to starting at college." I was due in New York in only a week.

"I'm going to miss you," she said. "It'll be strange to be in Billings without you." Mara was going to Montana State University to become a teacher. She wasn't excited about it but it was the best of her three career options.

"We'll still talk," I assured her. On gushi. No one could avoid it completely and expect to function in 2063. The trick was not to let it swallow you. But my thoughts had already started to drift back to Seneval and my meeting with Isaac.

I was so wound up about what he'd tell me that I had my trans take me to Wyldewood straight from school and was hours early for my meeting with Isaac. I let a guy twice my age show me patio furniture and twenty different pairs of shoes. Then I went and sat on the beach in the swimsuit I'd just bought, one the personal shopper had assured me utilized the latest technology.

The advantage of the false sun they used at Wyldewood was that it was never too strong. Everyone else on the beach with me was much older but looked a decade or two younger than the sixty or seventy-year-olds from 1986. They had their Bio-nets to thank for that. I dug my toes into the sand and noticed it wasn't the weird fake stuff they usually had other places, the kind that wouldn't stick to you. If you weren't thorough about brushing the Wyldewood sand off it'd still be clinging to your skin when you got home.

Because Kinnari and I had been to the beach in Lewistown and West Glacier with our moms on all-clear days a few times, I knew Wyldewood's beach experience was a couple of shades closer to reality than gushi but still not entirely right. The seagulls never shit, the wind never blew sand in your face, and the waves had a programmed uniformity to them, something you'd only realize if you'd been staring at them for twenty minutes straight like I had.

I don't know how Seneval knew I was out on the beach but she stalked over to me, tearing my gaze from the water as she looked me quickly up and down. I felt at a disadvantage in my swimsuit and the sight of her filled my nostrils with the imagined scent of cloves. To this day the thought of Seneval or anything to do with art class still conjures the smell for me.

"You're early," she noted, plopping down next to me. "Minnow's not ready to see you yet." Seneval's hands were making circles in the sand. "He's finishing up a shift."

I nodded like I was in no hurry. "And you—are you in the middle of a shift?" I'd been hoping to see her but hadn't expected it. She looked tired.

"I'm done for the day," she replied, one of her fingers brushing accidentally against mine in the sand. If it'd been Mara I wouldn't have thought about it twice, but this was Seneval, and my hand jerked.

"Nervous?" she asked. "You don't have to do this, you know. You can just go to New York and leave us all behind. You haven't done anything irreversible yet."

Both of our faces were pointed at the waves. It seemed easier to speak that way.

"I think you're really brave," I admitted, knowing that she wouldn't want to hear it. "Losing your parents, having to take care of your sister in the camp, and then dedicating yourself to this gateway work. I want to be like that. I want to know I'm doing something good."

In the distance two seagulls swooped down low over the water, their paths crossing in a graceful arc. For a split second I forgot none of this was real.

"I'm not so brave," she said. "My life took a turn that woke me up, that's all. I might've stayed a sleepwalker, like Silas described, if my parents hadn't disappeared."

"Lots of people have hard lives," I countered. "It doesn't wake them all up. There's something inside you that made you choose this."

"You're idealizing me." Seneval smiled out of one side of her mouth. "It's nice but it's not the whole story. Just be careful, okay? Don't try to be a hero. I'd feel bad if something happened to you."

I scratched the back of my neck. I knew I couldn't be getting a burn under the false sun. It only felt that way. "You should be careful too."

I risked a look at Seneval and saw her head bob. "We can wait upstairs in the domestic quarters, if you want. You can see how the other half lives. Minnow will come get you when it's time."

I slipped into the changing room to put my clothes back on. Then Seneval led me upstairs, to the floor where the majority of Wyldewood employees lived. Most of the doors were closed—unlike in the social welfare camps, people had their own rooms—but Seneval showed me a communal kitchen area. Someone had tried to make it homey by decorating the walls with food-related artwork. One of the pieces was a vintage-style poster of a food group chart complete with illustrations of things like a block of cheese and head of lettuce.

My stomach rumbled in response and Seneval reached into one of the lower cupboards to pull out a jomange for me. Popular and highly nutritious, the scientist-created fruit looked like a courgette but had a sweet citrus taste. I chomped into it as we edged down the long corridor, wiping away the juice that ran down my chin.

"Here," she said, stopping beside a door identical to all the others except it was labelled #43. She pressed her left palm flat against the door, a DNA scan unlocking it. I caught a three-second glance of Seneval's room—a simple assortment of light brown living room furniture contained within a space of what couldn't have been more than sixty-four square feet—before Isaac Monroe's voice carried along the hallway.

"Let me take this guy off your hands," he said with a business-like smile.

I turned to Seneval to say goodbye. "Go on," she prompted. "I'll see you on Friday."

"Right. See you then." I moved away from her room and heard the door close behind me.

"I'm at the end of the hall," Isaac said. "The luxury suite." His stiff smile began to loosen into something more genuine. "That's a joke. By the way, Cleo Dixon was happy to get that plate. She wanted me to thank you. Malyck's back at the camp now with her. He couldn't believe you'd come to Fairfield to bring the dish back, not even knowing who he was." We'd reached Isaac's door and he raised his hand for scanning. "Most people wouldn't have done that."

My shoulders bounced as if to say it was nothing. I followed Isaac into a room no larger than Seneval's. Because I had more time to examine it, I was able to spot the rectangular section of wall, about three feet from the ceiling, where Isaac's bed would emerge from when he required it. A lot of smaller properties were set up with retracting beds to make the best use of space. Seneval's room was likely the same.

Although I wasn't hungry anymore, I took a second bite of my jomange as Isaac urged me to sit down. "What happens when I get to New York?" I asked impatiently. "Who do I have to talk to?"

"There's still the vote." Isaac furrowed his brow. "Seneval didn't tell you that?"

"She told me." I'd just assumed Isaac's desire to talk to me meant the vote would swing my way and he wanted to discuss the next step.

"And then it could be some time before you're called upon to do anything," Isaac added. "The warren doesn't rush when it comes to who they can trust."

The warren. I'd heard that name for one of the core groups responsible for retaliations against the U.N.A. government on the Dailies, but it had never been directly mentioned in the gateway classes. Up to now I'd half deluded myself into thinking I was involving myself with some shadowy but more benevolent organization.

Hearing Isaac say otherwise made me feel like I'd been pushed out into the elements during a cyclone. This wasn't a game. If I threw my fate in with the warren I'd always be at risk.

"How do I know I can trust them?" I asked. "They've killed people." Two civilians had died at the Ro factory bombing three and a half years earlier. The government had lumped the warren's actions in with foreign-led attacks, terming the bombing 'terrorism.' Security forces later captured one of the women responsible and wiped and covered her before shipping her out to a radioactive spill site in Arkansas the government had been attempting to clean up for over a decade. Either the woman had one foot in the grave by now or she was already dead.

Isaac calmly shook his head. "Only ever in self-defence. The Dailies twist the truth. It's what they do. By definition, taking action can't be without risk. Every cause worth fighting for has casualties. You've already said you didn't want to be responsible for hurting anyone, and no one will ask you to. People do what they can and everyone is comfortable with different things. So if you want to go back to the official grounded movement campaigns and their slow-motion crawl towards change, that's what you should do."

"I didn't say that." The jomange was turning brown in my hand where I'd bitten into it. "I want change. I don't want to live in a police state. That's not what this country was meant to be."

"That's not what any country is meant to be." Isaac's hands covered his kneecaps. "You want change, but you don't want it to be messy. Don't you think we all feel that way? Maybe there's just not enough at stake for you personally to involve yourself. It was different for me."

I waited for him to explain. There was Wyldewood sand in my shoes, caught between my toes, and for a second I wondered if New York and law school might be enough for me, learning to help people the way Michael Neal did. But what if I didn't live long enough to get my law degree? Another nuclear attack could spell the end at any moment. Maybe that meant ultimately nothing mattered, but I didn't feel that way.

"My father's David Bruck Monroe." Isaac cocked his head. "You know who he is, don't you?" Of course I did. His company had built the Zephyr as well as Montana's commuter train lines. But if David Bruck Monroe was Isaac's father, what was Isaac doing working in Wyldewood, and why did he look the way he did? It didn't make any sense. He should've been born perfect.

Puzzled, I nodded slowly.

"What you wouldn't know is that my mother was an illegal," he continued. "My father didn't realize it either, when he first got involved with her. She'd told him she was a college student from Kansas, completing her degree out of state. But without the Bio-net to protect her, she was soon pregnant."

So that was why Isaac was so short. No one had fiddled with his DNA.

Isaac hunched over in his chair. There was no window in his room, but the lighting mimicked daylight, his eyes shining as if a hazy late afternoon sun were wafting down on him. "When he found out, he reported her. He wasn't in love with her—he just had a taste for grounded sex—so it meant nothing to him to have her disappear. But the government case worker who was assigned to her got a high-profile lawyer involved. Because of my father's money, everything was decided in private. It was ruled that I had the right to U.N.A. citizenship. On those grounds my mother was allowed to remain on U.N.A. soil until I was born, at which time she'd either be wiped or expelled."

A familiar guilt crept into my ribcage. Isaac's story was even more tragic than Seneval's. I had everything; Isaac hadn't been so lucky. "What happened to her?" I asked.

"While she was in custody waiting for my birth, she tried to run. She fled north into Canada. It'd only been a part of the U.N.A. for a few years then and a lot of former Canadians didn't feel any loyalty to the U.N.A. government. They were known to harbour rebels and she thought she'd try her luck in finding a sympathizer. Which she accomplished. I was born on an Alberta farm where the family made a habit of harbouring illegals. My mother and I were there for another five months before the SecRos caught up with us. They might never have found us except a local from the town was suspicious of the family she was staying with and turned in their names."

What he'd been describing had happened so many years ago, but an old pain whistled through the words. "I've never been able to find out where they sent her after that," he added, his voice like wood worn smooth. "The government handed me over to my father to bring me up. I was raised by a succession of Ros and human nannies he hired. I was ten before I even found out who my mother really was. My father had told me she'd been killed by a terrorist virus—he said that's what had made me the way I am."

The air in the room had grown stale. We each paused to slowly inhale. "Are you still in touch with him—your father?" I asked.

"I can't write him off entirely. His name has influence. How do you think I get into the camps on a regular basis?"

"But why are you working here, then? Obviously you don't need the money."

"*Obviously.*" Isaac echoed. "You could say it's more window dressing than a real job. It has its organizational advantages too. And my father gave up trying to make me into anything he could understand a long time ago. He's more than happy to forget about me most of the time. But enough about me, I need to know about you."

"I don't want to talk about my family. I don't want them involved in this."

Isaac inclined his head in a sign of understanding. "You don't have to tell me about them. I want to know about *you.* Why and what you think you can do for us."

"I've already told Seneval and the other gateway voters that."

Isaac's jaw set like I was beginning to try his patience. "It doesn't matter. Now you're talking to me."

Was it a bad sign that I hadn't done any work for the organization yet and was already wondering if I could completely trust them? They hadn't given me any solid reason not to. It would be impossible to help the movement in any meaningful way without having to trust someone at some point.

And so I told Isaac about the indelible feeling inside me that said things weren't right in the U.N.A. and that they hadn't been for decades. I told him if we were bound for destruction I still believed it was better to look the reality of the planet in the eye than to check into gushi and absolve ourselves of responsibility. I even described what listening to Arlette Courtemanche make people cry had done to me. Her, Malyck Dixon's broken plates, and hundreds of other things I'd seen.

Then I repeated what I'd said at the classes about wanting to help exchange information and keep eco-refugees safe but that I didn't believe in bombing and violence. Isaac listened without interrupting, and when I was out of breath and didn't have an unsaid thought left in my head that related to the grounded movement, I stopped and stared down at the bruised remains of the jomange Seneval had given me.

"Okay, then," Isaac said with a finality that told me I'd never see him again. "Thanks for coming to see me, Garren."

"That's it?" I wanted a hint in one direction or the other—were they going to accept me?

"For now. You might hear more in Friday's class." Isaac pointed at my jomange. "I'll take that for you if you're finished." I let him ease the fruit out of my hand before taking a step towards the door.

Alone in the corridor I shook my head, annoyed with myself and Isaac. Me for not being more certain about what I was doing and him for not giving me the thing I wasn't positive I wanted.

Head reeling, I staggered towards Seneval's room. I wanted to talk things over if she'd let me. Let her vouch for the warren. There were still hours until curfew.

Seneval's door was ajar. I noticed before I reached it and thought I must have had the wrong room. But no, it was #43. I knocked as I pushed the door open. It caught on something and I peeked inside, simultaneously saying Seneval's name and spying the body crumpled on the floor. *Hers*. It was Seneval's left foot that the door had snagged on. She was lying on her side with her head tilted at an unnatural angle, one of her arms folded underneath her torso and the other splayed to display the inside of her thin wrist. I dropped to my knees and gazed into her eyes. They were open but showed no signs of life. It was like peering into a pitch-black room that had no windows, no lights. She wasn't breathing, either. I'd never seen a body that still. I held my hand to her mouth to be sure, the way I'd seen people do in old movies.

Nothing. No warmth or flow of air from her lungs. Technically, she was dead. My ears started ringing and white blotches danced behind my eyes as I slipped into shock. The loss wormed its way into my stomach, making me choke.

No. This had to be a mistake. People didn't die easily in 2063. Not if they had Bio-nets and as a U.N.A. citizen, Seneval surely had one. There was no equivalent of the early twenty-first century anti-vaccine movement in the future; even the most fanatical grounded members didn't risk their lives by denying themselves a Bio-net.

Where I'm from, the first thing people did in an emergency was dive into gushi to contact the SecRos. No matter what you thought of the Ros, they put 1986's emergency services to shame. But the shock had turned my brain to pulp; the Ros didn't even occur to me.

Seneval had smiled at me on the beach. She'd made me believe I could be something more. She'd been right here, alive and well, when I'd walked down the corridor with Isaac.

Instinctively, I pushed back through the doorway and sprinted for Isaac's room. My shoulder hurt where it had collided with Seneval's door and I winced as I raised my hand to knock wildly. *How had this happened?* It couldn't be true; despite appearances I must have been wrong.

Isaac opened up for me, his eyes wary. "What now, Garren?"

"It's Seneval—" My unfinished sentence sliced at the air, my throat closing in distress.

We careened back to her room, my mouth and eyes gaping and her door still ajar like I'd left it. Isaac shut it firmly behind us and knelt beside her body. He took Seneval's wrist, feeling for her pulse while I crouched behind him.

"Did you send for the SecRos?" he demanded, turning to glance at me over his shoulder.

"No. I'll do that now." I cursed myself for letting precious moments elapse.

"Wait." Isaac smoothed his right hand over each of Seneval's eyes, gently closing them. Then he swivelled on his knees and stared at me with a pained expression. "She's gone. They can't help her."

"But they need to investigate." My voice cracked like a dead branch about to catch fire. "Someone her age doesn't just keel over dead."

"I think someone snapped her neck," Isaac said quietly. "Spinal shock. It must have happened fast; otherwise she would've sent for the SecRos." He paused and sat pensively back on his heels. "I've heard of something like this happening before."

"Look, just let me tell the SecRos. We're wasting time. Whoever it is could be getting away." If it'd been anyone but Isaac next to me, I wouldn't have stopped to debate the issue. But his opinion had weight; Seneval would have listened to him. That knowledge made me pause.

"Unless it was you." Isaac's unblinking stare turned cold.

Desperation ricocheted through my chest, sadness immediately surging in to cover it. "Come on, you know it wasn't me. I left here with you earlier."

"And obviously you came back to her room. I'm just telling you how it looks. Or how it could be made to look. Don't you see?"

No, I didn't. Did he expect us to just walk away and leave her body sprawled on the floor?

Isaac bowed his head. "You have to trust me on this. I've heard about other murders like this one. Security forces could nail you for her death if you're not careful. You need to get out of here immediately."

I didn't move. My shoulder had stopped throbbing. Either the Bio-net had already healed it or I hadn't hit it as hard as I'd thought.

"Look, I'm going to spell it out for you and then you need to stay away for your own safety." Isaac folded his hands in his lap and said, "I believe someone's infiltrated the movement. This is the third death like this I know of in the last couple of months. In one of the other cases, security took someone from the Sidney camp and framed him."

"How do you know he wasn't guilty?" My eyes kept flicking to Seneval's face. The room was so small there was nowhere you could look and *not* see her body. I couldn't believe she was gone.

I was ready to snap the neck of whoever had done this to her. So much for wanting to avoid violence.

"Because I knew this guy," Isaac said. "He wasn't the type. Didn't have an ounce of aggression in him. And the likelihood that there's more than one person running around Montana breaking the necks of members of the grounded movement is slim. I don't know who is doing this or why but I'm making it my business to find out. And you"—Isaac stood to his full height. From my position on the floor he looked as imposing as any politician I'd ever seen—"you need to go now or you might not be able to go at all."

"What about you?" I couldn't think straight. I'd probably never have seen Seneval again after Friday's class but I'd have known she was somewhere out there. The thought of that seemed so hopeful that its opposite crushed a part of me I couldn't name.

"Don't worry about me. I have an important name to protect me and people who will be happy to give me an alibi if I need it." Isaac watched me stand up next to him, nodding his approval. "I'm sorry we couldn't work things out. Maybe we'll catch up with each other down the road, but for now you need to steer clear." He flinched as his gaze drifted down to Seneval's body on the floor. "This should never have happened to her, of all people. She was so generous, so intelligent."

I didn't need to add that she was brave. He knew that too.

"I can't leave her here like this," I whispered. The second I left the room, her fate would become real and irreversible. As long as I stayed, Seneval was only dead to me. Isaac and me. The idea didn't make sense, but it was all I had.

"Yes, you can. It's what she'd want."

Even in my shock, I thought I knew the truth when I heard it, and I fought to find my voice. "Goodbye, Isaac."

As I spun to leave he said to my back, "You should call me Minnow now. I'm Minnow to my friends." It was the last thing I thought I'd ever hear him say.

EIGHT: 1986

"Freya?" Scott repeats, puzzled as he follows me into the living room. "Who's Freya?"

"I mean *Holly*. Freya's her real name. We had to—"

Just then Dennis reels into the room in a light linen suit, asking, "What was the ruckus?" His expression changes from annoyance to alarm when he sees me. "Robbie, is everything all right? We got a phone call from Holly a little earlier telling us about her concussion. She's not worse, is she?"

"Not worse, she's gone."

"What?" Dennis and Scott ask in stereo. They stand close to each other while I face off against them, hurriedly telling them about the men who took Freya. The whole truth would only make me sound like someone in need of a rubber room, but from the sketchy details I offer, Dennis says he assumes that Holly and I somehow got ourselves involved with criminal elements back East.

"We're not criminals," I counter. "But we know things they don't want to come out. And now that they have her I need help finding her."

Dennis's eyes widen. "We have to call the police. You two should've been under their protection already. You would've been safer."

I shake my head. "Not from these people. You don't understand what they're like. And now they'll question Freya and try to find out what she knows."

"But the worst has happened," Dennis insists. "These people

have gotten their hands on Holly. There's no advantage to keeping secrets from the police anymore."

Under my jacket my sweatshirt is clinging to my skin, damp with sweat. "No one would believe us," I say truthfully. "That's one of the reasons we never told. The things we know...the police would think we're crazy."

Scott's left foot is twitching. He leans anxiously forwards, one hand smearing at the beads of perspiration on his forehead. "If you'd never be believed why are these people so worried? It doesn't add up."

"So I'm lying, is that it?" My heart can't beat any faster but my voice spikes. It's just like with Isaac that time in Seneval's room. *Accusations punching at my ribs.*

"No, of course not." Dennis reaches out to grip my arm. "You said you need help and we're just trying to figure things out."

"I need help *now*." The director's people would be travelling in a pack. They'd have money and weapons and they'd be secretive, but they'd have to have dealings with someone over here at some point. Somebody must have an idea where they are. "We don't have time for this."

Scott's sagging jaw and bewildered eyes say it all. I should never have come here. Dennis and Scott probably think I killed Holly and buried her body in Stanley Park.

"Do you have cash?" I snap. "Can I take one of your cars?" Somehow I need to find the men from my apartment and follow them back to Freya without being taken myself. Dennis and Scott won't help me; they don't even believe me. The enormity of the job ahead of me sucks the air from my lungs.

Dennis and Scott trade wary looks. "I'll get you my keys," Scott says woodenly. "They're upstairs." He slips out of the room, leaving Dennis and I staring at each other.

The sound of Scott's halting footfall on the steps flashes me back to the afternoon Freya and I visited the man we thought was our grandfather. He went upstairs, leaving us in the living room too. He went to call someone that would take us away. "Is Scott calling the police?" I growl.

Dennis's hands compulsively smooth down his linen blazer, like I'm scaring him. "He's only getting the keys like you wanted," he says, his watery grey gaze flitting away from my face.

Upstairs I hear a door close. *Dennis is lying.* There's no doubt in my mind that Scott has a phone in his hand. "Holly told me you guys were like uncles to her," I say. "If that's true you should be able to tell that I'd do anything for her." I never had fathers but everything Freya said about Dennis and Scott led me to believe that if I had, I'd have wanted my fathers to be like them. The probably think they're doing the right thing by Freya but I can't help feeling disappointed in them.

"*Freya,*" Dennis corrects, like he's trying to trip me up. "You said her real name was Freya."

"I probably shouldn't have told you her real name. And you wouldn't believe the story of who she really is, either. But what you should know is that she hasn't done anything wrong. She doesn't deserve what these people will do to her."

Dennis freezes like I've begun to get through to him. If I had more time, maybe I could convince him to help me. But with every moment, Freya's likely carried farther away from us. I watch him extend his arms, palms up in a show of helplessness. "You have to understand how this sounds," he murmurs.

Before I can respond we both hear a creak from the stairs. "Just do me one favour," I plead. "Don't tell the police anything about Holly and me when they get here. Tell them you thought you saw a prowler or something."

I stalk into the entranceway and snatch my duffle bag from the floor. "Wait!" Scott cries from behind me. I swing around to catch sight of Dennis grabbing Scott's arm.

"Just let him go," Dennis advises. Scott stalls next to me, suspicion hanging heavy in his jowls. "What if there's truth in what he's saying?" Dennis continues.

"And what if there's not and the police could find her?" Scott fires back. "What if he's made the entire thing up and—"

My fingers reach for the front door at the same moment we hear a series of sharp raps from the other side. Just my luck. The cops must've already had a cruiser in the area. Dennis taps his lips with his finger and glowers a warning at Scott. The three of us ease away from the door, Dennis whispering, "You can go out the back. I'll show you the way."

"This isn't right," Scott complains, stopping in his tracks.

"Just give him a chance," Dennis begs on my behalf. "You know as well as I do that Holly's never had a bad thing to say about him."

Dennis leads me through the kitchen and to the door to the backyard, Scott remaining behind. Without a look back I race out through the doorway, past Dennis and Scott's tulip bed, garden furniture, and barbecue. Nearby, a lawn mower's running and kids at play are shouting into the night. It's the end to another normal day for some people.

I hoist myself over the back fence and into a laneway composed of household garages. Scott could be pointing the police my way already. I snake down side streets at first, then make a run for Cornwall Avenue where I'll have half a chance of catching a cab or a bus.

On Cornwall a couple about my age are out walking with their hands fused together, the girl in threadbare denim shorts and the guy in a Dire Straits concert T-shirt. The girl looks sideways at me as I pass, probably because I'm moving too quickly not to draw attention. For almost every piece of bad luck I've had today there's been a good piece to counter it, and down the road I see a city bus. It doesn't matter where it's going; I just need to get out of here. I head quickly for the closest bus stop, only twenty feet away. Within thirty seconds I'm climbing the steps and dropping coins into the fare box, no police or thugs to stop me.

I wasn't intending to go back to the apartment, anyway, but

now I have to assume that Scott's made that impossible. If the police start searching for me, Greasy Ryan's and Il Baccaro won't be safe either. I'm on my own. It's exponentially tougher than when Freya and I were on the run together. All we had to do then was get away, Freya's sixth sense our early warning system. Even then we wouldn't have made it without old Freya. It took two Freyas to get us clear.

For the first time since they snatched Freya I wonder just how they were able to do it. She should've sensed them coming. The night a junkie tried to jump me outside the bar after closing I was able to dodge him and get away without a scratch because she'd called to give me the details of the attack before it'd happened. In February she saw Scott clip a cyclist with his van. The woman's leg was scraped up where she fell on it but she was otherwise unharmed, just like Freya had seen in her vision. And there were less important things she sensed all the time. So many that I got the impression she didn't mention half of them.

But she would've told me if she'd seen any danger on the horizon. The concussion must have stopped her premonitions, at least temporarily. Either the director knew that or he got lucky.

Because it's long after rush hour, the bus quickly nears downtown. I jump off at Powell Street, my brain itemizing the only solid facts I know about these people.

1. The two Toronto addresses where Henry Newland (the man who they had pretending to be my grandfather) lived up until the end of February, 1985.
2. Nancy Bolton's employer, as of February 1985: Sheridan College, Brampton. Nancy was the one Freya met at the Eaton Centre. Nancy swore she was followed and that she hadn't turned Freya in. The money Nancy gave Freya helped land us that shitty first apartment and get on our feet.
3. The address and phone number of my "aunt"

Beverley as of February 1985.

4. The work address for Doctor Byrne (who acted as family doctor to both Freya and me) as of February 1985.

With Henry, Nancy, Beverley, and Doctor Byrne pretending to be fixtures in our mothers' lives, it's possible that they're still playing their parts in Toronto. Worry for our mothers has kept me and Freya from calling home or contacting any of these people, but now I have to take the risk. Beverley and I were never what you would call close, but she seemed to care about me and Rosine, which only makes her fraud feel like a bigger slap in the face. Henry isn't interested in helping; I learned my lesson with him last time. According to what the director told Freya, everyone here working for the U.N.A. is biologically incapable of sharing information about the future. If they try, a wipe sequence will be triggered by their Bio-nets, clearing their memory. But I don't need anyone to tell me about the future, I only want to know where Freya is.

Beverley's is the only number I know by heart so I decide to start with her, squeezing into the nearest payphone and feeding it a chunk of coins. On the third ring the woman who'd been pretended to be family to Rosine and me picks up.

"Are they listening to us now?" I ask, trusting that she recognizes my voice.

Silence.

"Did you know they've taken Freya?"

"I didn't know," she replies tonelessly. "I'm sorry."

Sure, she is. She sounds like someone who couldn't give a fuck. Almost like a SecRo. "Why would they want her when we haven't said anything to anyone?" I press. "And where would they take her?"

"I don't know the answers to those questions, either," she says.

Outside the phone booth, two women in stilettos, short

skirts, and bleached blond hair totter by. *Working girls.* I'm on the border of the bad side of town. Everybody needs somewhere to be and in Vancouver the Lower East Side is often where the troubled people end up. It's just as gloomy a place as the U.N.A.'s camps for the Cursed.

A short guy with a hoodie pulled up over his head speeds up to overtake the women and as I begin to steer my gaze away from the sidewalk scene, something about him makes me give him a second look. In the fraction of a second it takes to refocus I lose the brief opportunity to look the guy in the face. Phone pressed to my ear, I watch the man stride away. There's a confidence and sense of purpose to his gait that seem at odds with the direction he's walking in. He doesn't look like a guy on his way to buy drugs or rent a body. He looks like…

The scent of cloves overcomes me. I drop the telephone. It dangles by its cord as I race after him, zooming by the prostitutes. He begins to speed up as the distance between us closes. Maybe I'm wrong about him. Most people will run if they feel like they're being chased. But after what happened today I'm not about to let him go; I can't afford to second guess myself.

The rage and helplessness I've bottled up inside me erupt into action. I hurl myself at the guy's midsection on the sidewalk, my arms closing around him and my weight plummeting us both to the cement.

I rip the hood from his head as I flip him over. The prostitutes have caught up with us but give us a wide berth, lowering their voices as they pass. A lone raindrop lands on my ear and in the street a car roars past, the strains of INXS's "What You Need" spilling from its open windows.

Isaac's Monroe's baffled eyes stare up at me. "Garren," he says incredulously, "is it really you?"

NINE: 2063

Because no one but the killer, Minnow, and I knew Seneval was dead yet, I was able to make it safely out of Wyldewood, back to my trans, and onto the I-90 without attracting any attention. The sight of Seneval's lifeless eyes had been burnt into my mind and I was cold all the way home. When I walked through the front door Rosine took one look at me and wanted to know what was wrong.

"Nothing," I lied. Rosine's disbelieving gaze spurred me to revise my answer. "Mara was getting emotional about me leaving for New York."

"I thought you were at Lior's."

"I was." My friend, Lior, was the cover story I'd used. "Mara dropped by there to talk to me."

"Oh." Rosine's eyes popped. "I didn't think you two were still as close as you used to be. Are you upset about having to say goodbye to her too?"

"I don't want to talk about it right now, okay?" I just needed my mother to buy my excuse and leave me alone. "It's been sort of a rough night."

Rosine touched my arm. "Things will probably look better in the morning."

"Yeah. I think I'll just head up to bed." I felt Rosine's sympathetic stare cling to my shoulders as I walked away.

She must have warned Bening not to bother me because I didn't see either of them again for the rest of the night. Upstairs in my room I did a zillion push-ups, knowing I wouldn't be able to sleep unless I could trigger exhaustion. I kept trying to count the push-ups in my head and then losing track of what number I was on. Seneval had likely opened the door for whoever murdered her; otherwise the SecRos would've been on the scene as soon as a security breach was detected. That meant she probably knew the person who'd killed her.

Now her little sister would have lost her entire family. And my hands were tied; I had no way of helping her. I couldn't even finish my vetting process at the Billings Library and do my part for the grounded movement.

Then I started to wonder about the old people who might have seen me and Seneval together on the Wyldewood beach. Would the investigators try to track me down from their descriptions? Would they frame me like they'd framed the man at the Sidney camp?

I couldn't stop thinking. Seneval's eyes. The heavy smell of cloves. The feel of sand still trapped between my toes. The gritty thoughts and sensations washed over me all night long.

I didn't once turn my mind to Kinnari in Chicago with Latham. I had no idea anything had gone wrong until I woke up to the sight of my sister staring at me from a spot right next to my window.

Early morning light was wafting into my room, but I thought I must have been dreaming. Her eyes didn't look right. They were cold and barren, like Seneval's had been at the end.

"I'm sorry," Kinnari said, bursting into tears. "I shouldn't be near you. I just came to say goodbye."

"What're you talking about?" It wasn't a dream after all. My sister was unravelling in front of me. I'd never seen her look this upset, not even when we'd lost June.

"I have *something*," she cried, backing away from me. "There was an outbreak at the concert. People acting in ways I've never seen."

I sat up fast. "Are you sure?"

"I'm positive." Kinnari had begun to giggle. She scratched at the side of her face so harshly that her nails left two jagged red lines at her temple. "I'm sorry." She bit back her breath with a gasp. "It's hard to control. I can feel the sickness squirming inside me." She distanced herself further, her heels squeaking on my floor. "They quarantined the entire state of Illinois. They're going to try to kill everyone to make this go away."

"They won't do that," I argued. "The scientists will cure you."

"No, no." Kinnari laughed manically. The sound sent a shiver down the back of my neck. "You don't understand. If it wasn't for Latham, the Ros would have us now."

"Just to treat you. Not to hurt you." She was acting completely irrationally and I needed to calm her down. Besides, I never thought the government would take it that far. The Denver terrorist deaths were an anomaly; them aside, the scientists had had the terrorist-engineered Mossegrim virus under control for years. Even the newest strains could usually be cured if the virus was detected within the first forty-eight hours. Whatever Kinnari had, reason told me there was a fair chance the scientists could heal her.

"No, no, you're not listening," Kinnari hissed. "They'd be chopping us up into tiny pieces if they had their way and maybe they'd be right."

"Have you talked to Rosine and Bening?" I slowed my words to counter her panic.

Kinnari shook her head with an abandon that sent her hair twirling in multiple directions. "You do it for me. Tell them I'm sorry!" She ran out the door and into the hall, me bounding out of bed to chase after her.

"I'm sorry," she kept screaming. "I'm sorry."

And none of it was her fault. All she'd done was go to Chicago to see a concert.

I knew I'd be able to catch her. I had longer legs and on top of that, she was sick. But Kinnari made it easy for me when she flipped on the stairs, landing in an awkward arrangement of her own limbs on the first floor. She winced and cradled her hand like it'd been broken or sprained. As I caught up with her she shoved her face towards the hardwood floor. "Don't get close," she shouted.

I heard footsteps charging down after us. The commotion must have woken Rosine and Bening.

"Stay away from her!" I yelled, twice as loud as Kinnari had been. I hadn't listened when she'd said it to me, but now that my mothers were at risk, I needed to keep them safe. "She's infected with something. She was at the Hendris concert in Chicago. The terrorists must have released a new virus."

Rosine tried to edge past me but I held her back. "We can't, Mom. We don't know what she has. It's not safe."

"He's right," Bening said. "Kinnari, honey. I'm going to get in contact with some people who will help."

"No one can help," Kinnari said into the floor, her voice guttural and strained. "It's got me and it won't let go."

"That's just the virus playing tricks with you, honey," Bening said, stepping down to stand beside me but keeping her distance from my sister. *"Don't listen to it.* You fight, okay? Don't let it tell you what to think." Maybe inwardly Bening was in a state of panic, but you'd never have guessed it. Outwardly, calm always prevailed. She wouldn't have known anything about the nature of the virus yet—how it would spread at light speed, how the scientists wouldn't find a cure fast enough and the government would be forced to kill its own infected citizens to stop the plague's transmission—but she was already making pronouncements like she was a bona fide expert.

"Okay," Bening continued soothingly, "this is what we're going to do, Kinnari. You try to get up for us if you can, but don't run. If you run we'll have to chase you and you know what could happen if we get too close. We could get sick too."

"I know," Kinnari choked out. "I'm sorry."

Rosine's eyes were red-rimmed. "It's okay," she chimed in. "We're all going to be fine. Just listen to what Bening tells you."

"Right." Bening laced her fingers and squeezed. "Kinnari, you stand up slowly for us and walk a couple of paces into the hall. Then we'll file past you so that you can turn around and go up to your room."

Kinnari whimpered. I wasn't sure if it was because of the virus or her aching hand. It was painful to watch my sister struggle to her feet and shuffle away from us. Bening grabbed my shoulder and pulled me towards her. The three of us forged a wide path around my sister, whose limp hair was hanging in her face, her injured hand held out delicately in front of her.

A low, moaning laugh slithered from her mouth. In the past there would have been people who'd described the sound as unholy.

"That's perfect," Bening praised. "Now you go to your room and lie down, all right?"

Kinnari raised her head, her eyes landing squarely on mine. There were beads of sweat on her forehead I hadn't noticed when she'd been talking to me in my room. Fever setting in. "I'm glad you didn't come with us," she said, lucid for a moment. With that, she passed out, knocking her head on the floor underneath our feet.

I automatically bent to pick her up. Bening yanked me back so hard that my elbow thumped against the floor just like Kinnari's head had seconds earlier. It was Bening, too, that sent for an on-call domestic Ro to move my sister upstairs. When Kinnari woke up later she was worse, and the biologists Bening conferred with had dire news. Two biological weapons had coupled to create a bastard son, a catastrophic plague that could wipe out most of the U.N.A.'s population. The sickness was rampaging through the streets, changing the infected into people we didn't recognize. There was no cure in sight and nothing we could do for my sister.

The knowledge emptied me out. We were going to lose her.

I stayed home from school, venturing back and forth to Kinnari's room to stare at her from my side of the force field, my blood running cold at the sight of her. I didn't understand it then, but now I realize that Kinnari's apology wasn't for what she'd *done*—it was for the horrific things she knew she could soon be capable of. The nightmare creature that she'd turn into. Beyond psychotic, beyond anything you'd want to think about.

I don't want to think about the specifics now, either. How she curled up in the corner of her room, scratching the skin from her arms when she thought we weren't watching, and how she charged the force field to try to reach us when she saw that we were. How my mothers couldn't get another dog license after June was taken and had bought my sister a bird instead. How no one had thought to ask the domestic Ro to take the bird out of Kinnari's room until it was too late and she'd crushed its tiny head and yanked off both its pretty yellow-and-blue wings.

My sister slipped away from us while in plain sight, her heart still pumping blood and her mind seething. I mourned Kinnari even as she lived, my loss just one of millions. Across the nation, Toxo was swallowing us one by one, tearing families and cities apart, pulling them under and trampling them into bone. The government had no choice except to take grave action. They could order the infected put down or ultimately watch us all die, the U.N.A. drowning in plague.

The solution made me sick. But it was the *sole* solution. Like amputating a gangrene limb to save the rest of the patient.

The past doesn't want to let go, but the future demands to be born. Only sacrificing what had already been lost would save tomorrow. No one should have to face such miseries, but the next day the SecRos came for my sister like they'd begun to come for everyone who was sick with Toxo. A part of me died that day. But neither my mothers nor I tried to stop the Ros. We knew it was already too late. There are things you can't stop, and things you can.

The last thing I remember is Bening telling Rosine and me that the three of us were going to be evacuated. She didn't say where we were heading and I didn't ask. I was too broken to care.

And soon, the entire time I'd known as home was history, and my sister and everyone else I'd known were history along with it.

TEN: 1986

"Where is she?" I ask, my hands on Minnow's throat. "Where did they take her?"

"Who?" he asks, struggling against me.

"Freya Kallas. Where the fuck is she?" I crack his head off the sidewalk with enough force to make Minnow wince and stop struggling. Meanwhile, cars are sailing past in the street. I glance up at the flow of headlights, thinking that it will only take a single driver or passenger to report me. The police are probably already looking for me, anyway. We need to get away from the road.

"Get up," I command, jumping to my feet and forcing Minnow up with me. "Don't try anything. I have a gun."

"You don't need a gun to get me to talk to you," Minnow says. But I keep pulling him along, searching out an alley to yank him down—somewhere I can take a few minutes to question him thoroughly. So far all of the dilapidated buildings around us line up shoulder to shoulder, dirty bricks meeting grungy cement.

I know Isaac never gave me any reason to distrust him. He even helped me get out of Wyldewood so I wouldn't be framed for Seneval's murder. Or so he told me at the time. I don't know what to believe now, except that Minnow's presence in Vancouver can't be a coincidence. His father's David Bruck Monroe, one of the most powerful men in the U.N.A. And Minnow *remembers* me. He hasn't been wiped. For all I know he's the one who had Seneval killed and then pulled the necessary strings to get sent through the chute, away from the crime.

"I have a room not far from here," Minnow volunteers, his face more sad than afraid. "We can go there if you want."

"How can I trust you?" I ask, glimpsing a small parking lot across the road on my left. Half of the eight spots are filled. If we hunkered down beside one of the cars, it would be tough to see us from the street. "You could have a bunch of guys back at your place waiting to take me out."

"Nothing like that. I'm not with the people you're talking about."

"That's exactly what you would say, though, isn't it?"

"What is it these people have done to you and Freya?" Minnow sounds clueless but I'd be an idiot to take that at face value. In 2063, he made a habit of fooling people. The question is, was he ultimately tricking the warren, who seemed to have absolute faith in him, or was it the U.N.A. government he was faking out? "Why would they take Luca Kallas's daughter?"

I push Minnow into the street ahead of me when I see a break in the traffic. He doesn't fight me; he's anticipated where we're going and walks willfully towards the parking lot. "I know you won't believe me when I say this," he says, "but it's good to see you. Official records say you and your sister were infected with Toxo and euthanized."

"She was," I admit. "They sent me back here." On the other side of the road we stumble into the lot together. I pull Minnow around the passenger side of a black Pontiac. "Sit down," I command. "Tell me what you're doing here."

"Same as you." Minnow kicks at a pebble as he settles himself on the pavement. "Surviving."

"Not the same as me. You knew who I was. Only the directors and the people working for them aren't wiped and covered before they're sent through the chute."

"Not if you came the way I did." In the darkened lot I can't read Minnow's eyes. "If I really meant to run I could've disappeared already. I'm not your enemy."

I don't know that. "You're the only thing I have right now. I'll do anything to find her."

Minnow stares at the moving shadows on the wall across from us created by the car lights on Powell Street. "It's a dangerous way to feel."

I'm crouching, balancing on my toes and ready to make a move at any second. "If you want me to believe you, start talking. This is taking too long."

He pulls up his hood and rubs his mouth. "I'll tell you what I know if you do the same." I nod in agreement. "Some time back, the warren received a communication from a group of people who had travelled through the chute in 2071."

"When was this—the communication?"

"The first was in September 2063. Just after Toxo hit."

"Just before you arrived here, you mean?" I keep my hand on the zip of my duffle bag, in case he decides to run after all. It wouldn't help me to shoot Isaac dead but I have no issue with aiming for one of his arms or legs.

"No, no. I only arrived a few days ago."

I feel the ground disappear beneath my feet for the second time today. *Minnow just came from the future.* He knows the outcome of Toxo. Maybe he knows what happened to Bening too.

"You were just…just there—the U.N.A?" I stammer. "What year was it when you left?"

"2065. January first."

I motion with my hands. "Tell me—the communication." He needs to talk faster. I have to hear this, but Freya's still missing.

As Minnow clears his throat a burning craving for a cigarette blasts through my cells. Even a couple of drags would help me concentrate.

"The communication came through at the very top levels of the warren," he explains. "It'd taken this group a very long time to work around gushi defences." The U.N.A. ran gushi like a fortress. No civilians from outside the country's borders could communicate with anyone inside them. "They'd hoped to get through to us before the Toxo outbreak, but failed. Their larger warning, though, was about the time they originally came from. They said on September 19, 2071, a group of Doomsday cultists in France gained control of the country and its arsenal, firing nuclear warheads at the U.N.A., China, Russia, and then at themselves."

Nuclear destruction. That's what everyone in the U.N.A. feared for a long time. It's what even the people of 1986 fear. And still it feels like a shock to hear Minnow say it. That's how the world ends: We poison ourselves with a rain of bombs.

"The first U.N.A. bomb was shot down by DefRos off the coast of New York," Isaac continues. "But there were many others on the way. Warnings went out to key government and defence personnel. Up North, in Lake Nipigon, your mother and her team were ordered to retreat to the underground shelter that had been built there decades earlier."

"My mother?" I repeat urgently. *Bening.* "She survived the Toxo?" After Freya and I found out the truth about our identities, it was clear that Bening must have been one of the main scientists secretly researching the chute. That would've made her indispensable to the U.N.A., like Luca Kallas was. It would've given Bening the pull to have me sent back in time, saving me from Toxo. She could never have guessed that I'd remember my real identity and be hunted for it.

Minnow nods. "I saw her just before I came back. She was one of the people who sent me through the chute. She relocated to Northern Ontario permanently after you and the rest of your family had supposedly succumbed to the plague, and it seems that in 2071 she was still there." Isaac pats the back of his head, probably feeling a growing bump from the whack I'm already starting to regret. "Your mother and her team made their own local broadcast informing people in the area of what would be catastrophic radiation levels once the bombs dropped, and urging them to come to the Nipigon shelter. Because their remote area wasn't a primary target, Nipigon had more time to evacuate than lots of other areas. Your mother and her team went out in rescue choppers searching for families they could save. And they did save people. Probably quite a few at the shelter, but they sent families with children through the chute. The survivors came through in Western Australia on February 9, 1993, most of them settling permanently in New Zealand."

I'm not surprised to hear of Bening saving so many people. It was like she was just waiting for the moment when she could make the greatest difference. Now she has. For a moment or two my stomach puffs up with pride.

But Minnow hasn't finished yet. "The survivors who communicated with the warren were only children when they were sent through the chute," he says. "They said they'd hoped this time things would be different, but as they saw event after event, including the Toxo virus, unfold in the same way it had before, they felt they had to warn us."

It's such a wild story that I can't doubt him. People tumbling through time, from a point in the future that even I haven't seen yet, in the hopes of avoiding disaster. *Insane.* It makes me feel like a speck of dust caught in the wind. "But I still don't understand what you're doing here," I say. "How can you stop a 2071 nuclear disaster from 1986?"

The rain's getting heavier, trickling down my forehead and my neck. I slick my hair back and listen to Minnow reply, "Not *prevent.* The causes of the attack are too many and convoluted for that." He pauses, scraping his shoe along the pavement. "Our plan was to evacuate as many people as possible. It took us over a year to get key people into place in the Nipigon facility. The warren have undercover people in various government sectors but the chute was top secret. We knew they were hiding something big but we didn't know how big until the 2071 survivors got word to us. They didn't trust the government who would've left them to die the first time around, and so they came to us. When everyone was in position we forced your mother and her team to begin sending people back."

"Your own people," I venture. "Members of the grounded movement."

Minnow shakes his head. "Not just them. People from the camps. I was one of the first sent back to help clear the way."

"What do you mean, clear the way?"

"The people at the other end of the chute—the ones in Western Australia—they killed some of the 2071 survivors before the survivors began to fight back. Apparently they didn't believe the survivors about the nuclear attack. Communication between the future and the past is difficult. The people in 1986 depend solely on the word of U.N.A. officials sent through the chute, and it was obvious to them that the 2071 survivors hadn't gone through regular channels. And so there was a team of us— me and several others—sent through to deal with the people working at Lake Mackay."

By 'deal with' he obviously means kill the people at the Australian end of the chute. How can we ever hope to save the world when everybody is still ready to kill each other to ensure their own survival?

There's another problem, though. Somewhere along the way Minnow lost me; things don't quite add up. Even if the warren could disrupt security on both ends of the chute for long enough to send several submarines filled with people through, defense forces on the Lake Nipigon side would soon kick in— more SecRos than the warren and its people would be able to fight. That means they did this for the sake of a few thousand people at most, and possibly many less, when they still had six more years to work out a way of saving a greater number.

"Now tell me what you know," Minnow prompts. "You said everyone here from the U.N.A. not working for the director is wiped and covered, but you seem to remember everything."

"I didn't at first. It was Freya who started to remember. She saw me in Toronto by chance and wouldn't leave things alone."

I explain that I only know the barest facts about the director's operations—that a number of well-connected U.N.A. civilians were wiped and settled in Southern Ontario, the director's people playing the parts of their friends and family members, while the larger operation is focused on the United States political scene in an attempt to stop global warming before it reaches a tipping point.

Isaac's blank expression tells me I'm not revealing anything new. "Where are all the people from 2065 who came back with you?" I ask, squinting at him in the dark. If I can put the puzzle pieces together, will it help me find Freya?

"We scattered. I was with a smaller group and we got separated. It was mayhem in Australia. I'm hoping they'll catch up with me here." Isaac appears restless and unhappy as he says, "Come back to my hotel and I'll tell you the rest. With what you've said about U.N.A. security forces operating in this area today, we're not safe out here."

From the sound of things, we're not safe anywhere. No one is.

"I still haven't told you about the results of the Toxo outbreak," he adds. "Or do you already know the outcome?"

"I was sent back at the very start of the plague. I don't know anything." And I've gone from believing Minnow could be my enemy to swallowing his 2071 story and boomeranging back to suspicion within mere minutes. But I don't have time to sift through all my doubts. "Look, if you're *not* with them I need you to help me find Freya."

"How?" he says.

I get up, motioning for Minnow to do the same. "Where are you staying?"

"Just a couple blocks from here. A hotel room in the Lower East Side."

Walking through the Lower East Side is like taking a stroll through hell. It's swarming with lost people and dangerous vibes. "Lead the way," I tell him. The sooner we reach his place the sooner we can start formulating a plan. By now the director must know about Minnow and his people coming through the chute. They'd want him even more than they'd want Freya. In fact, they must think she's somehow involved with the warren's plan. I don't know how they hope to contain the situation. They can't possibly kill or wipe everyone who came through time with Minnow.

"This way," Isaac says, hanging right. "It's on East Hastings." People are milling around us on the sidewalks—some of them wild-eyed, some dejected, and others simply without enough money to be anywhere better. "You know, I think I may have received some intelligence about Freya just before I went through the chute. One of our undercover people in high level security forces learned that an archivist had found a photograph of a girl in British Columbia that was causing quite a stir in the upper echelons. The info didn't mean anything to anyone in the warren at the time, but now I wonder if they were talking about Freya."

"They must have been." There've been tons of press people and tourists snapping pictures at Expo. It just opened in May, which could explain why the director's men didn't find us earlier. Maybe Freya's picture got in a newspaper or magazine without us realizing it and seventy-eight years from now a U.N.A. archivist finds it. "What else did they say?"

"That was it. The woman we had on the inside only happened to overhear the scrap of information. She had no idea security were looking for someone in the past."

I still have my hand on the zipper of my duffle bag and I see Minnow's gaze flicker towards it. "You still don't believe me?" he asks.

"Just being cautious. Trusting anyone right now would be a luxury. But if you help me find her, I'll owe you."

"You'll owe me a few times over, then," Minnow says. "This isn't the first time I've helped you out." He points down the street to a five-story building that resembles a cement bunker with windows. A woman with a shopping cart loiters out front, while two others stand idly by the doorway. A Vancouver Canucks towel flaps from a second story window, partially obscuring a sign that proclaims the ground floor venue 'Vancouver's Premiere Country Music Pub.'

The air between Minnow and I feels charged with static electricity and I slow my pace as we draw near his hotel. I can't help thinking that if Freya were here, she'd be pulling us in a different direction. Without her I'm forced to rely on my own instincts and they're warning me not to go inside with him. "What happens if I walk through that door with you?" I ask.

"Look, you either have to trust me and let me help work out how to get Freya back or go find her yourself. I'm not picky about which option you choose. I've already been through enough to last me another hundred years." Minnow juts out his chin, his face dripping with rain.

In the last hour and a half or so I've lost everything; I need to have faith in someone. But doubt keeps trickling inside me like a leaky faucet that can't be ignored.

"Tell me what happened with the Toxo," I say. However this goes, I want to know what happened in 2063 and I'm still working the angles, searching for any overlooked pieces of information that could help me find Freya. "Did many survive?" My lashes blink in double time, fighting the onslaught of rainwater.

"We lost almost forty percent of the population before they cured it," Minnow says. "CHC quadrupled their Ro production rate to make up for the extreme population drop. The U.N.A. is like an android nation now." I hear the disgust vibrate in Isaac's throat. "And the Cursed camps still aren't empty, figure that out."

Ros work cheaper and faster than humans and have no will to defy orders—we both know that.

"I guess some things never change," I tell him, relieved that he sounds like the same old Minnow Seneval spoke so highly of, because, let's face it, in the end I'm not going to walk away from the only person who might be able to help me because of a bad feeling.

I nod, shifting my hand away from the duffle's zipper and taking a definitive step towards his hotel. Isaac smiles faintly and bows his head, graciously accepting my show of trust. Then a flash of lightning illuminates the night sky, catching us both by surprise. It's almost funny that you can slide backwards through time by nearly a century and still be momentarily awed by a common act of nature.

Thunder crackles. A white van skids up behind us in the rain, the two men from my apartment building spilling out of its back door. Minnow's reflexes kick into gear faster than mine. He sprints for the building. Seconds behind, so do I, the men's arms closing around me and something sharp pricking my shoulder. East Hastings Street begins a slow fade to black, my legs disappearing with it and my head too heavy on my shoulders. What's left of me can only watch as I'm dragged under, the sound of thunder the final thing to be swallowed up as I slide away from Vancouver and towards a darker place.

ELEVEN: 1986

O ur first winter on the West Coast was pretty gloomy. Don't get me wrong; we were happy to be alive. Sometimes so ecstatic that we were almost giddy with it, acting like kids half our age, throwing ice cubes down each other's backs and tickling each other until we couldn't breathe. But March and April were full of grey skies and rainy days and our apartment didn't compare to the comfort the Resniks' house had offered when we'd been in hiding in Toronto. In Vancouver we were afraid of own shadows, nervous that anyone who looked at us twice could be one of the director's spies.

It took us about ten days to get up the courage to go out and look for jobs. The first one I scored was a landscaping position, under the table, and then Freya picked up housekeeping work at a nearby motel. Our employers worked us too hard, treated us lousy, and paid us even worse, until we were ready to take a risk and use the social insurance (the Canadian equivalent of social security) cards old Freya had scored us to land better jobs. We figured she wouldn't have given them to us if they weren't safe.

By the beginning of June, Freya was at Il Baccaro, and two weeks later I landed bar work at Greasy Ryan's. Suddenly we had money to do things like whale watching and kayaking, and we still read to each other at night sometimes, only we were branching out from the creepy stuff and on to the bestseller's list, crime novels, and trashy romances that made us laugh out loud.

The first day it was nice enough to go to Kitsilano Beach, I couldn't stop staring at Freya as we lay on the sand. Although I'd seen her in less, I'd never seen her in a swimsuit. Hers was red with white polka dots, and the bikini bottoms tied up at the sides so both the left and right were decorated with looping bows of string. I kept reaching out to poke my finger through the nearest loop; Freya humoured me and assigned me the job of applying sunscreen. Here and now most people still want a tan, but Freya knew better; she said she was going to stay pale.

She lathered me in lotion too, and we made out under the sunshine on and off for hours. In between we'd walk down to the waves and swim. The water was cold compared to what we were used to at home and every time we plunged in, our bodies registered the shock all over again. During our third dip, a boy and girl on floating lounge chairs drifted near us. They looked ten years old or so and the boy grinned brazenly and burst out with the question, "Are you two boyfriend and girlfriend?"

The girl, her hair in a wet ponytail, grimaced like she was mortified. "You don't have to answer him," she said quickly.

Freya, who'd been treading water with her arms slicing through the waves, smiled at the girl. "Is that your brother?"

"My cousin," the girl replied, a scowl in her voice. "My completely immature cousin who still doesn't know that he's not supposed to ask strangers things like whether they're boyfriend and girlfriend."

The boy ignored his cousin's dismissive comments and said, "So *are* you?"

Freya took a couple of strokes towards me so that our legs were touching underwater. "He's my grandfather," she replied playfully.

"Her great grandfather," I corrected, skimming Freya's thigh under the surface. "She's my favourite great granddaughter."

"Very funny," the boy scoffed, beginning to steer away from us. "You two are such liars."

We'd irritated the kid by not taking him seriously and before he could get far, Freya shouted after the boy, her tone light and teasing, "Okay, nosey, he *is* my boyfriend. Happy now?"

The girl cousin, who was still bobbing in her lounge chair nearby, stared at Freya. Emboldened by Freya's response to her cousin's question, she said, "I hope I'm tall like you when I grow up."

"Thanks," Freya said. "But how do you know I'm tall?"

The girl folded her hands across her midsection. "We saw you on the beach before he piggybacked you into the water. We have a Frisbee back there. If my cousin promises to be less annoying, do you want to throw it around with us after?"

Freya and I smiled quickly at each other. It was like we'd accidentally picked up two strays and for some reason neither of us wanted to disappoint them. "As long as it's okay with your parents," Freya said.

"*Her* father," the boy offered. "And he won't mind."

A few minutes later we were tossing a Frisbee around Kitsilano Beach with two kids who'd been strangers to us moments earlier. Out of the water, the girl, Heather, was a bit clumsy, but the boy, Jeff, could catch and throw with ease. The father, an aging hippy, looked on from behind sunglasses, refusing our invitation to join in the fun. I did the math while I was watching Jeff race along the sand and figured out he and Heather would be about eighty-eight years old in 2063. That was something I tended to do a lot—calculate the ages of people when the future I'd experienced would come to pass again.

Eighty-eight doesn't seem nearly as old in the future as it does in the 1980s. The kids could easily have lived that long and been around to go shopping at Wyldewood, have their own domestic Ro servants, and develop addictions to gushi. Or maybe they'd be grounded members dedicated to saving the world. Maybe in the future a younger, different version of me would meet Heather and Jeff and never know there'd been another me who'd encountered them before.

Anything could happen.

Later, when Heather's father told them it was time to go, Jeff gave me what he called an 'Indian sunburn,' grabbing hold of my right arm and twisting the skin in opposite directions while Heather shook her head, embarrassed afresh by his behavior. "I told you he was immature," she said.

Freya and I waved goodbye to them the way we'd seen people do to departing relatives in TV shows. Freya's arm was around my waist and as Heather and Jeff walked away, she said, "Do you think that's what we'd be like if we were growing up in 1985?"

"We are growing up in 1985," I reminded her.

"I mean if we were natives of the time like they are. They seem so young for their age."

That was what it was like before the world went to rot—innocent, at least in places. "I guess we probably would be a lot like them," I agreed. "Would that be so bad?"

"At their age, no. But the entire place seems so clueless about the things they're doing and where they're being led." *To long-term disaster.*

"Maybe the directors and their people will smarten them up," I said dryly. We were in the bizarre situation of hanging our hopes for the world on people we didn't trust. It was impossible to think about the directors and what they represented without feeling a complex mix of gratitude and fear.

We strolled over to our towels and lay next to each other with our hands linked, too tired from running around after the Frisbee to do much else. In the distance, under the sound of the waves and people's voices, I could hear a drumbeat pumping out from a boom box, and intermittent dog barks and seagull cries. Under the warmth of the June sun, and surrounded by people that had no reason to want to hurt me or Freya, I felt safer than was prudent. No one can be on guard all the time, and I'd only slept for three hours the night before.

I drifted off right there on the beach, holding Freya's hand. When I woke up my forehead smarted and I sat up to reach for the sunscreen, knowing I was singeing. Freya's towel was empty and I scanned the horizon, looking for her polka dot bikini and tall form. The temperature seemed to have risen while I was asleep, and I uncapped the sunscreen and coated my face, arms, and chest while my eyes searched her out.

In the beginning I wasn't worried. Her flip-flops were missing but the plastic bag with our street clothes in it lay in the spot beneath our towels where we'd left it. Freya had probably just gone to the bathroom or to get a drink. But five minutes later there was still no sign of her and I started to get restless. On my left sat a couple who hadn't been there when I'd closed my eyes earlier. The girl, olive-skinned with straight black hair, was wearing a striped T-shirt over her swimsuit and caught me looking at her. "Excuse me," I said. "Did you happen to see the girl I was with?"

"We just got here," the guy next to her replied, crossing his legs at the ankles. "You were the only one here when we sat down five minutes ago." The guy had beefy arms and a face you wanted to trust; I remember noticing both those things right away. "I'm sure she'll be back in a minute."

"Sure," I echoed. "Thanks." I remained on the towel three more minutes, reminding myself *they* wouldn't have taken her without taking me. When the three minutes were up, my mind began to allow in other alarming possibilities, and I stood up and shoved my feet into my flip-flops. "If she shows up could you tell her I'll be back in a minute?" I asked the couple.

"No problem, man," the guy said.

"We'll watch your things for you," the girl added.

"Thanks." I stalked off to find Freya, my eyes darting in three hundred different directions. The beach was so crowded that day, I probably could've walked right by her and missed her, so I went slowly, my head stinging where the sun had gotten to me. A woman in a tube top and racoon eye makeup collided with my shoulder and then glared into my face, expecting me to apologize. Paused by the crash, I heard a new sound on the wind, one that bounced me back to the summer of

2063: Arlette Courtemanche inciting the crowd.

I muttered an insincere "sorry" as I turned to the right, following the music to a guy with a mullet sitting with his back against one of the long pieces of driftwood scattered across the beach, his arms cradling a battered acoustic guitar. The tune was the very one I'd heard Arlette sing on Du Monde Day but the lyrics were different—Canadianized. Where Arlette had sung about the Redwood Forest and Gulf Stream waters, this guy crooned about the Arctic Circle and Great Lake waters. The variations didn't dampen the power of the song and I stopped about fifteen feet from the man, a chill running through me as the tune pulled me simultaneously forwards and backwards in time.

For a moment, I forgot everything else. I even forgot to search for Freya, until a pair of hands clutched both my shoulders and a familiar head nestled between my shoulder blades. "Boo," she said softly. And then: "I heard you were looking for me."

Back in the present, I turned to look at Freya. "Where'd you go? I was starting to worry."

"Sorry," she said. "I was coming back from the bathroom and thought I saw someone."

"Someone?"

"Remember Ms. Jarrett from school?" Freya's skin was pink around her hairline. Like me, she hadn't been careful enough about sunscreen in that area.

Ms. Jarrett had taught me history for two years and I nodded. "Here?" It wasn't impossible. The U.N.A. had resettled the families of other important people before us and possibly even after. Maybe Ms. Jarrett knew someone with clout. "And you went after her—how do you know we can trust her?"

"I don't," Freya admitted. "I did it without thinking. It wasn't her anyway. When she took off her sunglasses her eyes were totally different."

"Good. It's better that it wasn't her." She could've been

working for the director or had her real memories triggered by seeing Freya (things normally didn't seem to work that way—usually a wipe and cover lasted forever—but we were proof that wasn't always the case) and who knows what danger that could've brought us? "It's like the past can't leave us alone today." I pointed at the guitarist and then threaded my fingers quickly between Freya's to lead her away, not wanting to be reminded anymore that afternoon of all the good and bad things we'd left behind.

Freya broke free and made me chase her down to the water, splashing cold seawater at me until I was forced to laugh and haul her into my arms. I waded out a few more steps before throwing her in. The look on her face when she hit the water was priceless. Then she was bounding up and wrapping her cold body around me, retaliating by pulling me in with her.

When we got back to our towels, the both of us wet, the guy stretched out next to us happily observed, "You found each other."

"We did," Freya said, equally cheerful.

Maybe it was because the day was disarmingly beautiful, or because throwing a Frisbee around with Jeff and Heather had helped make us less wary of people in general, or because I was more relieved to find Freya again than I'd let on, but we struck up a long conversation with the guy and his girlfriend. This was back when I was still stuck at the shitty landscaping job and our neighbour on the beach, Sheldon Ostil, listened to me complain about my boss, offered me a cigarette, and told me they were looking for someone new at the bar he worked at.

A few days later I followed up on the lead and when Greasy Ryan's hired me, Sheldon and I became friends. Probably none of that would've happened if Freya hadn't wandered off after someone who happened to look like Ms. Jarrett. And maybe I wouldn't have started smoking, either, but regardless, that day on the beach was one of the best we'd had in Vancouver up to that point. It's the day my head falls effortlessly towards when my legs vanish from under me and I stop fighting my own disappearing act.

For a while, events unfold just as they did that June day in 1985. We're hopeful, safe, and happy out on the sand, Freya and me. 'Holly' and 'Robbie' making new friends in a brand new life in an era that was once well behind us. Then the sky fills with clouds and the wind blows cold. Freya and I burrow into each other for warmth on our towels as thunder claps behind us. Sheldon sighs and stubs his lit cigarette into his palm. Like magic, he begins to disintegrate, his hand crumbling to dust that gusts away within seconds, leaving a void where his fingers and wrist should be. Next it's his entire arm. Then a portion of his shoulder. Each of Sheldon's dissolving parts is carried on the wind like ancient remains suffering from high-speed erosion. I shout, "Hold on!" and clutch his leg, desperate to keep him with us.

"I can't," Sheldon says calmly back. "Neither can you."

Sheldon's girlfriend has already vanished. So has everyone on the beach but the three of us: Sheldon (fading fast), Freya, and me. Beyond the shoreline, Kitsilano houses have been replaced by an impenetrable grey fog. For a moment, a sliver of it lifts just enough to reveal a familiar mushroom-shaped building. Then the clouds open up. They pelt us with stinging hail that instantly transforms the sand beneath us into mud. One of the shards clings to Freya's scalp and sends a thin river of red spilling down her forehead and her cheek. What kind of industrial strength precipitation can do that? I reach into her hair, clamping my fingers around a tiny shard of fine china.

The clouds must hate us with a passion to abuse us this way. I shield my eyes with my hand as I stare up at the falling fragments of china. They litter the beach like seashell slivers.

Next to me, Sheldon says, "This is nothing. Lots of worse things happen out there than some smashed china."

"I know," I tell him, the entire right half of Sheldon's body gone now. "But fight, damn it. Don't let them do this."

"*You* fight," Freya urges me, her face awash in blood. "It's your turn. Come find me. "

"I'm coming," I promise, my voice halting and mechanical. My teeth are turning to steel inside my mouth and my jaw…I've lost the power to open it. Control's been snatched out from under me. My will, my strength, my identity. *They've* poured my essence out. I'm not even human anymore. That's how it feels, like I'm nothing more than an empty carton of milk, and that should make it easy to give in, except that Freya's aqua eyes are staring at me with a tenacity I've never seen in anyone else.

"Find me," she demands. "You're so close already."

I must be. Sensation's returning to my mouth. My tongue tastes medicinal. The inside of my nostrils reek of it too. My body aches all over, like it's been folded accordion style. But although I'm zoning in on consciousness, I can't open my eyes. My lids remain firmly shut, no matter how I struggle. Behind them, Sheldon completes his disappearing act, even though part of me knows it's not real, and that it hasn't been June 1985 in almost a year. In my dream, sand blows into my pupils and seals my eyes closed. Someone laughs as I wince.

"He's waking up," a voice notes.

I shiver and shake, my body contorting as my lashes flutter and give way. My pupils stare headlong into a blinding white light. No…nothing quite as dramatic as that, after all. Just a flashlight they're shining on me, and in the same second I realize that I understand why I couldn't control my jaw. They've gagged me so I can't scream. I try anyway. I thrash around on the metal bars they've caged me inside, making muffled sounds of aggression while the flashlight holds me fixedly within its spotlight.

"There's no point," the voice behind the glare tells me. "You might as well save your strength."

"Let him scream, if it makes him happy," someone else says. "What's it to us?"

My hands are cuffed behind me; I feel that now too. Thirst,

rage, and helplessness. Only as something moves close by in the darkness does my head snap to the left and take in the shadowy image of a second cage, a man crammed inside it. In the dark I can only guess it's Minnow. Moonlight shines through the rickety slats of what appears to be an old barn, a cavernous space carpeted with hay and filled with forgotten things—a trough, wheelbarrow, and what could be old cans of paint. I panic when the flashlight swerves to illuminate Minnow instead. The square cage is too small to allow him to stretch out; he's lying unconscious in the fetal position with his kneecaps pulled in close to his chin. My cage is the same size, only I'm almost a foot taller than Isaac. I've never felt claustrophobic before but my body automatically rebels against the cramped conditions, my legs trying to stand as my head bashes against the top of the cage and knocks me straight back into oblivion.

TWELVE: 1986

The second time I wake up, the barn is bathed in the dim light of camping lanterns. Someone's uncuffed my hands and taken the cloth out of my mouth. Those are the first things I notice. Next is the water dispenser that's been hung inside the cage with me like I'm some kind of animal. I look past it, over at Isaac—still fast asleep—this time sitting up with the side of his head resting against the metal bars of his cage. A couple of months ago I saw a news report about a couple of police officers who had squeezed a black bear inside a cage roughly the same size. It'd been spotted wandering around Port Coquitlam and people were worried it was becoming aggressive. The bear didn't look any more comfortable trapped inside the metal bars than Isaac does now.

In front of the barn door sits a man on a red folding chair, staring dispassionately my way. As the sleep clears from my eyes I see it's the thin man in acid wash jeans who chased me out of my apartment yesterday. "Where is she?" I ask.

The man doesn't answer. His eyes settle in a spot behind me and it takes me a second—with my knees pressed up to my nose—to jerk around in the cage and see what he sees. A second man, one I don't recognize. This guy's wearing a plaid shirt and muddy Kodiak boots and says, "You don't ask the questions here. We do."

In Toronto, the guys who came after us were in suits, trying to pass as Canadian intelligence officers and businessmen-on-lunch types, but these two are definitely going for the rural look.

"I don't know anything important," I tell them, Minnow stirring at the sound of our voices. "Freya doesn't either. We haven't said anything to anyone. And we won't. It's been over a year and we haven't said a word."

Both of the men have walkie-talkies down beside their chairs, and as they crackle to life the men reach for them in tandem, a female voice commanding, "Bring Monroe in."

The man in the plaid shirt stomps towards the cage, sliding a key into the padlock and unlocking it. The thinner man is directly behind him and once the cage door has swung open he reaches past the first man to yank Minnow forwards. Isaac falls onto the hay-lined floor, his hands splayed out in front of him, while the man in the plaid shirt stands with a tranquilizer gun drawn.

"Up!" the thin man demands.

Minnow attempts to obey, staggering to his feet only to collapse to his knees. I don't know if he was injured when they abducted us or whether he's just stiff from spending the night folded like a newspaper. "Up," the man repeats, one of his hands gripping Minnow's arm to force him into a standing position.

Minnow's expression is blank as he successfully reaches his full height and stumbles forwards with the man. The guy with the tranquilizer gun keeps his distance, his weapon still at the ready. I watch in silence as a second duo—a man and woman—burst through the barn door and take charge of Minnow. As the newly arrived man reaches for him, Isaac recoils, nearly falling again. "What are *you* doing here?" Minnow says.

The woman, holding her own tranquilizer gun, aims it at Isaac. "Be quiet," she tells him. But as the trio walk out of the barn I hear Minnow questioning the man further. "It was you, wasn't it?" he says sharply. "You were the one who got to her."

The thin man in the acid wash jeans that haven't been relegated to fashion history yet closes the barn door behind them, and he and the other man return to their places on either side of my cage.

"Just tell me if Freya's okay," I plead. "What can it hurt you to tell me that?"

The guy in plaid sighs as he drops into his chair. "We already told you we don't answer questions."

I flex my knees and arms. They're numb like Minnow's must have been and if I get the chance to run I'll have to be ready. "I'm the one in the cage," I remind him, my head aching where I whacked it. My fingers skim over the top of my skull and find one hell of a goose egg. "It's not like you have to worry about what I'll do with the information." I swivel so I can see both men at the same time just by turning my neck. The thin man's sitting tall in his folding chair, his eyes as expressionless as if he were alone.

Before I'm even aware that I'm going to do it, I'm opening up my lungs and roaring, "Help! Fire!" That's something I learned from TV too—people are more likely to help you in cases of fire rather than personal attacks. I shout the words over and over with a vehemence that makes me cough. But neither of the men react to my outburst with anything more than a blink of their lashes or slight shift in their seats. There must be no one around to hear us. Because I don't know what else to do, their apathy doesn't stop me; I scream until my throat's raw and I'm forced to lean my head towards the water dispenser and suck on it.

The humiliation of that sticks in my throat. I never got the chance to help the warren, but I wish I had. All I am to the U.N.A. is an obstacle. And then I remember what Isaac said about the French nuclear bombs in 2071. The future has no future. Not the way it was unfolding back in 2063 or 2065 anyway. Now is the only chance anyone has. Will what Isaac tells the director's people change their minds about their plans for us? Will they even believe him? And where are they keeping Freya? There must be another building close by. Or maybe they took Minnow somewhere in the van.

I choke on nothing, my throat still dry, and then gulp down more water. No one says a word. Outside, an owl hoots. I twist and turn, trying to get comfortable, trying to get full feeling back in my limbs.

"Are they going to kill me or just fuck with my mind?" I ask.

The man in muddy boots taps his left foot idly on the floor, one of his thumbs folded over the other as they lie flat against his plaid shirt. "What did you have to do to get back here?" I prod, smugness colouring my tone. "Oh, right, you can't tell me, can you? That's how much control they have over you. They're in your head." But these guys have been U.N.A. trained. They're not about to fall for my mind games.

Minnow's already been gone about ten minutes. I can't depend on him to help me form a plan; I'll have to come up with one myself. For the next few minutes I absorb as many details about my surroundings as I can see. If there were only one camping lantern I could make a break for it and throw us into darkness, but four are placed in select spots around the barn. There's a ladder leading up to an empty loft but not much to use as a makeshift weapon; every advantage is theirs. Somehow I'll need to run for the door and hope they can't get a decent shot at me with the tranquilizer gun. I picture the moment of freedom in my head and try to make it play out neatly. If I can duck behind one of the men at the right moment, maybe the other will shoot him instead. Then I can use his limp body as a shield or…I don't know. Logically, I doubt any play I make will work. But I have to try. I'd rather die trying than give up on Freya.

No one should be able to destroy what we've had this past year. We never said forever but it was there underneath everything we did. Our old world was taken from us, for better or for worse. But we had something new, something still growing. We were meant to see this world together and make the best things in it a part of us.

Ronda and the Puente Nuevo have been waiting for us. The

whole world's been waiting, and I can't bear to think that maybe the waiting's finished with for good and they've already broken her.

Back in Toronto the director told Freya they couldn't perform the new wipe and cover as well as they'd done in the U.N.A. It sounded like a hatchet job that could render us vegetables. In the best-case scenario, a completed wipe would steal me from Freya's mind, in the worst she'd be a faint shadow of her old self. I've been losing my mind since I got home and found the apartment in shambles and Freya gone, but now I begin to go to pieces, my eyes burning and my feet kicking at the cage door like I don't care if I break a bone doing it.

"Maybe we should give him another shot," the thin man says. "Put him back under."

No. If they do that I'll never get out of here; I'll lose her for sure. I squeeze my eyelids shut and pull my legs towards me, out of breath. To calm myself I start counting the seconds, trying to calculate how long Isaac's been gone. Less than thirty minutes, likely, but every second counts. I need them to let me out of the cage. If Freya's here, I need to get to her and see what they've done.

"I need the bathroom," I announce, locking eyes with the thin man.

He hunches silently in his chair. I hear the other man get up and jerk my neck to look at him. He's wriggling something out of a knapsack—a collection of paper cups, the kind you'd find in a doctor's office.

"No," I protest. "*Come on.* Just let me out for two seconds."

"How many of these do you want?" the man asks, ignoring my request. When I don't answer he approaches the cage, scrunching two of the cups up small and shoving them through the breaks between the horizontal and vertical bars.

I don't really need to relieve myself yet. What I *do* need is for the men to believe I won't try to escape. I wait another two minutes and then smooth out the cups, pull down my fly and force out nearly a cup's worth of fluid. "Now what?" I ask, holding up the cup.

"Just set it down next to you. We'll get it later."

Later. Later when they plan to move me?

I don't complain. I just set the cup down and pull my legs up tight to my chin like I'm giving up inside. Meanwhile my ears continue scanning for sounds from outside the barn. Every few minutes an owl hoots or wind gusts. Aside from that it's terminally quiet. No cars or machine noises. No voices or sign of Minnow. Whatever they're doing, they're saving me for last.

When I think I've waited long enough, I try again. "I have to go to the bathroom," I mutter. "And it's not something that's going to fit in a cup."

These two are cold; they act like they haven't heard me.

"I'm serious," I tell them. "I'm human. It's a biological need."

Finally, the guy in plaid gets up. "If you think this is going to be your big getaway attempt, you can forget it. But if you're serious, we can take you outside for a minute." He glances at the thin man. "We'll cuff him and gag him again." He sweeps up his walkie-talkie and tells whoever is on the other end of it they're preparing to take me outside for a bathroom break.

It sounds harmless when he puts it that way. Kids at school have bathroom breaks. Office clerks. Everyone.

But my brain's rattling from the tension. This could be my only chance.

"Take the piss first so he won't toss it," the guy in plaid directs.

If they were two normal guys from 1986 the one in acid wash jeans might protest that he didn't want to touch the cup of piss. Instead he strides over to the knapsack and retrieves a pair of plastic gloves. He slips them on and then approaches my cage, the other man handing him the key. I watch the thin man jab it into the lock and gingerly retrieve the cup, placing it on the floor directly to the left of my cage.

A spider—free and independent from whatever's about to unfold—scurries by the cup and under a small pile of hay. It reminds me of how Kinnari used to talk about reincarnation. You'd think coming back as an insect would be a punishment, but maybe it's easier. Humans have more power than they know what to do with. They fuck even the simple things up.

The guy in the plaid shirt and Kodiak boots was right. I was going to throw the cup. I could still try to reach for it, but now that they expect it, that doesn't seem like the smartest move. I breathe slowly as the thin man reaches back into the cage for me, the other man standing with his weapon aimed our way. If they just wanted to kill me they wouldn't be using a tranquilizer gun. That's something on my side.

I don't know how I'll be able to sense the right moment to break away. If Freya were here she might be able to tell me, but she didn't always know either. Sometimes the future is like the toss of a coin. Things could go either way.

I don't fall down like Minnow did. I let the guy yank me to my feet while the other stands aside with his weapon pointed at me. The man holding me has to let go for a few seconds to pull the gag, cuffs, and a roll of toilet paper from the knapsack, but this isn't the right time, either. I'd never make it out of the barn. *Wait until we get clear of it*, I tell myself. *Wait until you've had a few more seconds to really get your balance.*

When he snaps the cuffs on and pushes the gag into my mouth I shoot the guy a dirty look that makes him say, "You might bite."

I might. I might do fucking anything to get to Freya.

With the restraints in place, the guy marches me out of the barn, the other man overtaking us. If he wants to stand in front of me, it must mean they're more afraid I'd run in that direction, and I can see why. This farmer's field hasn't grown anything edible in a long time. It's all prickly weeds, wildflowers, and reeds, but there's an old two-story farmhouse within walking distance up ahead. Too far for me to overhear any noises from it, but reachable. I can't see a road from here but there has to be one closer to the house.

I'm nearly as sure as Freya would be that the place must be manned by more security people. They wouldn't keep me in the barn if there were civilians within sight. It would make things too messy. They depend on flying under the radar.

In the darkness the moon seems gigantic. The way you imagine it would look if it broke free from its orbit and started hurtling towards earth. Low and off to my right, something glimmers in the night air. Fireflies. Hundreds of them. I've never seen one before, let alone so many. They flash like miniature fireworks.

I wish Freya could see them.

"Left," the thin man commands, guiding me roughly towards the side of the barn. He has one hand around my arm and the other's holding the toilet paper. It's the cheap, scratchy kind they always put in public bathrooms. The main thing is that his hands are full and the minute he gives me the toilet paper he'll have one hand free. I glance at the other man, who hasn't lost an iota of his focus. When he sees me look at him, he says, "Hurry up."

And this is it. I try to speak. With the gag in my mouth, my words come out sounding like I've swallowed a blanket. The man nearest me hesitates. I've given him one of those old Churchill quotes that they used to play on the U.N.A. Dailies: "It is more agreeable to have the power to give than to receive." I watch the man's struggle to translate my grunts into meaning play out in his eyes.

For me, it's always a surprise to be reminded of the future by external things. It trips up my brain for a couple of seconds before I can get a handle on the present. Immersed in a society passionately in love with oil-fuelled cars, French fries, and suntans like leather, it's as if the whole continent is throwing a party that will never end. The world of 2063 doesn't seem possible and although I never forget, it's as if that future only exists in my head—mine and Freya's. I wasn't sure if the shock would be the same for the director's people, who were never wiped and covered like I was. But it seems that it is, because the man's eyes glaze over for a moment.

I'm lucky that he cuffed my hands in front of me this time. I spin as I pull away, my joined hands soaring up together as a single entity. I crash them down on the arm that was clutching me. The action brings the man's head cascading down towards me, and I bend and hit his chin with the hardest part of my skull. It's the part I banged on the top of the cage earlier and it probably hurts me as much as it hurts him. He groans but reaches for me, the toilet paper spilling from his hand and unrolling like a red carpet.

The guy in the plaid shirt is already firing but can't get a decent shot off. With me and the other man grappling, I make a lousy target. Plaid puts down his gun and races for us. I try to hurl the thin man at him—use him as cover—but it doesn't work. The guy has an iron grip on me that sends us both stumbling into his partner. Feverishly, I swing my chained arms around, my legs kicking at air and flesh, and when the grip on me eases, I run. Away from them and towards the house, my feet trampling wild grass and tripping over nothing. I've run this way in dreams, cursed with slow motion and leaden legs. You know you'll never escape what's coming after you but you keep running because there's no choice.

I feel the men hot on my heels. Then the prick of something sharp in the back of my neck. They got me. It's only a matter of time before I'll fall. The house is still too far. I imagine I see the curtain in the back window flutter. Before I hit ground, a third man appears from out of nowhere. He must've been watching us the entire time, and because I'm unsteady on my feet, he doesn't have to hurry. There's no danger of me going anywhere except down.

THIRTEEN: 1986

It must be a different drug than the one they gave me on the Lower East Side. I don't pass out this time; I just can't move. Not even to blink. Two of the men heave me into the house, one of them holding me under my arms and the other lifting my feet. I can feel their hands on me, neither rough nor gentle. But I want to yelp with the pain screaming from my wrist. I tried to break my fall with it and that was a bad move.

Inside the house an elderly couple sit on a tan leather couch in lamplight, the woman knitting a purple scarf and the man staring blandly at the TV. The two of them look so ordinary it feels as if this has to be some kind of mistake. Maybe I'm unconscious and dreaming after all. Or maybe they have no part in U.N.A. business and are just in the wrong place at the wrong time. If only I could move my lips and ask them for help, but my tongue and lips are as paralyzed as the rest of me. I have to wonder if I'm even breathing. This is no vision of heaven, though—the old woman's forehead creases as she looks at us. "I thought they were finishing with the other one first," she says.

One of the men carrying me adjusts his grip as he replies, "He tried to run and fell hard on his hand. Someone should probably have a look at him."

The older man nods and reaches for his radio. I don't know what he says into it; my attention's focused behind his shoulder, at a lone door ajar in the hallway. A trio promptly emerges from the room, a heavy-lidded Minnow at its centre with each of his arms draped leadenly around his captors' necks. The men flanking Isaac drag him down the corridor towards us.

"They're done with him for now," the old man with the radio says. He scurries ahead of us, swerving into the room Minnow just exited from. The men carrying me follow, angling me into a strange, narrow staircase. We descend slowly, moving into a downstairs corridor of bare drywall. Between the angle my head's slumped at and the position of the men on either side of me, I can only make out a fraction of the room ahead on my left. Through the open door, I spy the lower half of a wheeled bed with a drab blue blanket spread across it. A lump under the covers signals that the bed's not empty but I can't see the patient's face.

It's Freya's hands on top of the blanket that give her away. I watched her paint her nails purple while she was listening to one of her Spanish language tapes this afternoon. I'd recognize her hands without the purple nails anyway. Long, thin fingers that are stronger than they look.

My brain fights the paralysis, wanting to jump out of the men's arms and rush to Freya's side. I think I feel my nostrils flutter. It could just be my imagination; it doesn't make any difference because I can't move anything that matters. The men shuffle past the room, moving ever farther from Freya. Inside a second room with a wheeled bed, they begin to set me down. The blanket looks identical to the one covering Freya, like one you'd find in a 1986 hospital or nursing home.

My arm with the injured wrist flops as they lay me down. Funny how it hurts more than the gunshot I took in the Eaton Centre last winter and how the people who are ready to tear holes in my memory and fill them up with confetti are concerned about the way I fell.

The trio of men recedes from view, several people in lab coats taking their place. One of them is holding an IV in his hand and another reminds me a little of Bening, not physically, but in her calm yet in-charge aura. *Damn, here it comes.* First the IV and then an FM helmet. A *functional magnetic resonance imaging machine,* technology that was in its infancy circa 2010 but that the government was using to read people's minds only a decade later. I grew up hearing stories about antiquated technologies like this from Bening, and now the technicians are fitting one of the helmets snugly over my head. I feel my brain begin to bend to U.N.A. will as whatever's in the IV flows into my bloodstream. A truth-teller probably. They started using the drug in conjunction with the FM machine when people started fighting the procedure.

Initially I try to battle the truth-teller the way I fought the paralysis—with pure mental conviction. I draw a line in the sand I swear to not to cross. A line that begins to blur…and blink…and forget its own existence.

"Let go," the woman says softly, her brown eyes reaching into mine with a certainty that has no need to depend on brutality. "There's no enemy here. We're on the same side."

And then…then nothing seems wrong. Nothing's worth fighting for. Those ideas are gone. In the spot where they used to exist there's only a swirl of intoxicating emotions and flickering images. Things like…a shade of pink I never noticed before, the most beautifully delicate shade Monet or Renoir could ever hope to capture on canvas. Seawater splashes from a breaching whale out on the Pacific Ocean. Eternal love. Legions of dancing fireflies. Profound gratitude. Wrapping my arms around Freya and holding her close. Her hair. Her pale eyes. Her long fingers. Her voice singing in my ear. A sense of calm I never want to let go of. Better than the first cigarette of the day. Better than anything. Peace. Hope. Surrender. Winston Churchill standing at the end of my bed with his arms crossed over his belly as he lectures, "Attitude is a little thing that makes a big difference."

Winston means it as a joke, I think. And I would laugh in appreciation but the paralysis makes that impossible. Not that it matters. Not that anything does except the woman's words. She says, "We've given you something for the pain and something else that will allow you to speak. You should begin to feel their effects any second now. Then I'm going to ask you a series of questions I want you to answer aloud as fully as you can."

The woman smiles at me with a kindness I'm helpless to resist. "We're trying to help everyone in the best way we know how, and this is your chance to help *us*."

In my mind's eye, I nod, the pain in my wrist fading. She's already helped me. It's going to be all right, no matter what happens. I don't know why I was so worried before. It's almost laughable how anxious I was, but now she'll take care of everything. The world is in good hands.

I try to smile back and I think it works because the woman's grin deepens in response. I feel as if I'm smiling her smile and she's smiling mine. There's no separation between us. I want what she wants. I believe what she believes.

Because of that I gladly answer every question she poses as soon as I regain control over my mouth, tongue, and lips. I tell her about my past with Minnow and about running into him on the Lower East Side by chance. Then I repeat what he told me. 2071. The Doomsday cultists. My mother helping families go through the chute. At times it doesn't feel as if either of us is communicating out loud. Thoughts seem to flit effortlessly back and forth between me and the woman. It's like a Vulcan mind meld out of *Star Trek* with added peace and love and I chuckle at the thought, or at least I think I do. It's difficult to tell what's real and what's not. The fireflies flickering to the beat of Peter Gabriel's "Sledgehammer"? Winston Churchill in a one-piece swimsuit standing directly behind the woman, twirling a hula hoop around his wide waist?

One of the guys in lab coats frowns and mutters something about the addition of the pain killer on top of the truth-teller and paralyzing agent making me punch-drunk. "Drug interaction," he grumbles.

I laugh at that too. I've never in my life felt so right. The colours in my head are greens now. I taste lime on my lips as a particularly tasty tropical shade bobs behind my eyes.

"We'll have to work quickly, then," the woman tells him, returning her attention to me. "Try to focus on what I'm saying, Garren. This is important."

"Your voice sounds like music," I muse before eagerly confessing all the remaining things she wants to know—details about Freya and me. Our plans to see elephants, giraffes, and rhinos on safari in Africa. The Puente Nuevo. Our surprise at President Reagan's second shooting and our hope that the U.N.A.'s plans will change history but that they'll leave us alone. I feel almost ashamed remembering that. This woman and the people she works with are striving for the greater good. I should've understood that they couldn't allow me or Freya to stand in their way. We don't matter in the scheme of things. "We were never going to tell anyone about the U.N.A.," I vow. "Never ever ever." The words roll off my lips like honey. I can't stop their sweetness; can't stop myself from repeating them. "Ever ever ever ever ever."

The woman frowns, her disapproval echoing inside my heart.

"I'm sorry," I splutter automatically. The last thing I'd ever want to do is make her unhappy. She's doing so much for the world and I only want to help her, like she deserves. Even so, the syllables bubble insistently up in my throat. "Ever ever ever ever ever," I stammer.

"Shhh," she commands. "I understand. Let's get back to Isaac Monroe. You said he told you the only reason he came back through the chute was to help evacuate people from 2065 in advance of this 2071 nuclear attack from the Doomsday cultists."

"Yeah," I murmur. "To kill your people stationed in Australia before they could kill the evacuees." *Never ever ever ever ever ever.* The singsong echoes in my head but I try to keep it there. It would only upset her to hear it again.

"Monroe never mentioned another purpose?"

"Noooooooo." The protest stretches out like an interstate

highway on my tongue. "What…what do you mean, another purpose?" It's getting hard to think. My mind feels crowded and sludge-like. Too many colours and sounds closing in on me. It's overpowering. "Ever EVER!" I blurt out compulsively.

Winston Churchill points at me and erupts into a belly laugh, the hula hoop whirling faster around his hips. "It's not funny," I counter, glaring at him.

"Oh, but it is, my boy," he says sagely. "Very much so." The hula hoop comes to a sudden stop and crashes to the floor. "Everyone has his day and some days last longer than others. Yours, my boy, is coming to a close."

"It doesn't matter if it is," I tell him, my voice feverish like a true believer's. "They'll do what's best."

"Will they indeed?" he asks, his face ponderous and long. "I've always believed if the human race wishes to have a prolonged and indefinite period of material prosperity, they have only got to behave in a peaceful and helpful way toward one another."

With so much pink in my head, there's no room for anything else, like comprehension. I wish I could understand what he's trying to tell me, but he might as well be speaking another language. "Make him stop," I beg the woman. "It's too much." Freya spinning to the music, her red locks flying. Kinnari scratching the skin from her arms, her poor wingless pet bird with the smashed head lying on the floor next to her. Pink like a dusty sunset, the inside of a conch or a puppy's tongue. Pink everywhere. The smell of it in my nostrils, like a field of wildflowers.

"Who?" the woman in the lab coat says, her disappointment with me dulling her eyes.

"Him. *Him*." My pupils shift to indicate the portly man's position behind her. He's back in his dark three-piece suit, a handkerchief in his top left pocket and a bowtie around his collar. He eyes me wryly as he flashes the peace sign with his fingers.

The woman gazes blankly over her shoulder and then expectantly back at me.

But I'm too weary to explain. I can't even remember his name.

"I think that's all we're going to get out of him right now," one of the men in lab coats says to the woman.

"No," I choke out. Because I still want to help the U.N.A. Answering the woman's questions to the best of my ability is the most important thing I'll ever do. But my eyelids have other ideas. They begin to close, the technicians slipping away from me.

"We should be able to try again soon," the same man says apologetically.

"We will," the woman agrees, her voice beginning to fade.

I force my eyelids open again to see if the man in the three-piece suit is still standing behind her. Strange relief drips down the back of my throat when I confirm that he hasn't gone yet. In fact, he's watching me with the weight of an expectation that seems almost parental. I may not remember or understand much, but there's this: "The empires of the future are the empires of the mind." I say it slowly and in a muffled voice, every consonant and vowel a battle.

I'm not sure why I say it. Only that it signifies something important I've forgotten.

"Precisely," the man bellows in his mossy, weathered voice. "Never forget that."

I can't promise anything; I can only try. In the meantime, I close my eyes and let sleep take me.

* * *

When I first open my eyes again, I don't know where I am, my old bedroom in Billings or the one I share with Freya in Vancouver. My lashes feel like stinging stalks of straw and my left wrist is constricted by something wrapped tightly around it.

The ache of it brings everything back in a flood. They took Freya. Then they took me. I told them *everything*. I fill with rage at the thought of them poking around in my brain again and making me feel things that were a lie.

Blinking, I raise my head and struggle to take in my surroundings. Directly beneath my face, stray pieces of hay litter the ground. I'm back in the barn, the camping lights lending it an eerie glow that means it's still night. My jacket's gone, leaving me cold in just my sweatshirt. My wrist is in a plaster cast, probably broken, and the twin bear cages squat empty in front of me. I blink again, wondering if I'm seeing this right: my two original captors lying next to the cages like overturned turtles. The man in acid wash jeans has a thin trail of blood dripping from one of his nostrils and the other man's eyes are open but motionless. Neither of them appears to be breathing.

"Garren," Minnow says, crouching down beside me. "Snap out of it. We need you with us."

I groan and pull myself into a seated position. A tall black man with a pointy chin is hovering around near the barn door, his handgun drawn. No tranquilizers this time. "What happened?" I croak.

The black man glances impatiently down at me. "Maybe I didn't give him enough to counter the other drugs," he says to Minnow. "We might have to leave him."

Minnow reaches into the back of his jeans, tugging out the roll of bills and set of IDs from my duffle bag. "They took these from you," he says, handing over the documents and emergency money. I ram them into one of my own pockets as Isaac reaches for a gun down on the ground behind him. He presses it into my bandaged hand, gets to his feet, and then leans down to hoist me up by my good arm. I'm woozy, swaying like I might fall, as Minnow stares into my eyes and says, "Tell me if you can't do this."

"What's the plan?" I mumble, steadying myself.

Minnow motions to the black man. "Luis is with us now. He

helped me get free."

Luis solemnly shakes his head. "I wish there was another way out of this."

"There's not," Minnow says abruptly, anger squaring his jaw. "There's too much at stake *not* to do this." His eyes zing back to mine. "We'll get Freya. She's in the house with the rest of them. The man who killed Seneval is with them too. We take Freya and put a bullet in everyone else. It's the only way we'll be free of them."

Luis begins to say something but Minnow cuts him off. "We'll discuss everything else after. We need to get in there before they realize we're missing."

"Seneval's murderer?" I say, mentally a step behind. "Are you sure?"

Minnow crouches by the barn door, grabbing a weapon in each hand—one of them lethal and the other a tranquilizer gun. "He worked at Wyldewood with me. He was in the movement. One of us. It would've been easy for him to get to her. He must've been working for the U.N.A. the entire time."

Why would they do that? Luis and Minnow are waiting for me; there's no time for more questions. "We took care of the sentry already," Luis tells me. "There'll be no one watching the field. The first people we'll see in there will probably be the older couple. Don't be fooled by their appearance. They're not civilians. Far from it. They just look that way in case of surprise visitors."

This is what it comes down to: People will die and I'll be the one who killed them. But it's us or them. Who knows how much damage they've done to Freya already? "We have to make sure Freya doesn't get caught in the crossfire," I say. My brain jumps back to the image of Seneval's lifeless body. If I knew what her killer looked like, I'd start with him.

"How many of them are left?" Minnow asks.

"Eight, including a director," our new ally replies. "But the scientists likely won't be armed."

We creep into the dark, Luis bringing one of the walkie-talkies with us. The fireflies put on a dazzling lightshow as we pass, making the moment seem even more wrong, like a summer patio party instead of a gun battle. We hesitate about six feet from the back door the men carted me through earlier. It's too quiet and the lights are off. If I hadn't been inside the house before, I'd think we had the wrong place. Something's not right.

Luis reaches for the walkie-talkie, his eyes gleaming with suspicion. He freezes and looks to Minnow for guidance. Isaac shakes his head; a hail of bullets sailing through the door. One of them carves out a space in Luis's cheek. It turns crimson and drips flesh.

Minnow careens fearlessly towards the right side of the door, shooting back. Luis returns fire too. I raise my gun and pull the trigger, a bullet whizzing by my ear. I don't think about what it could do to me. All I can think about is Freya inside, and when Minnow, hunching low, moves to open the door, I fire over his head.

Inside, figures scramble in the blackness. One of them is the old woman, I think. As I follow Minnow into the house I see her on the carpet, clutching her leg and moaning. She reaches for her gun down beside her while we continue deeper into the living room and Luis finishes her off with a bullet to the head. One of his hands is holding his cheek together and from nowhere, a bullet tears into his protective hand. Minnow's head whips around, searching for the source of the fire. I watch him lift his weapon and take the target down. The old man drops like a log. I wince as I see him hit the ground and then I'm running for Freya's room, my gun pointed in front of me like a shield.

Upstairs, the floorboards creak. More of them coming for us. *Six left.*

I don't know where the stairs to the upper floor are or how many more bullets I have. I just keep honing in on Freya down the unlit hall. The door to the basement is closed and I reach for the doorknob, expecting to find it locked. Instead it turns in my hand, revealing a small bathroom with a compact shower. I have no memory of a bathroom—just the stairwell that led me to Freya. But I'm sure this was the room and I drop, shove my gun down the back of my pants, and begin running my hands across the ceramic tile floor and then dive into the under-sink cabinet, searching for a hidden hatch.

It's like I hallucinated the whole thing. There's no way down. Just the regular things a couple of old people would stick in their bathroom—pink toilet paper (reams of extras in the cabinet along with a bottle of Pepto-Bismol and tube of Ben-Gay), miniature soap in the shape of flowers, and embroidered hand towels.

Unless…

I tug the shower door open. The grout between the porcelain tiles is convincingly stained. I grab at the flooring anyway, my fingers catching on an uneven edge. As I yank at it, a large, square-shaped section of the flooring pulls up in one piece. There's a stainless steel handle attached to the underside of it and—where the shower pan should be—a stairwell leading into the depths of the house. *The hatch.*

I climb in, shut it after me, and race down the steps. Freya's room was on the left. This time her door's closed and opening it brings me face-to-face with a man in a lab coat. He's the one who put in my IV and his face melts with dread when he sees me. "What have you done to her?" I ask, raising my gun to point it as his forehead.

I can't risk taking my eyes off him, but an out-of-focus Freya lies motionless in the hospital bed behind him. She's hooked up to a mess of wires and my chest starts to cave in, my fingers trembling around the trigger. "Is she going to be all right?" I demand. *Have I made it in time?*

Upstairs, another exchange of bullets peppers the air. The scientist's shoulders jerk in response. "What are you doing?" he asks, his tone matching the shock in his face.

"We're leaving," I tell him. "And we're taking her with us."

I shove the door closed with my bandaged arm. It doesn't hurt like it did before I lost consciousness. They must have frozen my wrist or given me something powerful for the pain.

The man in the lab coat backs up as I step closer to him. "You don't have to hurt anyone," he implores. "We know you weren't working with Monroe."

What does that even matter now? They saw inside my head and it didn't change anything. They were never going to let us go with our memories intact, otherwise Freya wouldn't be lying here in this state. My eyes flicker over to her on the bed. Physically she looks identical to when I said goodbye to her so I could get my bike at the hospital. Her eyelids are shut tight and I could almost believe she was just sleeping, if it weren't for all the wires and monitors.

"I wasn't," I tell him. "But now I am. Tell me how she is. *What did you do to her?*"

"I don't understand," the man says. "Why bother taking her? If Monroe's promised you a vaccine, he's lying. There isn't one. We could see that much on his scan. He doesn't have the power to protect anyone. Do you think you and the girl are just going to be a lucky statistic? Because the odds are you won't both make it."

I'm lost. Is he talking about the Toxo? Doesn't he know it's finished with? And what do Freya, Minnow, or I have to do with the virus?

Before I can ask him, the door swing opens behind us. I switch my aim from the man in the lab coat to the unknown person at the door and come within a hair's breadth of shooting Minnow, who lurches inside with his handgun and tranquilizer weapon at the ready. "Get her and let's go," Isaac barks, his head grimy and his hand smeared with blood.

I turn to ask the man—for the third time—what they've done to Freya, but there's no time for that, either, because Minnow has his finger on the trigger. The first bullet hits the man in the neck, the wound spurting like a garden sprinkler. The second burrows into his chest and transforms him into a corpse. He falls forwards, his chin hitting the bed. The weight of the rest of his body drags him to the floor, a pool of blood fanning out beneath him.

FOURTEEN: 1986

"Why did you do that?" I shout. "We need him to unhook her and tell us what her condition is."

"We don't need him for that," Isaac says, his eyes hard. He stalks over to the far side of the bed, lays his weapons down on top of the blanket, and pulls the IV from Freya's arm. "Watch the door. They'll keep coming."

I instinctively obey—my eyes shift to the door—but I'm slow to react when a middle-aged woman in a black skirt and long sweater opens it seconds later. Her eyes widen as she takes in our presence. Then she's off like a shot, the closing door separating us as she scrambles along the hallway. In the brief moment it takes me to pursue her, hurl my left arm around her neck and drag her back into the room to help us with Freya, another man has slipped inside. Bullets volley swiftly between him and Isaac, Freya lying unconscious beneath the gunfire.

My arm instantly releases its grasp on the woman, who sprints for the door. Standing directly behind the man in the open doorway, shooting him through the back of the head would be effortless. But I can't bring myself to do it—the act would feel like an execution.

He's already wounded, blood seeping through one of his sleeves and the lower part of his shirt. I absorb all that in an instant. The moment slows in my mind, seconds stretching like a rubber band. I'm the one who finally ends it—snapping myself back into place with the bullet I fire into the man's shoulder.

I wrestle his gun from him as he bends at the middle, his

body folding inward in reaction to the pain. Then I shove him to the floor, Isaac yelling, "Have you lost your mind?" Minnow's eyes are fierce on mine, one of his legs oozing blood. "We can't let them live. None of them. But he deserves death more than most. That's Demian Hoch in front of you. Seneval's murderer."

Isaac sweeps across the room, points his gun down, and delivers a bullet straight into the man's chest. The man lies wheezing on the ground, his fingers clawing futilely at the floor. I flash back to the image of Seneval's lifeless body in her room at Wyldewood as I bend down next to him, my veins pulsing with hate and my mind filling with darkness.

But shadowy things have begun forming in the blackness. Questions, doubts. Why would someone on his way back to the past want to kill Seneval? And what did the man in the lab coat mean about Isaac offering Freya and me a vaccine? What am I missing?

"Why?" I ask the dying man. "Why did you kill her?"

Demian struggles to project his voice. "You...should understand...to keep some things safe, others have to be destroyed."

"He was doing their dirty work then, same as he is now," Isaac says, moving back to Freya to continue unhooking the string of wires attached to her arm and beneath her medical gown. "They wanted to break the grounded movement apart from the inside, pit us against each other. Make others turn away from the movement." I watch Isaac's fingers slip beneath the thin fabric of Freya's gown, unease growing as the shadows in my mind come into focus.

"Why would you...choose...death over life?" Demian slurs, his question aimed at me but his eyes turning inward. Blood bubbles from between his lips.

Demian's dying words puncture my brain. Dizzy, I force myself back up. Somewhere in the distance, more bullets whir into the air.

More U.N.A. security on the way. Four of them left now, as far as I know. Maybe less. There's no time for me to question him further and even if there were, his Bio-net wouldn't let him offer any concrete answers. He'd instantly be wiped blank.

"Take a step away from the girl, Monroe," a woman's voice asserts from behind me. "Put your gun on the floor, Garren, and then not one more move from you. Believe me, I'll still have time to get another shot off if either of you fire."

Isaac, still leaning over the bed, freezes. "Shoot her, Garren," he says in a voice like cold steel, his gun roughly a foot away on the blanket.

But in the time it would take me to turn she'd easily take me out. Or worse, fire on Freya. I lay my gun harmlessly on the ground, straighten, and then don't so much as flex my little finger.

"I don't want to hurt Freya," the woman says, her voice right by my ear. "Or you, either. It's in your interest to help me stop Monroe. Has he even shared what he's planning?"

My left eyelid twitches, giving away my ignorance.

"You know these people lie, Garren," Minnow protests. "It's as natural as breathing for them."

"And for you," the woman says to Isaac. "If you believe your own hands are so clean, why haven't you told him about the destruction you're planning?"

"What are you talking about?" I demand, my fingers icy and my mind whirling. My eyes bore into Isaac's skull, searching out the truth.

"We've had a look inside Monroe's head," the woman explains. "We know why he's really back here." Her words breathe into my ear again, the alarm buried within them, making me shiver. "He has his own virus to unleash. If he succeeds it'll sweep across the globe and take out sixty percent of the population within months."

"Are you going to listen to this fabrication?" Minnow thunders. "Look what they're doing to Freya. And how Demian destroyed Seneval. Manipulation is their specialty. They'd tell you anything one minute and steal your thoughts back the next."

He doesn't have to remind me they can't be trusted; I know how the U.N.A. operates. But this woman's the second of them to speak of a virus. Could it be a story they constructed to divide us? But they couldn't have known we'd break free and come for them. And the woman has a gun pointed at the back of my head. She could've put a bullet in my skull already if she'd wanted to.

"Pure deceit," Minnow intones, reaching for his gun on the bed as I stare at him in confusion. Without a moment's hesitation, the woman behind me fires on him. I bolt out of the way. Their bullets pass in the air as I storm towards Freya on the bed, the horror of the woman's statement repeating inside my head. *Sixty percent of the population within months.* I finish yanking out Freya's remaining wires, gathering her in my arms. There's no pain in my injured wrist yet but no power in it either. I can barely support Freya's weight. Willpower alone will have to carry us back upstairs. Looking up, I see Minnow's made it out of the room, a hail of shots ringing out from the hallway.

The woman I grabbed earlier—the one who looked as if she were dressed for a day at the office—stands tall, one of her ears seeping blood from a chunk of missing flesh and her gun trained on Freya and me. "We're no one in the scheme of things," I tell her. "You must know that. Isaac's the one you need to take out if what you say is true."

"It's true," she confirms.

I don't want to believe it. But why did the man in the lab coat say those things about Isaac not having a vaccine? Why did Demian ask why I'd choose death? Neither of them explained themselves because they thought I already knew about the new virus.

From the first moment I saw Minnow on the Lower East Side, my instincts told me he was hiding something. Now the knowledge writhes inside my veins like a poison.

It all fits.

When Luis said, "I wish there was another way out of this," Isaac stopped him from elaborating on why he'd abruptly changed allegiances. *He didn't want me to hear anything that would stop me from helping the two of them.* Then there was the horror, the fear, in this woman's voice as she told me about the virus, and the questions I was asked about Minnow while I was in the FM helmet. *He* was the one they really wanted to know about. Him and his virus. Freya and I were just a subplot.

So how much of what he told me actually happened? Did Doomsday cultists start a nuclear war in 2071? Did my mother save families by sending them back to 1993? Has humanity been racing around in circles in time, playing out the same fate over and over? Why would Isaac, who had always placed such importance on human lives, want to destroy so much of the population from 1986? And why would anyone want to help him do it? Has he been pushed into insanity by losses he witnessed during the Toxo outbreak?

"What can Freya and I matter when faced with a virus of that magnitude?" I ask, unable to wrap my head around this new threat. It's like the Toxo all over again. Too big for me to fight and win. All I can do is try to reason with this woman. Try to save Freya here and now, so we have some kind of chance as our intact selves.

The woman is silent, the two of us picking up on the sound of footsteps from the hall. She swings her gun in the direction of the open door, her shoulders relaxing when the brown-eyed woman who questioned me earlier steps into the room with us, armed with a Beretta 9mm. The last time I saw her I would've done anything to help this woman. Now she's an enemy again and she frowns as she commands, "Put Freya back on the bed, Garren. *Now.*"

Everyone here knows my name and I have no idea who they are, just who they work for. Then it comes to me—since this is the woman who cross-examined me in the FM helmet, odds are she's the director. I'd been expecting the same one we encountered in Toronto but he told Freya there were a handful on either side of the border.

This director's seen into my head. She knows I wasn't working with Minnow when they kidnapped me. She must have assumed I've since sided up with him, virus idea and all. Or maybe whose side I'm on doesn't count for anything. Maybe I'm just a loose end to her, same as I was to Minnow. Someone to betray for the greater good without a second thought.

"Now," the director repeats. She and Minnow are more alike than either of them would want to admit. Both so ready to issue orders and bury the truth under layers of secrecy.

I hesitate before turning back to the bed, my wrist groaning under Freya's weight.

"I've got them," the woman in the skirt assures her leader. "I can handle this. Where's Monroe?"

The director inclines her head. "That's under control. We'll leave them all for the feeders. Too much has happened here to go unnoticed for long. It's time to abandon the site."

Feeders. Machines the size of rats that break down everything in their paths—metal, wood, biological matter—turning it all to ash. They're even capable of devouring themselves, when instructed, and in this case the U.N.A. obviously doesn't want to leave any evidence. For years members of the grounded movement insisted the U.N.A. government was using the banned technology in nefarious ways, to cover its tracks. It must be how they rid themselves of the submarines at the Lake Mackay end of the chute—the U.N.A. brought feeders back to the past with them. Builders—miniature construction robots— too, judging by the swiftness with which this hidden basement level would've had to have been created.

I set Freya gently down on the bed and stare at our captors, my eyes white-hot with anger. Time and again they've fucked things up and expected us to pay for it. The flame inside me rages to wildfire and I swivel on my heels, on the verge of charging towards the director like a rabid dog. Lucky for me, more gunshots erupt upstairs before I can take a step. In that instant my moment of insanity passes, simmering down to a controllable loathing.

"Take care of them," the director instructs the other woman before darting out of the room.

Surrounded by two dead and bloodied bodies, an unconscious Freya on the bed next to me, and my discarded gun on the floor, I've run out of moves. If I go for my weapon this woman will pump as many bullets into me as she can. And if I manage to take her out in return, my actions will ultimately only leave Freya as helpless feeder food.

"I was trying to help Freya," the woman confesses, watching my eyes dart back and forth between her and my gun. "We were performing the procedure as slowly as possible so it wouldn't damage her. There was every chance she would've been all right."

After everything we've been through this woman still expects me to absolve her; it's unbelievable. "Every chance," I repeat bitterly. "Even if it worked, Freya wouldn't have been herself anymore. And none of this is her fault. You know that. You would've broken her for nothing, just because they told you to."

The woman blinks under the weight of my stare. "You know what's at stake here. You know why we do what we do."

This is likely as much as she can possibly say without being wiped and I scowl. "And *you* know Isaac's changed everything with his plans. So why are we still the enemy?" I don't want billions of people to be killed by a virus any more than she does and my hope that the U.N.A. can succeed in preventing catastrophic climate change is probably as strong as hers is, but neither of those things makes our lives expendable. Freya and I have as much right to a future as anyone.

"You're not," the woman admits, a hesitancy and rational alertness in her eyes that make me suspect she's a scientist, not a security officer—someone accustomed to wiping and covering, probably, but not outright killing. Not on purpose, anyway. But she'll either have to shoot me dead, drug me, or tie me down to get the feeders to devour me. That's the thing about feeders; they won't attack a moving target.

Without warning the woman lets off a shot. It flies wide—well past Freya and me—embedding itself in the wall behind us. "Just take her and go," she says breathlessly, squeezing the trigger a second time. "This is your chance." The subsequent shot is wider than the first and, incredulous, I run for my gun, slide it down the back of my pants and scoop Freya into my arms. Staggering into the hall with her, Freya slips in my arms with every step, my damn wrist weak like a green branch.

We'll never make it this way. I stop and heave her over my shoulder, like a sack. Then I'm running for the stairs, running for our lives, my legs spinning like a windmill. Above me the hatch is open and I burst out of it with my gun in my good hand, at the ready. My heart's exploding and my mind's working at the speed of light. *Look right. Look left. Aim your gun ahead. Run like you've never run before. Stay alive. Save Freya.*

I don't know where they've gone—the director, Isaac, and whoever else is left—I just keep moving. Down the hallway and back through the living room, past the broken bodies of the elderly couple and another red-drenched form collapsed on the floor. A feeder's already devoured the unidentified person's head and is making quick work of the torso, incinerating as it goes. Bile shoots into my mouth at the sight.

Then I'm out the back door and careening in the opposite direction from the barn. My eyes find only darkness but there has to be a country road here somewhere, the hope of passing traffic. Behind me, another shot punctuates the night. The sound makes me move faster still, Freya bumping up and down on my shoulder. Ahead, a parked van, Volkswagen Rabbit, and rickety-looking detached garage come into view. A garage marks the end of a dirt road, its beginning point far enough in the distance to render it invisible from here. But all roads lead somewhere, usually to other streets. Tempting as it is, following this one directly out to what's bound to be a bigger road would make me an easier target when they come after me. I choose the long route instead, my breath growing short as I run into the long grass.

Surrounded by silence, the noise from each of my steps is amplified. Suddenly I'm not alone. Someone else's footfall is behind me, gaining on us. I turn to face them, holding my gun steady.

"Garren," Isaac says, relief sweeping into the air between us like all is forgiven. "You got her."

"And you got out." His face is bathed in red, his clothes torn in countless places, and his pistol down at his side by his bleeding leg.

"Did you get your hands on car keys?" Minnow coughs, his teeth looking like an animal's amidst all the blood.

I need whatever help he can give me and I shake my head, bile burning my throat for the second time in minutes. Knowing what I know, I can't let him leave here. But he has to believe I will, that I've convinced myself his virus was a lie.

In another life, we were allies. In this one, I'm forced to be his assassin. The dread of what I have to do mingles with fury at how he's betrayed me. Seneval's trust in him was marrow-deep and my anger sharpens as I imagine her disappointment. How could the same person who inspired her turn to a path of such destruction?

"We need to keep going," I mutter, veering back to my original direction. I stumble as I go, willing Freya to wake up and run with me. *If she can.* If she can even do anything anymore. If we make it out of here I don't know what to expect. I make an unspoken vow to the universe as I stagger onward: *You can do whatever you want with me, as long as Freya comes out of this okay.*

Unencumbered, Minnow is faster, even with his injured leg. "Wait!" I call as he surges ahead of us.

"Hurry up," he yells back.

A car engine revs from the general direction of the house. There can't be many U.N.A. personnel left but they're coming for us anyway. I run harder, tripping on an uneven piece of ground that sends Freya sliding off my shoulder. As I bend and turn to catch her, the pain from my wrist knocks me to my knees. A tear fights its way out my eyes as the Volkswagen slams to a halt behind me, its headlights illuminating Freya and me like stadium rock stars.

"Get in!" a female voice yells. In my panic and exhaustion I can't decipher the difference between a demand and a request. The woman opens the car door to show herself—the same woman who fired two gunshots past us so the director would believe her orders were being carried out. A bullet from Minnow's pistol wings over her head, narrowly missing her. She ducks back inside, unharmed.

No matter what this woman has done for me, I can't trust her. Isaac, either. Both of them have saved me at least once and I can't imagine what must've happened to Isaac—or the future—for him to believe setting a virus loose in 1986 is a sane plan, but I don't have the luxury of waiting for an explanation.

There are things you can't stop, and things you can. I can't allow him to set foot out of this field if it means he'll kill billions of people.

I drop Freya to the ground and swing to aim at Isaac. My finger squeezes the trigger and the bullet hits him square in the chest. A lucky shot. But for a second it seems to have no effect. Isaac's face falls but his body remains stubbornly upright. Then his shirt erupts in blood and he topples to the ground like a wooden plank.

Numbly, I haul Freya back over my shoulder and jog to the car, throwing myself into the backseat with her. As we peel into the field, gunfire crackles again. From behind us this time. Out the back window I see the director sprinting towards the car. A shot dings the back of the car but we're farther away from her with every spin of the wheels.

"Who's left in the house?" I rasp, my vocal chords brittle.

The woman shakes her head. "There were a lot of bodies. At least one of them was still breathing but he'd lost a lot of blood; I don't know that he'll make it."

At least two of them remaining, but maybe only one who could give chase. I set my gun down at my feet. As the car bumps onto the main road and races for safety, I lean back against the vinyl seat and inhale deeply, catching my breath before I bend over Freya. Resting her head in my lap, I kiss the end of her nose and caress her face. Her limbs look so thin and pale in the flimsy blue medical gown that all the oxygen is sucked from my lungs again. *I have you, Freya. Now it's time to come back to me.*

"It's okay," I murmur. "You're okay. You're okay." My mind falls backwards in time as I say the words. *Us in the Resniks' kitchen, Freya leaning against the counter in only a T-shirt, reminding me who I was.* "Because the night," she told me as the world folded in on me. "You always like this."

I'll remind her, too, if she needs me to. I'll do whatever I have to. My lips brush her forehead. I unfurl her medical gown where it's rolled up her thighs, forcing it to cover as much of her as possible. My hands rub warmth into both her arms and then each of her hands, trying to turn the ragdoll in the backseat with me back into the real Freya Kallas.

FIFTEEN: 1986

For a long time I don't look up; I keep my eyes on Freya, watching her breathe in and out in the darkness. "You told me she would be all right," I say to the woman.

"The process was interrupted," she replies stiffly. "It's impossible to say what the results will be now."

I glance up at the back of the woman's head. Her hair's covering the damage Minnow did with his gun—her missing bit of ear at the tip—but the side of her neck is streaked with blood. "Take your best guess."

The woman straightens her shoulders against her seat. "We've never pulled anyone out in the middle before. Give her time."

"Why won't she wake up? Is she in a coma?"

"She'll wake up," the woman insists, but there's no certainty in her tone. "She's strong and healthy."

"She had a concussion." Fighting with my lame wrist, I pull my sweatshirt over my head and drape it across Freya's chest. Outside, the light's turning a deep purple, night fading into morning. We must be breaking the speed limit; fields hurtle by us on either side, the woman making an abrupt left that seems to come out of nowhere. Soon we're closing in on suburbs, the spaces between houses tightening and subdivisions coming into view.

"I know," the woman says, holding her head unnaturally still. "I warned them that would make it riskier."

My heart sinks. She either outright lied when she said there was every chance Freya would've been all right or was just trying to make herself feel better. In reality, right here with me Freya might be farther away than she's been in fifteen months.

"There was another boy awhile back," the woman continues, voice wavering. "He had a benign brain tumour that resulted in some of his memories becoming unstable." She skips over the details, leaving them to my imagination. "He reacted badly. His cognitive abilities and memory were profoundly affected. I couldn't risk that again."

The other director warned Freya wipe and covers performed in the present would be more rudimentary, that they didn't have all the necessary technology in place to complete them as smoothly as they would've in the U.NA. Nausea coils in my stomach, bounding upwards as I struggle to hold it down. "You shredded his brain."

"I couldn't do it again," the woman repeats. "I was being as careful as possible but when I saw you and knew there was a chance for her..."

She took it. I'm surprised she can reveal as much as she has without triggering a wipe and I run my fingers along a strand of Freya's red hair and say, "Are you telling me you think it was safer to stop in the middle of the procedure rather than trying to finish the job?"

"In this case I think it might be, yes."

Then why won't Freya open her eyes and look at me? "There must be something you can do for her." I don't mean to shout but the words come out loud and uneven. "You're the expert."

"We shouldn't force her to wake up," the woman snaps. "I'm telling you, we have to *wait.*"

An overwhelming urge to hurl the woman out of the car surges through my arms. I focus on Freya and force myself to fight it. "Where are we going?"

"I don't know." The woman's arms tremble around the steering wheel. She was completely unprepared to become an enemy of the U.N.A. today and seems in danger of unravelling.

The car's slowing to a crawl and I point my gaze out the window, at a sleepy suburban neighbourhood composed of large, attractive houses with two-car garages. Tidy hedges separate most of the properties.

"I'm just trying to put some distance between us and them and stay out of sight," the woman adds. "Where do you think we should go?"

"I don't even know where we are."

"Surrey." Our eyes meet in the rearview mirror. Surrey's only a stone's throw from Vancouver. They didn't take us far. Somewhere in Delta or a more rural area of Surrey itself, probably.

"What would they expect us to do?" I ask.

She should know the answer to that better than I do, but the woman replies, "I don't know." One of her hands dives into her hair, twisting it at the roots. "They'll need reinforcements to looks for us."

Which gives us a window of opportunity, as most of their people seem to be stationed out East or south of the border. But first things first, driving around with a gun at my feet and a half-naked girl draped across my lap is a good way to get pulled over by the police. In the short term that might keep us from being taken again, but eventually the cops would give Freya back to her mother. Then the U.N.A. would have easy access to whatever's left of her. And I would likely be sent to prison for kidnapping.

"We need clothes for Freya," I say. Most stores won't be open for hours yet, which narrows our options. "And you need to clean up."

The woman eyes herself in the mirror, spitting on her hand and then dragging it down her neck. "I need something to stop the bleeding." She brakes, sweeping her hair back to examine the tip of her ear. I saw much worse inside the house, but we both wince at the sight of her bloody flesh. "Maybe one of these houses has a clothesline," the woman suggests breathlessly.

"I doubt it." The pavement's dry now but it was raining when I was taken last night. Most people wouldn't have had a chance to hang clothes and besides, this neighbourhood is too affluent to forego the luxury and speed of a dryer for a clothesline. On top of that, wooden fences obscure any view of the backyards. "What about a clothing donation box? There has to be one somewhere in the area."

The woman steers us swiftly out of the neighbourhood and we scour the surrounding streets for any sign of a charity box. Five minutes later I spot a bright blue cube marked 'DONATE' in an L-shaped strip mall. A realtor, fish and chips store, hairdresser, and fruit market skirt the parking lot. "On your right," I advise, the car tilting as we take a sharp turn into the lot.

Nothing's open yet and no indoor lights are on, but there's a single car at the far end of the lot. Either somebody left their car here overnight or showed up to work early. We need to do this quick.

"Is there a tire iron in the trunk?" I ask, lifting Freya's head from my lap so I can throw my sweatshirt back on and climb out of the backseat.

The woman cuts the engine and gets out of the car with me. "I don't know." Near the rear of the car, on the driver's side, I see where the director's bullet hit. We were lucky—it took off a section of paint the length of an eraser but looks more like a parking lot scrape-up than something sinister.

Next to me the woman slides the key in the trunk and pops it open. Sure enough, there's a spare tire, tire iron, and compact toolbox squeezed into the trunk along with wiper fluid and several plastic bags full of groceries that someone must have forgotten to bring into the house with them. At a glance I notice paper towels in one of the bags—something that could help stop the woman's bleeding.

I reach for the tire iron and toolbox, pressing the box into the woman's hands in case we need it. "Let's go," I tell her, not wanting to leave her with Freya. I don't trust her not to change her mind and drive away—she's so frazzled it wouldn't surprise me if she headed straight for the U.N.A.'s Ontario base and offered Freya back to them.

As we approach the charity box, I wish it was still pitch-dark out to offer us some cover. Unfortunately the day's fast closing in. I size up the box, noting it's structured like a mailbox. You can slide items in but not retrieve them. The top will have to come off.

I go to work with the tire iron, jamming its flatter end under the box's lid. But I need more leverage than I can get with one good hand. "Help me," I demand. "What's your name anyway?"

The woman grabs on to the tire iron with me. "You can call me Elizabeth," she says. Together we pry the nearest corner of the lid open. With our combined strength pushing stubbornly on the tire iron, the lid suddenly gives way and flies open. I jump onto the clothing slot and peer into the box's contents— it's full to the brim with garbage bags. I rip into one after the other, tossing usable contents for Freya down to Elizabeth: black jeans, sandals, a polo shirt, a frilly blue halter top, a pink miniskirt that Freya would hate but looks like it would fit, a white knit sweater that I'd bet has never been worn, and a mustard-coloured windbreaker.

"That's enough," Elizabeth says nervously. "Passing cars are taking an interest."

"One second." I ferret out a lime green headband for Elizabeth and leap down, leaving the lid open. We hurry to the car to deposit the tools in the trunk. I grab the gun from the backseat and toss it in along with them, burying it at the bottom of one of the grocery bags. Elizabeth tucks a wad of paper towels against her ear and holds it firmly in place with the headband. The lime green doesn't exactly match what she's wearing, but the headband's decent camouflage.

Meanwhile, Freya lies spread across the backseat like Sleeping Beauty, her lips parted and her face a mask of calm.

The light creeping into the sky returns some colour to her skin, making her appear a shade less delicate than when we sped away from the farmhouse. Hope swells in my stomach. Maybe she'll be all right. She remembered the truth the first time they tampered with her memories. Maybe she can do it again. Freya's not like other people.

I scoot into the backseat, Elizabeth burning out of the parking lot like we're being chased. "Be careful," I warn. "We don't want to be stopped for speeding."

"I know, I know," Elizabeth says anxiously. "Where do you want me to go?"

"Just drive." My mind lands on Dennis and Scott. What would they do if I showed up on their doorstep with Freya unconscious in my arms? Would they help me this time or would they consider Freya's condition further evidence of my guilt?

I pull the pink miniskirt up Freya's legs—over the one-piece medical gown—and then untie the gown where it drapes around the back of her neck so I can slip it down her shoulders before guiding her head into the polo neck. Once she's decent I reach under her skirt to tug off the medical gown. I didn't come across any socks or shoes in the box, but I strap her feet into the sandals, relieved they're only a size or so too big.

Finally, I prop her into a seated position and lean her head against the window. I'd like to stay close and keep my eye on her, but for appearance's sake I'm better off in the front seat. "I'm climbing up there with you," I warn Elizabeth.

She holds her arms in tight to her body and glances at me sideways as I thump down into the passenger seat, thinking over her question: *Where do we go?* We need money and a place to keep a low profile, but it's impossible to focus on those things when Freya's out like a light. People can live weeks without food but only days without water. If she doesn't wake up, she'll need an IV to replace fluids. And then what? Will Elizabeth be able to take care of her or will she need to be admitted to the hospital?

But I can't let myself think like that. *She'll wake up.*

Elizabeth's steering us east and for now I don't question her decision. Once Freya wakes up we could catch the ferry west to Vancouver Island and try to hide out in some sparsely populated patch of wilderness, but if they came for us there our backs would be up against the wall. Having run out of land, we'd be trapped.

I stare over my shoulder at Freya as I say, "Isaac told me a lot of things about 2065. I don't know which of them are true."

Elizabeth furrows her brow and keeps her eyes on the road. "I can't tell you that."

"But you told me about the boy whose mind you shattered."

"Carefully and incompletely," she qualifies. "The far future is..." she pauses, the skin under her eyes creasing heavily. "The future is strictly off-limits."

"What if I just ask yes-no questions?"

She shakes her head vehemently.

"You told me about Isaac's virus. Technically, that's the future."

Elizabeth swivels to look me in the face. In some other time and place her green headband would look comical. "Technically saying the forecast is calling for sun tomorrow would be discussing the future too, but the parameters are narrower than that." *And the parameters that would trigger a wipe would have been programmed before Elizabeth was sent through the chute, which could have been years ago. Then they wouldn't include Minnow's plans for 1986 so couldn't prohibit her talking about them.*

Fifteen months ago the Ontario director told Freya that if people working for the U.N.A. begin to transmit information about the future and what they're doing here, a wipe sequence is instantly triggered. Sharing some general information seems permissible but the U.N.A.'s existence, present aims, and reasons behind their goals are out-of-bounds. As is any knowledge of the future, which leaves me largely in the dark about Isaac's version of 2065 and 2071 events.

"What about the virus?" I probe. "Is it still a danger to us all? Was Isaac working alone or are there others out there who could unleash it?"

Elizabeth's cheeks colour, suggesting the news won't be good. "We had a difficult time with Monroe. He obviously had access to brand new grounded technology that helped him resist our methods." Probably a drug hidden somewhere on his body, something he ingested when they dragged him out of the barn. "We'd only begun to break through his defenses," she continues. "It was such a thorny undertaking, we were in danger of irreparably harming his mind, which would prevent us from obtaining all the information we needed. We discovered his desire to release the virus but not the details. We were forced to temporarily stop mining for information. To give him a chance to stabilize."

Stabilize and escape. With my help.

"Why would he want to decimate the current population?" I ask. "He wasn't like that, he respected human life." Guilt pierces my skin as Isaac's image shimmers behind my eyes, the feeling instantly driven away by his plotted massacre.

Elizabeth remains silent. We've crossed into forbidden territory. Isaac's reasons come from the future.

When I asked him out on the Lower East Side how he could stop a 2071 nuclear disaster from 1986, Minnow told me he wasn't trying to prevent it, simply helping people evacuate. But maybe he *was* trying to stop it, in some way I can't fathom. I'm feverish at the thought, my mind twisting and turning, sliding down a chute that never ends. Maybe humanity would be better off if no one had ever discovered the chute. Otherwise people might never stop insisting on second chances, constantly trying to revise the past and creating new dangers in the process.

"He couldn't have come through the chute alone," I continue, thinking aloud. "Not if he killed—or somehow got past—the people the U.N.A. must have stationed in Lake Mackay. He said he came with a team."

Elizabeth's face is stony. "We know he wasn't alone at the outset; we're not sure what became of any others. We believe he had the most important role in potentially spreading the virus but he wasn't in possession of it when we picked him up. I can't say more on the subject of the lake. You have to understand, my mind is a minefield."

She must not be capable of discussing U.N.A. forces in Lake Mackay and therefore can't tell me what happened there, but someone out in Australia would have informed their people in North America about what happened with Isaac and his crew. Otherwise they wouldn't have thrown him into the van with me.

"So you don't really know if we're safe from the virus," I surmise.

"No. We thought we'd break through Monroe's defences in the end, that there'd be time to uncover his entire plan. There wasn't. But I would've shot him myself, in the field, if you hadn't done it first. We couldn't let him follow through with his intentions."

There's little room for regret over my actions. It had to be done. Everything happened so fast back there. I didn't know if I could rely on Elizabeth to do the job. Minnow had proven he was good with a gun—he might have taken her out first instead. She's a scientist, not used to armed altercations.

And then it hits me, the realization descending with deceptive softness, like the first snowflakes of the season. My feelings of necessity are Minnow's feelings about the virus. He wouldn't do it unless he didn't see any option. The things he told me about 2071 were the cruel truth. Widespread nuclear destruction that would make the planet uninhabitable for years to come. It happened once already and in 2065 we were travelling down that same path to annihilation.

Isaac couldn't expect to kill the Doomsday Cultists in France who launched the bombs; they wouldn't be born yet in 1986. And preventing the birth of any single person responsible for the attack probably wouldn't change what happened on

September 19, 2071, either. But killing many, many people—billions of them—would alter human history. Losing sixty percent of the population would cripple nations. There wouldn't be enough people to keep basic services running. Infrastructure would crumble.

There'd be no place for an arms race in a world like that. People would be too busy trying to survive and take the first steps to putting civilization back on its feet. Carbon dioxide emissions would drop as a result of the culling, slowing global warming. I can't know for sure this scenario is what would have fuelled Minnow's decision, but there's a horrifying logic to it. Killing sixty percent of the population might well keep the planet clean, preventing animal extinctions and possibly our own, for years to come.

Ultimately we could end up making similar or drastically different mistakes regarding the earth, but there's no way a virus of the scale Elizabeth described could fail to make a dent in humanity's path. Minnow's virus would bring rapid change, causing ripples that would be felt all the way to 2071 and beyond. Killing people now could save the future.

But there's no guarantee of that, and why should the people of today be sacrificed on a gamble? Maybe the U.N.A.'s efforts to alter the future would have generated enough change to prevent the disaster of 2071. Minnow should've given their plans a chance to succeed.

He was wrong to attempt to wipe out the majority of humanity with a virus, even if his goal was to save the planet. Most of the population of 1986 would agree with me. And yet, I shot Minnow for the same reason. Does that mean only the vast number of people who would be affected by Isaac's virus make his actions wrong?

My eye sockets and forehead twinge, cobwebs of pain spinning out along my skull. It would be better not to know these things, not to carry these questions in my mind. I feel it trying to expand with the weight of them, and failing.

"There's nothing we can do about the virus either way now," Elizabeth says, surprisingly stoic. "It will happen or it won't. I was thinking about what you said—how you asked me what they'd expect you to do."

I nod bewilderedly, one of my eyelids pulsing again.

"Maybe Monroe's dead body will convince them you hadn't joined forces with him. If they believe you killed him, they couldn't believe you were involved in his plans for the virus. In that case they might leave us alone and concentrate on looking for others who are more dangerous."

The ones who came with him from the future, ones who might still have access to the virus.

I don't know how much the director saw and I say, "They might think Isaac was shot by one of your people in the house and that he bled to death in the field trying to get away."

Elizabeth sighs, her hands tightening on the wheel. "They could. We have no way of knowing how they'll regard the shooting or what resources they'll dedicate to coming after us. We need to get as far away as possible, leave the continent. We could drive across the border and fly out from the United States somewhere. They wouldn't expect that, I don't think. They'd be more likely to look for us at the Vancouver airport."

Freya and I were led to believe there are more U.N.A. personnel south of the border than there are in Canada, making it a riskier place to hide. We travelled across the entire country rather than slipping into the United States the last time they came after us. So Elizabeth could be right that crossing the border isn't something they'd expect of us, but considering Freya's state, what she's proposing is just as impossible as catching the ferry to Vancouver Island. We're only about twenty minutes from the Peace Arch crossing in Washington State, but it may as well be a thousand miles away.

"I'm not leaving her if that's what you're suggesting," I say angrily, my gaze whipping into the backseat. A lock of Freya's hair has fallen between her lips and one of her hands is folded under her head, acting as a cushion against the window. I didn't position it that way and my heart revs in my chest.

Catching my expression, Elizabeth glances over her shoulder at Freya. "I know you wouldn't leave her." Elizabeth flips her gaze back to the road, unaware of the change in Freya.

"She's moved." My skin tingles as I repeat myself. "She moved her hand. That has to be a good sign, right?"

Elizabeth nods slowly, her eyes springing back to Freya. "I hope so." But Elizabeth's tone isn't as optimistic as I'd expect. I'm on the verge of cross-examining her when a horn blares from the car in front of us. There's minimal traffic on the road and no disturbances that I can see, but for a moment the sound shakes me free of any deeper questions and sends my eyes scanning the area for the source of the driver's irritation.

I'm no wiser about what pissed him off when I watch him ease off his horn and push a cigarette between his lips. A body should know better than to yearn for poison but mine doesn't. I inhale deeply as the driver flicks a lighter in front of his face, my lungs filling with imaginary nicotine and smoke.

When I return my attention to Freya, her head's still settled sleepily against her hand and she's staring steadily back at me, her blue eyes pale and infinite in the early morning sunshine. I can't count how many times I've seen Freya wake up in the past fifteen months. Sometimes with a yawn or bleary eyes and sometimes with the energy of a child. In all those months I've never once seen this strangely detached expression in her face.

"Freya?" Joy and urgency coil in my voice. "Freya?"

Her eyelashes flutter shut, the invisible divide between us falling into place and sealing me out of her existence.

SIXTEEN: 1986

Elizabeth whips around to look at Freya, too late to catch her moment of consciousness.

"Her eyes were open," I say breathlessly. "What's going on—why is she asleep again?"

Elizabeth purses her lips and fretfully adjusts her headband. "She must be starting to come out of it, but that could be gradual. Listen, Garren, I just want to warn you not to expect too much. Pulling her out of the process before completion could've caused some unpredictable results."

"You said stopping the wipe was better than continuing." The desire to hurt Elizabeth rages through me again, pumping out from my heart and into every part of my body. Anger with myself charges in after it—I shouldn't have left Freya alone when she was least able to protect herself. It was stupid to think they'd forgotten about us.

"I believe that. But I can't say how what's been done so far will affect her." The remorse in Elizabeth's face has no impact on me. "I'm sorry. Just have some patience with her."

I have endless patience for Freya, if that's what she'll need. But the injustice of the U.N.A.'s actions burns. Reading someone's mind is invasive but butchering it with a wipe and cover is barbaric. Especially when we're talking about Freya, and the scientists don't have the technology to make a clean job of it. "You're the one who suggested driving across the border," I snap. "How can we do that when she can't keep her eyes open?"

"We can't." Elizabeth's mouth sours around the

disappointing syllables. "We have to wait."

But we can't stop moving—that would give them a better chance to hunt us down. We'll have to keep going until Freya's fully conscious. "How much cash do you have?" I ask. The eight hundred dollars in my pocket could keep me and Freya going for a while but it won't be enough to buy us international plane tickets and fake passports.

"Only what's in my wallet. About ninety dollars." Elizabeth bites her lip as she slaps her cardigan pocket. I watch the realization sink in that her bank account and credit cards will soon be inaccessible to her; if she uses them the well-connected U.N.A. could track her through the information. "I saw a bank machine a few minutes ago," she adds hastily. "I could withdraw more before we leave the area."

My own ATM card is either being devoured by feeders back at the farmhouse or in the hands of the director, and the banks themselves won't be open for hours yet. Even if they were, my Robert Clark ID is gone. The only person I can pass for now is Chris Henderson, the name on my fake driver's license and social insurance number. And Chris Henderson has no bank account.

"I'm guessing you don't have secret ID under a different name they don't know about," I say. "Which means it's possible they could find out if we cross the border anyway."

"I didn't prepare for this; I didn't expect it." Elizabeth's look of exasperation makes me roll my eyes. "What about you—do you have any money or identification?"

She couldn't know that Minnow returned the eight hundred dollars U.N.A. security had stolen from me, and I lie. "Isaac gave me two hundred dollars back in the barn along with the fake IDs for me and Freya that your people had taken."

I don't owe Elizabeth the truth and I have to protect the money Freya and I have left. Besides, admitting to less might inspire Elizabeth to get creative about putting her hands on extra cash. I'm not going to carry her—she needs to pull her own weight.

Because the U.N.A. have seen my emergency ID the three of us will need new identities as soon as possible. I know a guy just outside of Chinatown that puts together convincing documents, but heading into Vancouver now would be lunacy. Maybe hopping over the border is our best option after all. Even if the U.N.A. discovers we've crossed into the United States they won't know where we're going. A population of 240 million should give us a fair opportunity to blend into the background in the short term, until we can get enough money together to book a flight.

I tell Elizabeth to head for the ATM and we pull off the Fraser Highway and double back to the bank. Ten minutes later we're in an otherwise empty Surrey parking lot and Elizabeth's climbing out of the car. She trudges to the bank machine wearing the expression of a moving target while I hop into the backseat with Freya.

I know she's not exactly in a coma and that Elizabeth said I shouldn't force her to wake up, but maybe her subconscious can hear me and needs encouragement. "Remember all those horror books we used to read when we first got here?" I ask, my voice hushed.

A quote from *The Picture of Dorian Gray* springs into my head: "The basis of optimism is sheer terror." What I'm feeling now is too complicated to be only one thing, but sheer terror is part of it. I have to believe she's reachable—that the Freya I knew is still in there.

"I don't know what we were thinking," I continue. "We should've been reading happy, hopeful things. Stuff like *A Christmas Carol* and Jane Austen novels. *The Lord of the Rings* books even—at least they would've had a positive ending." I wish I had a book with me so I could read to her. Hearing something familiar could help bring her back.

Something like Hendris maybe. As much as Kinnari loved her, Freya was a bigger fan. I only know the lyrics to one

Hendris tune, her biggest hit, "Shade." I stumble over the verses as I sing aloud, fishing for some words and peppering my rendition with mistakes. But I know the chorus as well as anyone and that part I croon with quiet certainty:

We could live in the shade forever
I will take you there tonight
But first you have to learn how to let go
of the difference between darkness and light
The truth is a silence
The truth is a shadow
The truth is a memory
The truth is our right

The rhythm of Freya's breathing doesn't alter. Her brow is furrowed in her sleep, her posture unchanged. When Elizabeth yanks the car door open and gets in, I sigh to myself.

"I could only take out two hundred dollars," Elizabeth explains as she glances at me in the backseat. "It would've been less but I raised the limit this past winter." Anxiety carves into her cheeks. "We'll need more."

I slide out of the backseat and take my place next to Elizabeth in the front. "It'll have to come from somewhere else then."

Elizabeth nods unhappily and starts the engine. We turn out of the parking lot and onto the street. The day looks golden, like one that will draw people to the beaches although officially, summer is weeks away. I squint as I stare towards the sun. Out of nowhere a crow crashes into the windscreen, its body bouncing against the hood of the car and into the roadway.

A savage shriek rings out from directly behind me. Flinching, I twist to see Freya sitting bolt upright in the backseat, her hands on her thighs and her eyes drilling into the spot the crow collided with our windscreen. The sound spilling from Freya's mouth is raw and forlorn, almost alien. I didn't know a person could sound like that in real life and the shock delays my reaction.

"Freya!" I have to shout at her to be heard over the unending scream. "Freya. It's okay. It was just a bird."

But she won't stop shrieking. Elizabeth pulls over to the curb, an angry brown Chevette on our tail honking in complaint, and then whipping around us to zoom past.

"Freya," Elizabeth intones gently as she peers into the backseat. "Freya, dear, don't worry. It's done. It's over and done." Her tone is reminiscent of a mother addressing a child with a skinned knee and Freya presses her lips together and stares, wide-eyed and silent, at Elizabeth.

My own eyes interpret Freya's expression as fascination and now that she's quiet, her harrowing screams fading into the upholstery, I lower my voice and say, "She helped us get away from them." I cock my head to indicate Elizabeth. "But we have to keep going to stay safe."

The intensity of Freya's gaze unnerves me. The relief I want to feel at seeing her awake is halved. "Freya, are you all right?"

Elizabeth rejoins the flow of traffic as I wait for Freya's answer.

Her eyes don't leave mine but she remains quiet. "Freya?" I repeat. "Say something. I need to know you're okay."

With Freya sitting behind me in a stranger's clothes—the pink miniskirt that couldn't be more unlike her—and staring at me from familiar eyes that suddenly seem unknowable, I feel frantic. My instincts tell me to leap into the backseat with her again, but the more cautious side of me warns that any sudden movements might scare her, that after all she's been through I shouldn't violate her personal space.

"Hey," I say softly, deciding Elizabeth's approach was right. "It's okay. Are you thirsty? Is there anything you need?" I thought I saw some orange juice in the trunk among the groceries.

Freya won't even nod or shake her head for me and I stare

accusingly at Elizabeth, who avoids my eyes. Have they turned Freya's mind into a wasteland? My heart crumbles, but I try again. "Freya, listen, can you just...will you raise one of your hands for me?"

Freya glances down at the back of her hands, her face long. Then she lifts both her hands into the air and holds them about a foot from her face, gazing out at me from between them like she's awaiting further instructions.

My face explodes into a smile. She understood me. Her mind wasn't shredded like the boy with the brain tumour.

"Thanks," I tell her, my body filling with gratitude. Tears form behind my eyes. I want to say so much more but I remember what Elizabeth said about giving Freya time.

I watch Freya fit her hands back into her lap, her eyes darting between me and Elizabeth before settling on her own window. Riveted, she stares out at the British Columbia sunshine.

"What about the border then?" Elizabeth asks quietly. "Should we try?"

Break for the border. Like in a western movie. The smile's stuck on my cheeks like it was etched into them with a laser beam. But Freya's silence is a barrier to successfully crossing into the United States. If she refuses to speak to the border guard, he or she will have the car searched and question us in depth. "You know we're less than half an hour away," I warn. "She's not ready."

Elizabeth bobs her head and glances into the backseat. "Freya? How are you doing there?"

Freya switches her attention from the window to Elizabeth. I watch Freya's long lashes blink slowly, her posture frozen as though every bit of her concentration is centred on the sound of Elizabeth's voice.

No reply comes, though. Freya sees me staring and returns my gaze. There's a self-consciousness in her face that makes me feel I should look away.

"Freya," Elizabeth says, her tone as gentle as it was when the crow crashed into the car. "We're going to need you to do something for us soon." Elizabeth glances my way. "Do you have her identification?"

I fish Freya's fake driver's license and social insurance card out of my jeans. The day before our driver's license photos were taken we went white water rafting on the Elaho River. The valley was so unspoiled that time vanished. The effort of paddling was distracting in itself but it was the old growth forests, hanging glaciers, and water that ran wild, rough, and pure, that made me forget—for hours at a time—that I'd ever lived in another time and place. Later that night, as I was thinking back on the day, I remembered how Freya's expression in Elaho had reflected feelings identical to mine. In the middle of that ageless landscape we had nothing to hide. For once, we felt like exactly who we appeared to be.

Looking at her now, I have no idea what Freya's thinking or feeling. I peer at the girl in the photo and am flooded with memories. The real birthdays we celebrated in private because they didn't match up with Robbie and Holly's paperwork. Freya repeating Spanish phrases from the tapes she'd take out of the library. *No hay de que. Lo siento. Te extraño mucho.* Any smattering of Spanish I know is what I picked up listening to Freya.

Last October. When Freya won tickets to see The Cure at the Coliseum and she was so excited the feeling was contagious. I wrapped my arms around her as we danced to "In Between Days," her hands reaching back to grasp my legs and the voices of thousands of Cure fans ringing in my ears: "Come back come back come back to me."

In the present I glance at Elizabeth, wondering what she wants me to do with Freya's ID. "Give it to her," Elizabeth instructs. I reach into the backseat with it, Freya staring at my fingers for ponderous seconds before she lifts one of her own hands to take the driver's license and social insurance card.

"That's who we need you to be, Freya," Elizabeth explains. "If the border guard ask for your name and birthday, that's what you tell them. Can you do that?"

Freya's lips part. She drops her head to examine the documents made out in eighteen-year-old Amy Lewandowski's name, and then nods hesitantly.

I hope she understands, and that she means it. But I don't want to put her through this if it means we'll fail or the effort will strain her mentally. "Look, I know we need to get away from here," I say to Elizabeth. "But if we reach the border and she still won't say anything we're going to attract unwanted attention. Can she even handle this?"

"We'll do most of the talking for her," Elizabeth insists, laying out a back story for customs. I'll be Amy's boyfriend. Elizabeth will say she's Amy's aunt and she's driving the two of us to California for Amy's mother's wedding.

The second marriage story is a nice touch—countless people get divorced here and now, while in the U.N.A. the vast majority of marriages lasted. That doesn't mean the marriages of the future were necessarily stronger, only that gushi gave people a place to escape to where the state of their real life marriages often didn't matter as much.

"Why California?" I ask. Elizabeth's pulled herself together and is thinking on her feet—I'm relieved and surprised to see that, but I'm not sure we're ready to carry out her plan yet. A single look at the gunshot wound under Elizabeth's headband or one wrong word from Freya could push us into more trouble than we're capable of crawling out from under.

"In case the border guard reports back to anyone about us," Elizabeth replies. "We tell them Sacramento but stop in Seattle instead."

"Pick up new identification and book flights out of the country," I add, my eyes swimming to Freya. "Do you understand what we're talking about? Do you remember what happened to you?" I'm desperate to know how much damage we're dealing with.

"Don't ask her about that now," Elizabeth protests, her eyes harsher than her tone. "Save any complicated questions for later. You can see how fragile she seems. We don't want to risk upsetting her and we need to keep her focused on the basics of our story." Elizabeth's features soften as she gazes into the backseat. "We're heading to California for your mother's wedding on Saturday. I'm your aunt Elizabeth and this here is…" She looks to me for confirmation.

"Chris," I say.

"Chris," Elizabeth repeats. "We'll be gone five days. You're Amy Lewandowski and you're…"

"Eighteen." I point to the ID in Freya's hands. "Born on November 13, 1967. Just like it says there. You're Canadian and live in Vancouver. Can you remember all that?"

This time Freya nods readily, like she wants to please us. "Amy," she echoes. "Canadian. My mother's getting married in California on Saturday."

It's amazing to hear her voice. Like a genuine miracle. "Right," I say happily. "Good."

Freya's eyes zoom back to her window and stay there. I give Elizabeth directions to the border: Highway 99 South, which becomes the I-5 in Washington State. I've heard other people discuss the route often enough to remember it.

We pull into a gas station to fill up and so I can dump the gun and most of the groceries before we get on the 99. Then Elizabeth goes to the bathroom to clean what's left of her ear. While she's gone, Freya and I switch seats—if Elizabeth really were her aunt, Freya would be riding up front with her. Climbing out of the car, Freya seems steady on her feet and I want to throw my arms around her and hold on to her for a minute, but she slips nervously past me like I'm a stranger.

The drive down 99 is mostly quiet, punctuated every five minutes or so by Elizabeth's repetition of our cover story. Freya successfully parrots Elizabeth each time. I hold back all the questions I want to ask, and Freya offers no explanations of her own. She's lucid but like a deer caught in headlights.

Twenty minutes later we're at the Washington border, part of the convoy of traffic winding around the Peace Arch. Because of Reagan's death, both flags atop the monument are at half-mast, and although I've lived in Canada for fifteen months it strikes me as strange that the United States and Canada are two nations rather than one. Growing up I always knew them both as the U.N.A. Truthfully, they still seem that way to me. In my mind the border's an illusion that hasn't yet been erased.

There are only a few cars ahead of us in the rapidly shortening customs line. Four. Three. Two. One. We're next. Elizabeth turns expectantly to Freya. "Freya," she says loudly, her hand tapping Freya's shoulder. "*Freya.*"

I unbuckle my seatbelt and lean forwards in my chair to look at her. Freya's fallen back to sleep at the worst possible time. "You said we shouldn't wake her up," I counter. "We need to get out of here." I glance over my shoulder at the cars gathered behind us. We have to turn around somehow, go back where we came from.

But Elizabeth's driving onward. She's decided it's show time, whether we can pull it off or not. Elizabeth rolls down her window, the border guard in the tiny hut to our left gazing down at us. "Citizenship?" he asks.

"Canadian," Elizabeth says, handing him each of our driver's licenses. "All of us."

The border guard flips quickly through the documents. He smiles through his greying beard, pointing at Freya with his thumb. "Looks like you brought a sleeper with you."

Elizabeth pauses, her moment of reticence reeking of guilt. *We shouldn't have chanced crossing yet. Her panic to get away has ruined us.* Then Elizabeth's right hand flies out to stroke Freya's hair. "The poor thing isn't feeling well," she says. "A touch of food poisoning from the fish she had for supper last night."

Freya wriggles in her seat, gasping into consciousness like someone saved from drowning.

"Wakey, wakey," the border guard says in a tone midway

between comical and someone who enjoys the power that comes with his job a little too much. "So where are you folks going?"

"Sacramento." Elizabeth replies. "My sister—her mother—is getting married."

"And you?" He wags a finger at me in the backseat.

I tilt my head to indicate Freya/Amy. "I'm her boyfriend." That much is the truth and the words slide easily off my tongue. "Her wedding date."

"How long will the three of you be staying in the United States?"

"Five days," Freya blurts out in a dry voice.

The border guard chuckles at Freya's enthusiastic joining of the conversation. "Well, don't eat any bad fish." He hands Elizabeth our licenses and adds, "Have a good day."

My shoulders unknot as we leave the custom station in our wake. Elizabeth pulled it off but she shouldn't have rushed Freya. We can't afford to make mistakes, and I can't trust her judgement.

My fingers squeeze Freya's arm before I lean back in my chair and snap my seatbelt on. "Good job."

"Thank you," she says meekly.

Within minutes she's out again and my eyelids are heavy too. I need to stay awake, to make sure Elizabeth doesn't screw us over somehow or make a wrong move, and for a while longer I do. My throat's dry and I gulp down some of the juice I salvaged from the groceries in the trunk. Then I lay into Elizabeth, in barbed whispers, for defying her own advice about not waking Freya and being patient with her.

While Elizabeth's defending herself I drift away, her voice fading into the hum of the car chugging along the highway. Last night left me exhausted, and between glances out the window I dream snatches of dreams—visions of my mothers dancing together in a future life, of Freya and me paddling in Elaho, of the two of us having lunch on a roof terrace in Ronda, and of art classes with Seneval that end in her death.

Nothing's really over. Everything stays with you. The past. The future. Your dreams. Your fears. The people you've lost and the ones you're afraid to lose. Nothing is ever finished.

That's how it feels each time I wake up, that I'll be looping through my life forever. Until the last instance, when I catch Freya staring into the backseat, watching me like I'm an exotic zoo animal. Her eyes clear my mind of everything but her. "You're awake," I observe.

"Am I?" Her lashes blink with a rapidness anyone from the U.N.A. would recognize. It's what people of the future did at the moment of exiting gushi and returning to real life. An automatic reaction to clear gushi visions and adjust their eyes to reality. Only gushi hasn't been invented yet.

"Of course you are," I say gently but firmly. "You're wide awake."

The view from outside the window catches my eye, diverting my attention: tall buildings, long city blocks, and a monorail zooming almost directly over our heads. *We made it to Seattle.*

"We just arrived," Elizabeth tells me. "I don't know the city. Where do you think we should go?"

I don't know Seattle either. It was abandoned before I was born.

So we drive like the tourists we are, Elizabeth and I craning our necks as we cruise around in circles. We pass the Space Needle, the Pike Place Market, and an area that appears to be a business district. Then we swing around and head north again, crossing over the bay. On a nondescript street a few blocks from the University of Washington, we stumble across a motel. It looks like the kind of place we can afford and I instruct Elizabeth to give the person at the front desk a sob story about her credit cards and baggage being stolen. The same story worked for me once, but with her middle-aged office clerk persona, Elizabeth will be believed more readily than I would.

Left alone in the parking lot I finally return my gaze to Freya, who has stopped her rapid blinking but whose profoundly confused eyes worry me. "Everything's under control," I assure her. "Don't worry. We're going to be fine. The hard part is over with—we got across."

Freya grinds her lips together and glances down at her chipped purple nails. "I don't...I don't understand," she stammers. "What is this? How come I can't stop it?"

This is exactly what I was afraid of when I saw her eyelashes flutter in that telltale way. She thinks everything she's seeing and hearing is gushi, that she's somehow stuck. There hasn't been a case of gushi cementing since 2039 but I might suspect the same thing in her place.

"I'll explain everything when we get inside." I don't want her to go into shock and cause a scene before we can get her safely into the motel room. "It'll just be a few minutes now. But trust me, you don't have anything to worry about."

"The way you repeated that is making me nervous," Freya admits. "We're in a lot of trouble, aren't we?"

"Not nearly as much as before." I don't know how much she remembers about being taken but Elizabeth's advice to save the complicated questions for later echoes in my mind. Regardless, I can't resist asking the one that's been looping through my head since Freya first opened her eyes. "Do you remember me?"

Freya nods soberly. It's the answer I was hoping for, yet it still feels wrong. "Do you remember me?" she asks.

"I remember everything about you." My hand reaches for hers, closing tenderly around her cool fingers.

Freya peers down at our linked hands. Silence envelopes us. It feels strangely like the first time we touched. Like this is brand new again and together we're something not yet decided.

We're still holding hands when Elizabeth opens the car door and interrupts the quiet minutes later. "We're hours early for their regular check-in time but we're in luck," Elizabeth chirps proudly. "They had a room for us. I had to pay them a deposit because of the credit card situation but they'll refund it when we check out." Her chin slopes down as she takes in the image of our hands. "I told them you were siblings so you shouldn't do that anywhere motel staff could see."

Freya snatches her fingers back, two splotches of red forming on her cheeks. I feel the sensation of her fingers against mine even when they're gone. I grab Freya's charity box clothes from the trunk and Freya and I trail Elizabeth through the lobby and up to our room. Surveying its matching queen-size beds, I realize I should've stolen a change of clothes for myself too. My head fills up with things that still need to be done as I pile Freya's clothes on the bureau behind me. The fake passports. Money for plane tickets. Flying someplace new where they'll never find us and creating different lives for ourselves while hoping the threat of Minnow's virus has been neutralized by the very people who could be searching for us right now.

If Elizabeth thinks she can depend on me to scratch the first thing off our list, she's wrong. I'm not leaving Freya alone again.

"Stretch out and lie down, Freya," Elizabeth advises, motioning to the beds. Freya lowers herself tentatively onto the nearest mattress, her feet still solidly on the floor. She tugs restlessly at her miniskirt, trying to make it cover more of her thighs than it was designed to.

"You said you'd explain," Freya reminds me.

"I will." But first I turn to Elizabeth. "You need to go get us passports. I'll give you some money for ours."

Elizabeth's face pales. "You'd be better at that than I would. I have no idea how to find someone who could make us convincing forgeries."

"Or sell us doctored stolen passports," I add, gazing protectively at Freya on the bed. "You'll do fine. I can't leave her here."

"You can leave her with me," Elizabeth insists. "I'll watch out for her."

"Forgive me if I don't want to leave her in the hands of one of the people who were ready to do a hatchet job on…" I don't want Freya to overhear so I stop short, throwing my good hand into the air in a gesture of defiance. "She stays with me. It's not up for discussion."

Elizabeth points her gaze in Freya's direction and sighs soundlessly.

"Look, you got us through customs and you got us this room," I continue. "Dealing with the kind of people who can get us passports will be easy. They'll want your business. You just need to find them." My left palm itches under my cast. The cast itself feels heavy and looser than it should. 1986 medical technology is lousy and I haven't treated my wrist or the cast that surrounds it with the tenderness it requires. "When you get outside ask someone what the worst part of town is. When you reach it zero in on anyone who looks shady, like they could be dealing."

This is probably a tall order for someone like Elizabeth, who has likely never dealt with any 'bad guys' unless you want to include U.N.A. personnel in the category. Once she leaves the motel with a chunk of my cash in her pocket there's always the chance Elizabeth will skip town without us. But I have to risk something here and it won't be Freya.

Crestfallen, Elizabeth points out, "They'll need photos."

"They can leave that part for last. We'll stop into a photo booth later and then bring the photos in when we go pick the passports up. Freya needs to rest first."

Freya bristles at my suggestion from the bed. "Freya needs to know what's going on," she insists, her cheeks pinkening like they did when we held hands in the car.

Elizabeth clutches her abdomen. "I can't do this all on my own. Even if I can find someone to sell us passports, what are we going to do about the flights? We'll need at least fifteen hundred dollars to get us to Europe."

If that's even where we want to go. Having seen inside Freya's head, if the U.N.A. decides to widen their net beyond North America, Spain would be the first place they'd look for us. Better to avoid Europe entirely and head for South America.

But I don't plan to tell Elizabeth where we're going. Once we get to the airport our trio will have to divide into two parts. It'll be safer for everyone.

Unfortunately, more risks will need to be taken first. There's no safe, legal way for us to get our hands on anywhere near as much cash as Elizabeth mentioned. She and I both know that. We'll have to steal it. Hopefully from someone who doesn't need it as badly as we do. And when it happens, it will be one more thing I can't allow myself to feel bad about.

In the meantime I frown and nod. "I'll figure something out while you're gone. But it could be dangerous."

"We can't be caught." Elizabeth's frown is at least as deep as my own.

"I don't plan on it. But I'll probably need your help." I feel Freya's stare on my cheeks, the warmth spreading to my forehead and down along my neck. She's like a sponge, absorbing every word Elizabeth and I say but giving no indication of how she feels about any of it. "We'll talk about it when you get back, okay?" Before I can start worrying about coming up with clever robbery plans and the price to be paid if the police catch me in the act, I need to be alone with Freya. My arms are dying to hold her, and we have to talk. One night apart from her felt like forever.

"Okay," Elizabeth agrees reluctantly. "Give me the windbreaker at least. I'm still wearing the same clothes they last saw me in."

"They *who*?" Freya demands.

Elizabeth floats me a wary look as I hand her the windbreaker and a pair of hundred-dollar bills. She presses the extra room key into my hand before turning on her heel and exiting the suite.

With the door closed behind us, Freya's head wilts on her shoulders. "My head hurts and I'm so thirsty, so tired. What happened to me? Where are we and what kind of trouble are we in?"

Freya's skin is waxy and pale and she hasn't had any fluids since before I unhooked her from the wires back in British Columbia. "Let me get you some water," I say, zipping into the bathroom for glasses.

I upend one for each of us, turn on the faucet and fill two glasses of water. It doesn't take more than a few seconds but when I return to the bedroom Freya's asleep on top of the bedspread, her feet still hanging off the mattress. Elizabeth said coming out of the wipe process could be gradual and it looks like she was right. Freya's worn out.

I set her water on the nightstand next to her and gulp mine down. Then I gather up Freya's feet, sandals and all, and lift them slowly onto the bed. I fold the bedspread over her and lie down next to her, watching her sleep, so happy her higher reasoning capabilities seem intact that it feels like something close to what Kinnari was looking for in meditation and numerology. We didn't really have words to describe the feeling in the U.N.A. but I know what many people here and now would call it.

A state of grace.

SEVENTEEN: 1986

Outside, a woman's whistling "The Greatest Love of All."
Still half asleep, I roll over onto my left arm. It's the feel
of the cast around my wrist that makes me open my eyes.
In the first moments of wakefulness you can forget anything.
Freya was never taken. I didn't break my wrist or shoot Isaac
Monroe. My sister never died of Toxo. There's only this unseen
phantom woman whistling cheerfully from some undefined
place. One of the motel maids, maybe, I realize as I float closer
towards consciousness.

The bedspread has been folded over me the way I folded it
over Freya earlier and there's a space where her body should be.
I gaze sleepily at the closed bathroom door. "Freya?"

In the corridor, the sound of Whitney Houston's biggest hit
begins to fade. Since the future I knew is in the process of being
rewritten, Whitney Houston has another chance along with
everyone else. Maybe this time she'll live to be ninety-seven.

"Freya?" I repeat, my gaze flicking over to the empty glass
on the nightstand at her side of the bed. "Are you all right?"

I jump to my feet, take three long strides to the bathroom
door, and pull it open. *Empty.*

The U.N.A. can't have taken her—they would've grabbed
me too—and I curse as I fly into the hall. Where would she go?
I rampage through the motel with my face burning—the coffee
shop, the pool area, and every damn hallway in the motel—I
scour them all looking for her.

The extra room key is snugly in my back pocket, and I stand

in the lobby counting what's left of the cash Isaac returned to me. Minus the two hundred dollars I gave Elizabeth, it's all still there. Freya's fled with only the clothes on her back.

I don't know why she'd do it and I don't know who I'm angrier with, myself or her. But I have to find her. Jogging into the street, I'm breathless with worry. I circle the streets surrounding the motel, expanding my perimeter as I see no sign of Freya's red hair or pink miniskirt.

I run with a violence that leaves me gasping on the corner of Northeast Forty-Third Street and Eighth Avenue, my body bent and my palms on my lower thighs to steady myself. If I didn't know better I'd think I was in some not-quite-trendy urban Vancouver neighbourhood—the low-rise apartment buildings and modest houses look and feel West Coast familiar.

A wave of dizziness knocks me to my knees. After everything that happened last night—the drugs, the shootings, the shock—my body can't take much more. I need a minute. My knees ache from the fall and I stretch them out in front of me as I fill my lungs with oxygen. Exhale. Inhale. Exhale.

Freya said she remembered me but clearly she didn't remember the U.N.A. snatching her. There were holes in her memory that caused her to run off. Where would I go if I had gaps in my memory? Where would I look for answers? Is it possible she's wandered back to the motel and is waiting for me there?

I force myself up and half sprint, half walk to the University Motor Inn, fighting the sensation that I'm about to pass out. Inside the motel I race to the room and find it just as I left it. I knock back two glasses of water, hoping that will be enough to keep me upright, and head straight back into the street where I snare the first cab I see.

It smells like smoke and my lungs greedily suck in the bad air. "Where to?" the driver asks.

I have no clue. I'm out of my mind with worry. Can barely string together the words that will get the cab moving.

"Got an address for me?" the driver prompts, an edge creeping into his tone. He must've faced down a dozen varieties of weirdoes while doing his job. I'm just the latest.

"No address," I mumble. "I need to find someone." I tell him about Freya's pink skirt and red hair, say we had a terrible fight and she ran off.

The driver pushes at one of his sleeves. "Look, I'm no private eye. Your girlfriend will come back when she's cooled down. You're better to sit and wait it out."

"I can't do that. I need to find her now." Maybe he's worried I won't pay him. I pull a hundred dollar bill from my pocket, waving it frenziedly. "Take it. You can give me the change later."

The driver stares at the offered bill. "No American cash?"

I'd forgotten I'd have to change currency. Last I heard the Canadian dollar was worth a lousy seventy-one cents. "Sorry, I just got here."

The driver pinches the inferior Canadian bill between two of his fingers and gives me a tired look, like he's doing me a favour. "Okay, then. Let's go."

Because I have no idea where Freya could be, we begin by making a wider circle around the motel. Then we cross the bay and the driver takes me to the heart of the shopping district. I do a double take every time I see a girl with red hair or one poured into a pink miniskirt. The driver points out likely candidates. None of them are Freya and we continue to whirl around the city for close to an hour before the driver suggests I try the Space Needle.

"Everybody who comes to Seattle for the first time wants to go up the Space Needle," he says. "I bet that's where she went."

He could be right and I ask him to take me there. Relief lights up his face when we reach the Space Needle. He hands me American greenbacks in change, happy to be rid of me.

The disc section at the top of the needle reminds me of the one perched atop Vancouver's Harbour Centre. I can only hope

Freya feels the same way and that it drew her here. I pay $3.50 to ride the elevator up to the observation platform. The sunny morning has become a sunny day and the view from the platform is striking—blue water and blue mountains in nearly every direction, ferries, cargo lines, cruise ships, and buzzing city streets framed with skyscrapers. There's even a float plane coming in for a landing on the lake below while I roam the deck looking for Freya. I check the revolving restaurant too, and when I'm one-hundred-percent sure she's not here, I stagger into the street.

There's a bus approaching and I dash for the nearest stop. Since I don't know where to search next, public transit is as useful as a cab. Soon I'm heading south on Second Avenue, my eyes glued to the window and my mind filled with visions of pink and red. I can't think straight. Can't believe this has happened.

Fifteen minutes later I hop off the bus and start pounding the pavement, light-headed again. My feet carry me in random directions, zigzagging by late nineteenth century brick and stone buildings. Art galleries, cafés, nightclubs, and book stores dot the area but it's anything but gentrified. As I walk the people's faces become harder. Lower East Side people. People like the Cursed of 2063. Many of them homeless or otherwise down on their luck, like me.

It wouldn't surprise me if this is the spot Elizabeth ended up in search of passports. With her help, I'd have a better chance of finding Freya, and I wonder if I should head back to the motel to see if Elizabeth has returned, or at least call our room.

I've only begun scouting out a payphone when I spy a totem pole across the street. Accordion music wafts in my direction as I near the public square where the totem pole is rooted. I've seen these in Vancouver too—a collection of vibrantly painted totem poles nestled in the middle of Stanley Park—and I guess that's what tugs me towards the square, the eye's fondness for familiar things.

When I reach the square, which is really more of a triangle, the accordion player launches into "American Pie," his feet moving in time to the music. The man's wearing a fedora and brown plaid suit and he smiles jauntily as I pass.

I can't smile back.

Not in that moment.

Then everything changes. *I see her.* In that pink miniskirt she'd never pick out for herself, her red hair a beacon in the sunshine. She's sitting on a park bench next to a homeless man with a grizzly grey beard and oversized hood pulled over his skull, the two of them deep in conversation and unwrapped Big Macs in their laps.

The totem pole is directly behind them and I approach quickly, my eyes smarting as my world hastily reassembles itself. I stand in front of Freya, the man next to her noticing me first. "Can you spare any change, buddy?" he asks, his eyes leaping to my face.

I don't answer him. I sit on my haunches and touch Freya's knee. "What happened to you? Why did you leave?" It would be easy to shout at her now that I've had the good luck to find her again, but the anger's already dissolving. "You had me worried sick. How did you even get here?"

"You were asleep," Freya tells me, without the slightest note of apology. "I didn't think it could matter when none of this is real."

"This is real life." I say it with complete conviction. I should've made the point more forcefully before she had the chance to run away. "It's not a dream and you're not in gushi."

Freya's neighbour on the bench frowns. "She's a bit touched," he says under his breath. "I've been looking out for her. Got her something to eat." He glances at her half-eaten Big Mac, then back at me. "It seems you know her well."

"Very well. I'm going to take her home. Thanks for watching over her." I reach out to shake his hand.

The man pumps my good hand and then tips an imaginary

hat to Freya as she rises to accompany me, leaving the remains of her Big Mac behind. She waves goodbye to the man before turning to face me. "I don't understand any of this," she says, distraught. "It can't be real." She runs one of her hands over the hip of her skirt. "The clothes, the transportation. They must be nearly a hundred years old." Her gaze soars to the architecture surrounding us. "The buildings are even older. Like in Moss or parts of New York. But this is the West Coast—the *deserted* West Coast."

"It's not deserted. Not yet." I point to the first greasy spoon I see. No more waiting. I'll tell her everything right now, but I need something to eat while I do it. I'm wobbly on my feet. Feel like I could collapse at any second. "This is 1986 Seattle. Not a simulation or any kind of game, the genuine article."

"Not possible," Freya counters as the two of us slip into the restaurant. A waitress gestures in the direction of an empty booth with two menus in the middle of the table. I order sausages and eggs with French fries without looking at the menu and Freya asks for ice water.

Our eyes lock across the table. "Tell me the last thing you remember before waking up in the car," I say. The din from the other customers will prevent anyone from hearing us. Besides, who would believe the things we have to say?

Freya shivers and wraps her right hand around the salt shaker, pulling it closer. "Playing veloxball at Thomas Jefferson. In Gym C. You know, the one near the general auditorium."

Thomas Jefferson is the school Freya and I went to together in Montana before we were sent through the chute. *Veloxball*...I haven't heard the word in so long it freezes my brain. As it sputters to life, it's jerked nearly eighty-years into the future. Veloxball is essentially soccer played in a simulated low-gravity environment—much faster and wilder than traditional sport, which is seldom played in the future, except by people much older than us who aren't as aggravated by the slower pace. My mind yo-yos, crashing back to the here and now. Freya. Seattle.

1986.

"What year was that?" I prod. If she doesn't remember anything of her time in the 1980s it's no wonder she can't accept this as reality. There've been so many occasions, late at night, lying in bed sleepless, that I've found myself nearly losing grip on the truth myself.

"2061." Freya's voice bubbles with impatience.

2061: two years before Toxo hit, which means any of her surviving memories are from when she was fourteen or younger.

"So that's where you remember me from—Thomas Jefferson?" I think of the day we spoke about her family's domestic Ro being taken into custody. Freya would've been a couple of years younger than fourteen then. Her stares in the hallway came later. I can't remember exactly when —I didn't pay much attention at the time. But is that why she let me hold her hand in the car earlier? Had she already begun to develop an attraction to me in 2061? It's been a long time since Freya's crush on me was a secret, but she never pinned it down to a date.

Freya nods and swallows a mouthful of the water the waitress has delivered to the table.

I choose my words and tone carefully, remembering how difficult it was for me to accept the truth in 1985. "This is going to be very hard to believe, Freya, but try to keep an open mind." The waitress has brought me coffee. I forgot to order it but I must look like I need it and I loop my fingers through the mug's handle and gulp down caffeine before continuing. Then I begin with 2063, explaining about the Toxo outbreak—the convergence of biological weapon P-47 and the terrorist-created virus Mossegrim. Together they created too big a threat for the U.N.A. to neutralize and I hate to be the one to take Freya's brother from her this third time but she has to know.

Freya freezes when I tell her about Latham and Kinnari. She's motionless for so long that I wonder if she's going into shock. Then her shoulders quiver. She shakes her head, pounds the table with her fist and tells me to stop. "This is crazy!" she yells. "Latham's not dead. There's no such thing as *Toxo*. Latham's probably never even spoken to your sister."

Freya's eyes are wet and that makes it tougher for me to keep going. I tell her what I know about her and her family. Details about Latham and her parents that it would be impossible for me to know if she or Latham hadn't shared them. Freya's second sight too. The numerous times she forgave her father for being "too tired for children's voices." I offer it all as proof of our unbelievable story before confessing the most staggering part—the Nipigon chute, an unexplained natural phenomenon. Real life magic that hurtles anyone or anything that encounters it seventy-eight years, seven months, and eleven days back in time. And how the U.N.A. used the chute to save us from Toxo, giving the world a second chance but also making us victims of a wipe and cover.

"It was you that figured it out," I tell her. The food arrived a while back and I've finished most of it, so immersed in what I've been saying that my taste buds haven't registered a bite. The fat and salt have done their job, though. Filled me up and kept me from passing out. "You recognized me on some level despite the wipe. You wouldn't leave things alone until you found out the truth." A sliver of embarrassment roosts in the pit of my stomach as I describe our time on the run—the highlights of the last fifteen months, from Toronto to Vancouver to her being taken. The nature of our relationship seems natural to me but I can imagine how it would feel to a mentally fourteen-year-old Freya—someone who was never grounded like I was and who hasn't had the introduction to 1985 the cover gave her the last time she was wiped.

Freya's eyes are dry again by the time I stop talking. Pity battles with anger in her face. "You've thought of everything, haven't you?" she says. "Every minuscule detail. It's like a paranoid delusion from the old days. Is that what's the matter with you? Some kind of sickness?"

I've overloaded her with her information—it's too much to process at once. "How would I know about your second sight if I was delusional? That was your family secret. You told me your mother even made you hide it from your father later on because he wanted you to be tested. He thought you might be able to use your gift to help the U.N.A."

"Then this isn't real," she insists. "Something's happened to my brain. You're not here. I'm not here. There is *no* here. This place doesn't exist outside my head or gushi."

"What's happened to you then?" I challenge. "You know there hasn't been any gushi cementing in decades." And if we were in the 2060s, the Bio-net would correct nearly anything else that could be wrong with her.

"I don't know what's happened." Freya stands up quickly, knocking over her empty glass in the process. "But not the things you've said."

I stand up with her, blocking her way. "Don't run again." I grab both her arms and hold her in place. "I know it sounds insane. I felt the same way when you told me the truth last year. But if you take off again they might find you and try to finish the job they started. Even if they don't find you, you have no idea how to survive here. It's not like where we're from."

The two things I haven't mentioned yet are Isaac's virus—a threat that could still be out there—and the nuclear war of 2071. I can't tell her about either of them now. They would only sound like more outrageous lies and she has so much to digest already.

Freya doesn't struggle with me but her stare is stubborn and icy. "Let go of me."

I try using her own logic against her. Whatever will keep her safe. "If you think this is all in your head maybe I'm here in your mind for a reason, to look out for you somehow. You protecting yourself."

Freya breaks our visual connection and focuses on the table. "You'll say anything, won't you? It's like a game. If you get me to stay with you, you win."

"How does that fit with your theory about everything being inside your head?" I argue.

I have her there. Freya shrugs listlessly, her arms tense and her hair falling into her face.

"Please." I release her, our bodies still less than a foot away from each other. "Come back to the motel with me. We can talk more. I'll tell you anything you want to know. Just don't disappear on me again. I thought I lost you. Twice in two days." I'd drag her back to the motel by force if it wouldn't cause a scene. If I had Elizabeth's car with me I might risk it. Without it, we'd never make it that far. I know how tough Freya can be, even if she doesn't realize it herself yet. She'd scream her lungs out and fight me so hard that we'd attract police in no time.

Freya shifts her weight and brushes her hair out of her face. Out of the corner of my eye I spy our waitress behind her, waiting to be paid. I yank a fistful of cash out of my pocket, afraid to take my attention off Freya for even a few seconds.

"What happened to your hand?" Freya asks as I drop a couple of bills on the table, next to our dirty dishes. Her tone is muted and slightly curious.

"I think my wrist is broken. I fell while trying to escape last night." *Which she doesn't believe happened.*

"You look different," Freya allows. "Older than I remember."

"Because I am."

"Right," Freya says doubtfully, glancing at the café door. "I don't want to go back to the motel but I can walk with you for a while, if you want."

I'd rather we stay out of view indoors but at least she isn't making me chase her. As we head for the door together I'm acutely aware she might break into a sprint at any moment.

Outside we begin walking down First Avenue. Freya makes me explain, a second time and in greater detail, about the Nipigon chute and the many things that have happened since we were sent back in time—the man who pretended to be our grandfather but was an agent of the U.N.A., leaving our mothers behind for their own safety, the hypnotherapy that returned our authentic memories, our jobs and apartment in Vancouver, and our old plan to settle in Ronda after travelling the world to see the animals we'd lost to extinction.

"It's a good story," Freya tells me, not unkindly. By now we've found our way into a secluded walled-in park where tables and chairs are laid out near a waterfall. The setting looks like a fairy tale, which doesn't help my cause.

Freya's sitting next to me, her toes scrunching up in her stolen sandals. "These clothes feel weird," she observes, her fingers scratching at the fabric of her skirt.

U.N.A. fabrics had come a long way. As comfortable as a second skin; you were barely aware of them. I've grown used to the clothes here, along with most other things, but they must seem as rough and heavy as a burlap sack to her.

"That was one of the reasons they wiped and covered us, supposedly," I tell her. "To help us adjust to life back here."

A tiny bird lands on the small circular table between us. It hops towards Freya and the trace of a smile appears on her lips. The expression vanishes before it can take hold. "The first thing I remember is the trans hitting that crow," she says. "I was in the school gym before that. Then I was here. I must've suffered a head injury or been infected by something. A new terrorist virus like the one you told me about."

The bird takes flight, soaring away from us and into a nearby tree. We both watch it go.

"So you don't believe this is gushi anymore?" I ask.

"I don't know. I've never felt this tired in gushi." Freya hunches over, her elbows in her lap and her chin in her hands. She should be resting back at the motel, but at least we're well hidden here. The only other people in the park with us are a middle-aged couple sipping coffee out of paper cups and a college-aged girl with her head buried in a John le Carré novel.

"You don't have any virus. You're fine." I slouch in my chair, my legs sloped in front of me like fallen tree trunks. "We've both been through a lot. I'm tired too."

"The part of my brain that's protecting me is tired," Freya notes lightly. "I guess we need to get you an understudy."

I smile, a chuckle escaping from my throat. Despite her weariness Freya smiles back at me. "You sound the same," she says. "Not that we ever talked that much, but from what I remember. And in your…your story about us, you said we were *together*?"

"For the past fifteen months. Since just after we met back here and realized who we really were." I don't know what will become of us if the last three and a half years of her memories are gone for good. I'm practically a stranger to her. In Freya's mind, the things I remember so vividly never happened. Will she grow into that person I remember? Can we start over or will it be different between us this time?

"What was it like?" she asks. "What were *we* like?"

I hesitate. The thought of discussing our shared past with a different Freya is too surreal for words. Can't she see in my face what were we like? How hard it is for me to sit across from her like a casual acquaintance when I want to pull her into my lap and bury my face in the crook of her neck?

I push my lips into a rigid grin. "You won't believe me whatever I tell you."

Freya rubs her eyes, tiredness overtaking her again. "I don't know what to believe, Garren."

My name on her lips makes me shiver. "We fought sometimes," I volunteer. "But we were good together." Better than good. "I can't imagine being with anyone else." A shyness that shouldn't have any place between us steals into my ribs. I ignore it and continue. "I'm in love with you."

Freya flinches. Her hands balance on either side of her chair. Her expression morphs from sheepish to dispassionate as she stares at me from under her lashes. "I must have felt that same thing if I went back in time to save you."

She's referring to old Freya. The very first Freya. The one who watched me die in the street and then hurled herself into the chute to give us a second chance.

I can't tell if I'm making any headway with this Freya or whether she's still convinced the present is some kind of illusion, a joke being played out in her mind. But what she's just said couldn't be more serious to me, and I don't know how to respond. I hesitate for so long that she adds, "You don't seem like a bad person but I wish you hadn't said those things about Latham dying and the virus. Maybe you couldn't help it because you're only a part of my mind—some kind of manifestation of my deepest fears—but it was a cold thing to lie about." Freya glares at me indignantly. "You should take it back."

So far my patience with her has come naturally, but now it collapses under the weight of a grief that will never fully heal. "I won't take back the truth. And it wasn't just Latham who got sick, it was Kinnari too. If you think I'd lie about her horrible transformation—the inhuman things the Toxo virus did to her—then you're hopelessly in denial." My voice sprouts thorns. They slice into my throat as I describe the night I woke up to find Kinnari in my bedroom, scratching her face, laughing manically, and apologizing to me for something she couldn't have helped. *The infection.*

That was only the beginning and I explain the rest in anguished fits and starts. Kinnari's devolution. The monster my sister became while my mothers and I could only watch helplessly from beyond the force field. My eyes are searing and blinded with unspilt tears as I remember what Kinnari did to her pet bird, what she would've done to us if she'd had the chance.

I could've prevented her infection in the first place, but I thought I had more important things to do. Freya used to blame herself for Latham's infection too, back when she could remember it. We tried not to speak of the terrible details from that night and instead hold fast to our previous images of

Kinnari and Latham. The people they truly were. Not the puppets the Toxo made them.

But being forced to confront that night again after everything else I've been through in the past twenty-four hours breaks me. My vocal cords are slashed to shreds, my inner strength bleeding into the pavement underneath my feet.

Freya grips my good hand under the table, stopping me dead. Her fingers are warm, unlike the last time I held them, and her eyes are pink and pained. It's minutes before either of us says anything, and then Freya cuts through the silence. "You're too tired to do this anymore," she says, newfound tenderness in her tone. "I think maybe we should go back to the motel now."

I nod and push my chair back, our hands untwining. We stroll slowly out of the park together, probably looking, to any passersby, like two regular people who've been poking holes in their relationship and then trying to knit the pieces together again.

EIGHTEEN: 1986

know that Freya hasn't suddenly decided to take my story on faith or regained her memories from the last three and a half years while we were sitting in the park; it's only that she can't deny the truthfulness of my emotion and doesn't want to argue anymore. I understand all that as we step through Seattle streets together. I guess I was never going to convince her of the convoluted truth in one afternoon. It will take time. I don't know how long. Day, weeks, months. But as long as she doesn't run off again, we're heading in the general right direction.

I spy a drugstore window advertising passport photos as we walk, and I guide Freya inside the store with me. The woman who snaps our pictures says usually there'd be more of a wait but it's been a slow day and she can have them ready for us in thirty minutes. We wander up and down the aisles, Freya sleepily examining the magazines, headache and digestive remedies, and hair products. Sometimes she stops to read packages' small print and other times she holds the objects up to me so I can explain their function.

In aisle three I catch her eyeing up the sanitary napkins with a frown. The Bio-net made such things unnecessary in the future, but Freya makes no comment on their strangeness.

Soon we're in a cab on our way back to the motel and Freya tells me about the college student who gave her a ride into Pioneer Square and the homeless man, Jim, who befriended her there. "He didn't seem to have anything of his own," she says, "but he used some of his physical currency to buy me one of those Mac things because I was hungry."

"How did you like it?" Compared to what Freya was used to in 2061, the Big Mac would've tasted like salty rubber, as most fast food of 1986 does. Strangely, you find yourself developing cravings for it anyway. Sodium, trans fat, fructose, caffeine, nicotine.

Freya makes a face but diplomacy quickly replaces her expression of distaste. "It was really generous of him. I wish there was some way for us to help him."

"I do too." There are too many people with nowhere to go and I'm not sure what's worse, letting them live in the streets where they have to beg for whatever they can get, or warehousing them in camps the way we did in the future. Jim has his freedom but probably doesn't know where his next meal will come from. Malyck Dixon was fed every day but kept on such a short leash that my dog June, before she was stolen, had more liberty.

I don't ask Freya if her sympathy for Jim is another sign she's coming around to the truth, but I take it as one.

Minutes later we're settling into the motel room again. Elizabeth hasn't returned, which gives me something else to worry about. Maybe she took the two hundred dollars I gave her and put it towards a one way ticket to Belgium. She could've been lying about how much cash she had back in B.C., just like I was. She could be jetting over Washington State as I watch Freya unbuckle her sandals. It wouldn't surprise me.

For all I know, Elizabeth could've made a call to one of the U.N.A. directors and fixed a deal. Information about our whereabouts for a promise not to chase her. Putting my fate in her hands has gotten Freya and me this far but the last time I decided to trust someone it ended with me burying a bullet in his chest. So just how long should we wait for Elizabeth to return?

Freya's already crawling back into bed, casting an uncertain look in my direction. If she believes none of this is real, odds are she'll act more recklessly than she would otherwise. After all, bodies can be fit together for hours without any consequences in gushi or whatever kind of vision she thinks she could be having. But if she's not so sure, like her expression suggests, maybe she wants to keep me at a safe distance.

"I'll be over here," I assure her, dropping into the nearest chair. I want to stay awake, be ready for anything that might happen. And if Elizabeth isn't back soon, Freya and I will have to skip out. Catch a bus or train that will take us far away from here and acquire more cash in the quickest and easiest way possible. I'm not looking forward to it but that's reality. We've run out of options and stand at the point where I'll have to knock off a convenience store or some other place with minimal security in order to buy flights off the continent.

There's no time to raise enough money legitimately, and I'm running through robbery scenarios in my head, staring from the numbers on the nightstand clock radio to Freya's sleeping form, when a key turns in the door. Elizabeth bursts into the room in a patterned head scarf, the windbreaker I gave her earlier, and a pair of jeans that she's folded at the ankles. "Where have you been?" she demands, her jaw and shoulders taut.

"Where have *you* been?" I fire back, my fingers grasping at an inch's worth of air. "We were this close to leaving."

"I came back hours ago. There was no one here." Elizabeth's panting as she marches towards my chair, her left hand closed around a plastic bag. "I thought you'd either been taken or left. I've been driving around looking for you, hoping it was some kind of misunderstanding."

"She wandered off while I was asleep." I glance at Freya on the bed. Our shouting has woken her. "It took hours to find her. She was all the way across town. When we got back and you still weren't here, I thought you'd left Seattle without us. I was going to give you until six o'clock." It's almost six now.

Outrage blossoms on Elizabeth's face. "I wouldn't leave without you, Garren."

I'm glad to be wrong. "Why didn't you leave a note?"

Elizabeth unties her scarf. "In case they'd been here, taken you, and were planning on returning."

"But you came back anyway." She has more loyalty than I've given her credit for. I'm impressed.

"You could've written a note, too, you realize," she says testily. "That would've saved us the misunderstanding."

"I left in a hurry." I explain about Freya's three-and-a-half-year memory gap and the difficulty I had convincing her to come back to the motel while Freya looks on from across the room, her weight balanced on her elbows.

Elizabeth approaches the bed and begins quizzing Freya about dates and events. It doesn't take long to confirm her memories end partway through 2061, in the middle of that game of veloxball in Thomas Jefferson's Gymnasium C.

Freya's lips harden, her tone teeming with intellectual curiosity. "If what Garren told me is true, then you were one of the people who tried to wipe me."

Elizabeth bows her head. "I can't discuss it, except to say that we were wrong and I'm happy there wasn't more damage done."

I remind Freya that most people working for the U.N.A. are unable to discuss the future or their work because specific mentions of either activate a wipe sequence. "But never mind that now." I hurry the conversation along, afraid it could lead us to Isaac and the things I've intentionally omitted. "What about the passports?"

"We need to bring photographs in tomorrow morning." Elizabeth turns to take a seat in the only other chair in the room. "My first lead didn't pan out. There was no one home at the address. I waited for an hour and half before starting fresh. Then there was more waiting before I could meet with the second man. He took half the cost in advance and will attach the photos when we come in and pay the rest of his fee. There's some other potential good news. He has a contact in a repair shop and we might be able to get some money for the car."

A chop shop that will take the car apart and sell its pieces. "How much would they give us for it?"

"I don't know," Elizabeth replies. "He didn't say. We can wait and see before going ahead with other plans to pick up more cash. We might be lucky."

"Let's hope." If there's a way to get off the continent that doesn't involve having to commit a robbery, I'll take it. We have to wait until tomorrow to get our hands on the passports anyway.

"I almost forgot." Elizabeth dumps the contents of her plastic bag onto the circular table between us—a pair of tan pants and a long sleeve checked shirt. "I bought them at a second-hand store along with these." She taps a hand to her jeans. "I thought they looked about your size."

"Thanks." After forty-eight hours in the same clothes, I must be on the verge of growing mold. Wearing anything else would be an improvement. "Can you watch over Freya while I shower and put these on?"

"Of course." Elizabeth brightens like my request is a sign that I've forgiven and trust her. I'm not sure either of those things is wholly true but I'm genuinely relieved she came back for us.

Later, after I've thoroughly cleaned up everything but my plastered wrist, Elizabeth and I discuss our airport and flight plans while Freya sleeps. Elizabeth nervously agrees that going our separate ways at the airport tomorrow will increase our chances of eluding the U.N.A. She casts a philosophical look at Freya as she declares, "I think she trusts you even if she hasn't quite accepted what's happened yet. Aside from the sizeable gap in her memory, she seems cognitively healthy. I think you two are going to be fine."

"Hopefully we'll *all* be fine. Once we get away from here." Elizabeth and I are sitting on either side of the table again, me in my second-hand tan pants and checked shirt, periodically shifting my gaze to Freya's hair on the pillow—the only part of her I can really see.

"It could be they're not even coming after us." Hope crowds onto Elizabeth's face.

"I thought that once before and this is how it turned out. If they just let us go this time it probably means bad news." That shooting Isaac didn't end the virus threat.

"Don't think about that. It's beyond us."

"Take things one day at a time," I quote. It was probably some other time traveller who coined the cliché—a man or woman who knew firsthand the only way to get through life without being pulled under by its weight is to live moment by moment, freeing your mind from the dangers of the future.

Elizabeth nods like this is sage advice. Our fears about each of us deserting the other have been proven false and that's brought us closer. I lean across the table and whisper that I never told Freya about Minnow plan's for 1986 or the global disaster of 2071. "I don't want her to have to worry about that kind of destruction," I explain. "She's better off not knowing."

"Maybe so, but..." Elizabeth hesitates. "You felt otherwise about your own memories."

"This is different." I only want to protect her.

And the U.N.A. wants to protect the future. Maybe our aims aren't poles apart, then, but there's an important distinction. What I'm doing won't steal Freya's identity or past from her. Only hide dark shadows that may never touch our lives anyway.

"You might feel differently in the future," Elizabeth points out. "It could be a great burden for you, knowing these things and not having anyone to speak to about them."

"That's a burden you'll have to face too."

"I won't have any option. My choice that my life would be a secret one was made years ago." Loneliness falls around Elizabeth's shoulders like a cloak. "Anyway, everything doesn't have to be decided tonight." She stands, drawing her solitude snugly to her so it fits like a shield.

With that, we say goodnight. Elizabeth takes the far bed and I lie down next to Freya, on top of the covers and facing the other direction so I won't make her uncomfortable. I sleep fitfully, my mind unable to relax. If I dream, I'm not aware of it. But each time I wake, the shadows on the wall feel sinister and every sound is a potential menace.

It would be worse if not for Freya. Her nearby presence soothes me enough to drift off again. The last time I wake up she's bent over me, her hair tousled and the hem of her polo neck bunched up around her waist where the bed sheets have gathered too.

"What is it?" I mumble.

"Nothing." Freya backs away, her knees shooting up to form a tent under the covers. "Sorry. I didn't mean to wake you up."

"You didn't." I sit up next to her, yawning into the dark. "I don't think I'll sleep well until this is over."

"You think something bad is going to happen?"

I'm mindful that I told her there was nothing to worry about. "I just don't think we can let down our guard, that's all." I'll worry less once we're on a plane out of here.

"Because they might find us?" Freya asks, like she's repeating some often-heard wisdom she has yet to confirm for herself.

"Only if we're not careful and wait too long to leave, which isn't going to happen."

We're both whispering so as not to disturb Elizabeth, and Freya nods, her head slanting down to rest on her knees as she stares at me. "The way you say all these things is so persuasive, but how am I supposed to believe I'll never see my brother again? That everything I knew is just *gone*." She gasps as her tongue stretches over the word. "In one second. I was there and now I'm here, with you. And you and everything else here seems so solid and real, but…time travel…"

Her sentence dangles, twisting enigmatically in the hazy patch of moonlight seeping through the parted curtains. I remember my awe when Freya and I first learned the earth wasn't the transparent, finite place we'd believed it to be. In the last twenty-four hours that awe has transformed into dread—the fear that there will be no end of threats from the future rocketing along the chute towards us.

One day at a time. Don't think beyond tomorrow.

"I know how it sounds," I say.

Freya buries her head in her knees, momentarily hiding her face from me. When she turns to reveal herself again she says, "These people you say are after us, would you recognize them if you saw them again?"

"Most of the ones I've encountered are dead now." I never explained exactly how I escaped. "I had no choice. It was either us or them."

I watch shock at the revelation that I've killed people streak across Freya's face. "So these U.N.A. security personnel could be anyone, anywhere?"

"Unfortunately, yes." My system shifts into high alert mode. "Why? Did you see someone suspicious today?"

"No. Not how you mean." Freya raises her head, unease glimmering in her pupils. "I've just been having some strange visions. Everything I've seen today is exceptionally weird and maybe this other thing is only another part of whatever's going on with me but..." She wraps both arms around her knees, hugging them tight.

"Tell me, Freya." The concussion must've messed with her second sight—otherwise the U.N.A. wouldn't have been able to kidnap her—but it sounds like it's back. On one level that's good news. Despite what they did to her, she's recovered.

She releases her knees at the sound of my voice, straightening her spine. "The first time I saw him was when I woke up in the trans with you. In my mind there was an image of a boy crawling through a field. There was a lot of blood on his clothes and his face. He was hurt. From what I could see of him, he didn't look familiar. Normally my visions are of people who are close to me and things that are just about to happen to them or me, but this didn't work that way. There was just this bad, bad feeling attached to the vision."

Goose bumps erupt on my arms. "What kind of bad feeling?" Before she can answer I add, "You said the *first time* you saw him. There have been more?"

Freya's head jerks in agreement. "A few. Enough for me to tell he was a man and not a boy. A smallish man. I think there was someone helping him later. He seemed barely conscious but he was in some kind of trans, like some of the ones in the streets here. And then just now, before you woke up, I saw him again. Lying down with wires attached to him. The bad feeling was so strong it was almost as if *I* was the one feeling it. But I wasn't." Freya's hands run up and down her arms, like she's trying to warm herself. "It was coming from him."

There's no mistaking who she's talking about. Minnow isn't dead. He survived the gunshot.

"I don't know what it means—why I keep seeing him when he has nothing to do with me," Freya continues. "Unless I have brain damage and these visions, along with everything else I'm seeing, are because of it."

"You're not seeing me or any of the things you saw out there in Seattle today because of brain damage." I keep my voice level and calm, the opposite of how I feel. "They're real. I know it might take a while for that to sink in. The man you're seeing is real too. He's one of the people I thought I'd killed early this morning." Most of the U.N.A. personnel Isaac and I shot definitely weren't going to get up again. Their Bio-nets must have been modified before they were sent through the chute—the wipe sequence programmed in while advanced healing was switched off. Otherwise they could've attracted unwanted attention, seeming to be superheroes compared with the rest of the 1980s population. But Minnow's Bio-net wouldn't have been modified in the least. I didn't consider that when I shot at him. My single bullet should've been an onslaught.

Freya's teeth graze her bottom lip. "If what I'm seeing is

true, he doesn't look as if he's in any condition to come after anyone. And this feeling coming from him, I can't explain it but I don't think it's about us. It's like an all-consuming dedication. A darkness inside him. A longing for something I can't put into words. I don't know how, but I think something terrible is going to happen."

"The man—could you tell if he was under guard?" I've never known Freya's visions to be outright wrong, but they're not always entirely accurate either. The future is subject to change and in this case she hasn't actually seen destruction. Maybe it's only the strength of Isaac's intentions that she's picking up on.

"Why would he be under guard if he's working for the U.N.A.?" she asks, like she's trying to catch me out, looking for holes in my story.

"But is he being watched?" My heart thwacks at my ribcage. "Is he in cuffs or strapped down?"

"I don't know. I've only seen snatches of things. But nothing that gives me the impression he's being guarded. I think whoever he was with only wanted to get him to safety."

"Are you sure?"

"No," she says sharply. "I'm not sure of *one* thing. He just keeps popping back into my mind like a poison." Her fingers chafe at her forehead. "I wish it would stop."

And I wish her visions of Minnow had never happened in the first place. Because now that I know Isaac's alive, and there's a possibility the U.N.A. don't have him in custody, I have to go back. Cross the border into Canada and hunt him down.

Billions of lives are at stake. He can't be allowed to release the virus.

The future isn't written in stone. President Reagan's assassination proves that. Possible outcomes can be changed.

With the help of Freya's second sight there's a chance I might be able to find Isaac and succeed where the U.N.A. have so far failed. It will mean putting Freya on a plane with Elizabeth, so she won't be taken again. And it will mean I might never find her, because they won't be able to risk leaving a trail. But if I don't try to stop the deaths of so many, I won't be able to live with myself. So there's no real choice, no easy way out.

I didn't want Freya to be burdened with some of the things I know and now those secrets will be spilled in less than a day. A wisp of regret escapes my lungs. Maybe it's better if she doesn't believe me after all.

But then Freya's eyes vault to mine, her gift perhaps already warning her that what I'm about to say will change everything.

NINETEEN: 1986

Freya's face lengthens as she listens to the potential doom the chute has brought to 1986. Then she questions me about Isaac and the people who escaped 2071 only to see their nightmare begin to unfold anew. I hear the doubt and fear in Freya's voice and with every reply I give I'm afraid I'm offering her another reason to run away again. Worse, she can't see anything more about Isaac, even when she tries.

"I don't know how to bring on the visions," she says when she opens her eyes. "They usually spring out of nowhere."

Elizabeth's bed creaks. Freya's body is partially blocking my view but we both turn at the sound of the second creak. Elizabeth's voice rasps into the blackness of the room, "What is it?"

I explain quickly: what Freya's seen, what I believe it means, and what I intend to do about it.

"You can't go back." Elizabeth's tone is unbending. "They'll catch you if you show up anywhere near Vancouver again. They'll have reinforcements assembled by now and they'll be all over the area looking for Monroe. You're not even sure he's *not* in their custody. You heard Freya, she doesn't know anything else. There's not enough information for you to go on. No point in crossing back over the border. It'd be like looking for a needle in a haystack. They'd have more chance of finding you than you would of finding Monroe."

Everything Elizabeth said is the truth, but I can't let go of the catastrophe facing humanity. "Keep trying," I urge Freya.

Sleep has been chased away by the danger on the horizon and Elizabeth continues to argue with me about the uselessness of returning to Canada while Freya slips into the bathroom to shower. Someone from the neighbouring room pounds on the wall behind our beds, sick of the early morning bickering. We revert to antagonistic silence. I flip the TV on but switch the sound down. A scratchy black–and-white print of some John Wayne movie is playing. I stare at the moving images on the screen, not really seeing them.

Amorous sounds from next door begin to shake our shared wall. The people we woke up have decided to make the most of their wakefulness and I resist the urge to rap back in complaint. Everyone on the planet may not have long—why should anyone be quiet?

The wall's still rattling like an earthquake has hit Seattle when Freya rushes out of the bathroom in the black jeans and frilly blue halter top I stole for her yesterday, her hair dripping down her back. "I saw him again," she says. "He was on his feet. Weak but walking. Towards another trans, I think."

"Was anyone with him?" I choke out.

"I didn't see anyone. It felt as though he was alone." Freya grabs her elbows, cupping one in each hand. "The bad feeling's stronger now. Or maybe it's only because of the things you told me. It feels like devastation lying in wait. *Terrible*." She shakes her head, flecks of water spritzing the air. One of them lands on my bottom lip.

"I need details. Street names. Descriptions." Her memories of Vancouver have been erased. She won't know places by sight. That will make this more complicated. "Do you know where he's going?"

Freya's gaze leaves me. I watch her attempt to reach into the future, stillness surrounding her as the present begins to drift into the distance. For a minute we feel worlds apart.

Then her eyes return to mine. "I'm sorry. It comes and goes. I can't control it. Maybe as we get closer…"

"*We're* not getting any closer. You and Elizabeth are getting on a plane."

"You can't do this on your own." Freya's fingers anxiously thrum her elbows. "Look, I still don't know what to think about all the things you've told me—I don't remember any of it—but when I see this man you say is Isaac I know in my bones he's planning something that will touch us. Touch everyone. If there's a chance the horrible feeling I'm having is linked to a deadly virus the warren engineered, how can I get on a plane with someone I never laid eyes on before yesterday and run away with her instead of helping you stop it?"

"It's not running away," I protest. "You won't be safe if you come with me. You don't know anything about how this place works—you'd be a sitting duck." If it weren't for the kindness of the people of Seattle, she'd probably have been picked up by the cops minutes after wandering away from the motel.

"You'll never find him without me." The determination in Freya's cheeks sends a shiver up my back. "Like Elizabeth said, it would be the same as searching for a needle in a haystack."

"No." My hands have begun to tremor. I won't let her do this. "You have to get away from here. As far as you can so they won't be able to find you again."

"You're the only one here I recognize, Garren." Freya's tone pleads for understanding. "If this is the truth then it's just us, isn't it? Everybody else is gone. Years away from existing. Except my mother, and from what you've said I can't see her ever again. I can't afford to be wrong and stay out of this. Either this *isn't* real and it doesn't matter what happens to me anyway, or it's just you and me here. Us and the people on the planet with us right now. Did you see the little boy in the lobby with his mother earlier?" Freya doesn't wait for my answer; she knows I saw them: a moon-faced toddler in a jumpsuit who waved at us from his mother's arms when Freya and I arrived back at the motel late this afternoon. "If this virus does what you say it's designed to and kills sixty percent of the world's population, who would die—the mother or her son? Both of them maybe? Because I didn't help you stop the virus and ran away to hide. Do you really think I could do that?"

"We might not come out of this, Freya." Desperation hollows my words. "What if I tell you it's all in your head?"

"It doesn't matter what you tell me, I'm coming with you anyway." Freya's eyes beam my distress back to me. Her left hand moves tentatively towards my right, her fingers fitting between mine just the way they always have. "Like I said, if it isn't real there's no cost to me."

But it is real and it could cost us everything. I wish I could tell Freya I'll run away with her instead, let the world stand or fall on its own. But that's not the people we are.

Behind us Elizabeth noisily clears her throat. "If you really think there's a chance we can stop Monroe, I'm travelling back with you both." Minutes ago she thought trying to find Isaac was an act of futility and my eyebrows tug together in confusion. "I know I said everything didn't have to be decided tonight but now it looks like it does. And I've made up my mind."

Freya nods her acceptance and I think of what Elizabeth said while Freya was sleeping, about making a choice that her life would be a secret one. Does she feel responsible for us after what she did to Freya's memory or is it the rest of humanity she can't turn her back on?

"We should go now," I say, my puzzlement turning to respect. Whatever Elizabeth's reasons for doing this are, they hinge on self-sacrifice. "We don't know how long we have." With Isaac on the move it's possible we'll already be too late.

It's almost five o'clock in the morning and within eight minutes we're filing out of the motel room, each of us quiet and on edge. Elizabeth checks us out of the motel and I climb behind the wheel of the Volkswagen, Freya next to me and Elizabeth in the back seat. Seattle blurs into the distance, the morning sky grey and lifeless.

Twenty minutes from the border Freya has another vision. "He's surrounded by trees," she says. "And there's dirt at his feet. No people nearby, only nature. He's lying down to rest. He's not as badly hurt as before but he's not finished healing."

The damn Bio-net is doing exactly what it was programmed to. Saving human life. Judging by Freya's visions some uninvolved civilian must have found Minnow, probably after he'd been crawling wounded for hours, and called him an ambulance. Then he was likely taken to hospital but escaped as soon as he could, aware the U.N.A. would be hunting him.

"And the bad feeling?" I ask. My eyes are dry from lack of sleep and my wrist aches. I probably shouldn't be driving.

Freya narrows her eyes in concentration. "It's as strong as before. He'll do whatever he can to carry out his plans. But right now it seems as though he's waiting. For someone or something. I'm not sure which."

"We should check hospitals in and around Surrey," Elizabeth advises. "If Monroe was admitted to one, even for a short time, someone must have seen him."

I cradle my damaged wrist in my lap, my good hand on the wheel. "But we know he's not there now. And the U.N.A. will be checking medical facilities too. Maybe we're better off searching parks."

We agree to search heavily treed areas, beginning with any Surrey parkland. I pull over so Elizabeth can take possession of the driver's seat before we reach customs. She's composed a new border crossing story in keeping with the one we used yesterday. The three of us were en route to Sacramento for Amy's mother's wedding. When we stopped to spend last night in Oregon, Mrs. Lewandowski placed an apologetic phone call to our hotel. She'd had second thoughts and was cancelling the wedding to jet off somewhere secret by herself and ruminate on her life.

The female Canadian border guard grimaces sympathetically as Elizabeth relays the tale with just the right amount of detail, emitting a faint, unspoken embarrassment at having such a flighty sister. "And so," the guard says lightly, "anything to declare?"

"Nothing." Elizabeth's lips pucker into an uptight smile. "There wasn't time."

The guard stares pointedly as me in the backseat. "Not bringing back any alcohol or cigarettes?"

Is my thirst for cigarettes leaking through my pores? "No," I reply truthfully. "I'm trying to quit smoking."

The final thing the guard says to us before waving the car through is, "Welcome home."

I wish I'd never had to see it again, but the British Columbia landscape genuinely feels like a second home, as perfect as any spot on U.N.A. soil could be. In 2071, all this beauty could be destroyed. Blasted to bits. Irradiated. Ash from the burning destruction blocking out the sun and sending the planet into nuclear winter. If I was as certain this was the earth's future as Isaac seems to be, maybe I wouldn't want to stop him.

But from a place eighty-five years earlier, I have to believe there's time for humanity to change without being brought to its knees. The world isn't destined to be annihilated. There's no such thing as destiny. There are only the choices we make now.

Outside, it's begun to drizzle, the sky stubbornly drab. Once we reach Surrey we veer off the 99 and stop at the first convenience store we see. While Freya and I head inside to pick out a map, Elizabeth takes the car into the McDonald's parking lot across the street so she can use their bathroom.

I glance at the maps and tell Freya to look for umbrellas—as much to hide us as to keep us from getting wet. My throat's as dry as my eyes and I've shuffled to the back of the store to peer into the fridge when someone clasps my arm, fingers tightening into a steely grip. I jump in my skin, my neck snapping to the right. Freya's standing a half-step behind me, her blue eyes startled and enormous.

"Someone's coming." Freya's hand falls away from me.

"They recognized the trans and are turning around. Coming back to get us."

Freya and I race to the front of the store to stare out the window, our eyes searching the road. A mud-flecked station wagon with wood panelling peals into the McDonald's parking lot as Elizabeth steps out of the restaurant and nears the Volkswagen. There's no time to warn her. I see her body brace, grasping imminent danger. A thirty-something-year-old woman in an oversized shirt and teased hair jumps out of the station wagon and grapples with Elizabeth, trying to force her into the station wagon.

Elizabeth drops to the ground, resisting with every muscle in her body and screaming blue murder. The sound torpedoes towards us like a bull's eye, hitting me in the centre of the chest. *She's trying to warn us.* She doesn't want us to be taken too. I pull Freya slowly backwards, further into the store so we won't be spotted from across the street. A gunshot splits the air. The sound urges us nearer to the window again, to the sight of Elizabeth's inert body on the pavement. The woman fires a second shot directly into Elizabeth's temple, the barrel of the gun kissing her skin. If Elizabeth wasn't dead after the first shot, there's no hope for her now.

The woman spins to survey the parking lot and then reels towards the station wagon, her eyes scouring the immediate area. *Looking for us.* She leaps inside the open passenger door and the station wagon spurts back into the street.

Freya's fingers tighten around my arm again, yanking me in the direction of a door I hadn't noticed. The man behind the cash registers roars at us as we stream through it and into a crowded stock room. "They're still coming," Freya cries. "They think we must be close."

They're right. But between the well-stocked wire shelving units that line the walls, we discover a rear door. Freya and I burst through it and into the open air. A three-foot-tall cement wall edged with trees separates the back alley from a suburban neighbourhood. I clear the fence easily. Freya drops her hands onto the fence to push herself over. I reach for her with my good hand but she doesn't need my help. She drops into the line of trees with me, the two of us sprinting through them and into a road flush with semi-detached houses. An upended tricycle lies at the top of one of the nearest driveways and at the far end of the street a man with a long black ponytail is walking a pair of identical white dogs, talking to them like they're human.

The dogs bark excitedly as we fly past them. "Where are they?" I ask Freya, neither of us slowing.

"The store. But they're not following us through the stockroom door. I don't think the clerk told them which way we went."

We keep running, our clothes soggier and heavier by the minute. Even when Freya thinks the U.N.A. personnel have deserted the convenience store and are searching for us by car again, we don't stop. We sprint from street to street, and through cut-offs channelling us into adjoining neighbourhoods, avoiding busier roads.

The U.N.A.'s first choice couldn't have been to shoot Elizabeth. They would have wanted to question her—look into her head and find out where we are and exactly what our plans are. Us and Isaac. There's no question that they assume we're working together now. But Elizabeth caused too much of a commotion outside the McDonald's. They had to cut their losses.

They'll do the same to us if they get the chance. They'd never take our word that we're trying to stop Isaac just like they are. If they find us and we resist being taken, they won't hesitate to slash us out of the equation.

Only when Freya finally says, "I think they're getting farther away," do we slow to a walk. The thin materials of my shirt and Freya's halter top have been drenched through to our skin. The rain isn't torrential but we've been wandering around in it for at least forty minutes. Our other clothes are back in the car and we can't go back for them or it. Police will be on the scene.

Even the maps I was holding when Elizabeth was shot are slightly damp in my back pocket. Those maps and several hundred dollars are all we have left now. No car, no Elizabeth, no identification. There's nothing left for us to start over with. We're worse off than we've ever been, but we can't stop now. We have to find Isaac and end this.

"I don't understand these people," Freya says sadly, her chin tucked towards her chest. "Elizabeth was on their side. She spent years trying to achieve what they wanted and they killed her like it meant nothing."

Because she helped us. That made her a traitor and threw everything else about her into question.

I grunt in disgust. "They only think about the larger picture." Just like Minnow. The warren and the U.N.A. government both have their own ideas about what's best for the world, and no faith or trust in anyone who doesn't share their ideology. A cold war of a different kind.

With Freya's hair matted to her skull and droplets of rain slipping down her cheeks and the slope of her nose, she looks desolate. I don't need to hear her admit it out loud; I know she believes me now. Seeing Elizabeth shot and having to run for our lives has transformed the things I've told her from a possibility to reality.

"I think Isaac's getting wet too," she says. "I can't see him the way I did before. It's hazy. Water dripping onto his face like he's barely aware of it, coming in and out of sleep."

Completely vulnerable: asleep, alone, and out in the open. We couldn't have a more perfect opportunity. "We need to find him before he gets moving again," I say.

Freya and I venture cautiously out to one of the main roads to find a cab, huddling together under a bus shelter until a yellow taxi rolls gingerly towards us, veering around a giant puddle that couldn't have made us any wetter—only muddier. Inside, we question the driver about nearby forests. The closer to the Surrey hospital the better, since that's probably where Isaac was taken.

"Somewhere natural looking," Freya specifies. "Somewhere you can't see the roads."

The driver has one of those hula dancers stuck to his dashboard and he fixates on her hips, fondling his clean-shaven chin as he ponders our criteria. "Sounds like you're looking for Green Timbers. It has lots of nature trails, wetlands, fishing, that kind of thing."

"Take us there," I tell him, fumbling in my pocket for the maps. Unfolding the moist Surrey map, I zero in on the square green space between One Hundredth and Ninety-Second Avenue. The Fraser Highway cuts right through Green Timbers but judging by the park's size, the majority of it could be shielded from the sight of roadways if it's densely wooded enough.

"Are you sure you two aren't wet enough already?" the driver jokes.

Neither Freya nor I laugh; our minds are everywhere but here. I stuff the map into my pocket and lean back in my seat, automatically draping my arm around Freya's shoulders. It doesn't feel anything like summer today and her top is intended for tanning temperatures—she must be freezing. I'm the one who flinches when I remember my mistake. Although I've explained about our relationship, the only thing Freya can remember from our shared past before yesterday is a single conversation on the Thomas Jefferson grounds.

Self-consciously, I begin to reclaim my arm. I open my mouth to tell her I'm sorry, and Freya's voice is equally quiet as she says, "It's okay." She leans into me a little, news radio covering our silence. Walgreen drugstores in the U.S. have ordered Anacin 3 pulled from its shelves after a man died from taking a capsule that may have been contaminated with cyanide. Two cosmonauts spent four hours outside their orbiting station conducting construction experiments yesterday. Three thousand tourists are stranded in Darjeeling, India, by protesters campaigning for autonomy in eastern India.

So it goes. Good news running into bad. The world never pausing to catch its breath.

Freya and I don't separate ourselves until we reach the park's main entrance off One Hundredth Avenue. Counting out taxi fare, I hear the radio newscaster announce that newly sworn-in President Nelson is establishing a national emergency task force on global warming. "The president cited a 1979 landmark report by the U.S. National Academy of Sciences that linked the greenhouse effect to global warming," he continues. "That report warned 'a wait-and-see policy may mean waiting until it is too late.' The new emergency task force will be headed by Senator Al Gore, who held the first congressional hearings on climate change in 1976. According to President Nelson, the National Climate Program Act of 1978 had 'utterly failed in its aims and America's environmental concerns must be tackled with vigor and determination.'" The radio station plays a clip of Mitchell Nelson declaring, "We are all stewards of this planet and must demonstrate that Americans take that duty seriously. Our home is this earth. There is no duty more fundamental than protecting our home."

Before I was sent through the chute my knowledge of 1980s politics was patchy, but I don't remember any 1986 emergency task force on global warming. Later, Al Gore penned a book on conservation, became vice president of the United States, and raised awareness of climate change through a documentary about his global warming campaign. By then regular citizens had lost control of the country and corporations ruled from the shadows, most of them not thinking twice about the future of the planet.

Maybe this time awareness among common people will reach critical mass before it's too late. With U.N.A. power and money behind the environmental cause, maybe oil companies and other wealthy multinationals will be forced to consider something other than their own greed. It's possible. Real change within reach. Despite the virus threat, I feel light-headed as I step out of the taxi, Freya trailing behind me.

My chest swells with hope. I reach back for Freya's hand, the two of us running headlong into the rain—grassland meadows, hardy green forest, and a clear blue lake spread out ahead of us like a tapestry. Nature in all its glory.

TWENTY: 1986

We veer off the trails, searching for Isaac in the hidden places most walkers and bikers wouldn't spot easily from the paths. Weaving between trees, wet mulch squishing underneath our soles and knotted roots threatening to trip our tired feet, Freya and I hardly speak. We don't want to give Isaac any advance warning. He must think we're either miles away or locked up under U.N.A. guard with our memories being shredded. If he had help within easy grasp, he wouldn't be lying passed out in the dirt. What is he waiting for?

Because of the rain, even the trails are mostly deserted. Aside from a few Douglas squirrels, two women in hooded jackets who lecture us about being underdressed for the weather, and a guy with a hefty backpack, we don't see anyone. We're thirsty, hungry, wet, and cold, and wondering if it's time to cross Green Timbers off our list and try another park when Freya points out the crest of a khaki pup tent in the distance. With all the surrounding foliage I would've missed it.

We creep towards it, the weather-beaten tent looking ever eerier as we draw near, like it could've been erected in the park decades ago. A forgotten relic. I whip open the tent's front flap, ducking to look inside. Near the back of the tent, three or more plastic bags are piled neatly on top of each other, the transparent top bag containing a wool sweater, bar of soap, hair brush, and can opener.

"These aren't his," Freya says, disappointed.

There was no tent in her visions, which made any connection

between it and Isaac unlikely, but I'm disappointed too. Isaac is vulnerable in his sleep but unless he wakes up and offers us additional clues, finding him could be virtually impossible. There's no shortage of trees in British Columbia; he could be anywhere.

"Can we sit inside for just a few minutes?" Freya asks. "It's so cold." Her jeans cling to her legs like a scuba wetsuit. Neither of us has complained out loud up till now and I nod readily, scrambling into the tent behind her.

From inside, the rhythmic sound of the raindrops is soothing but the tent is so small, there's barely enough room for the two of us. When we sit down across from each other, hunched over our knees, our shoes touch. We'll need something to drink soon—we can't keep running on empty—but for the moment it feels good just to be sitting someplace dry. If only we could start a fire and really get warm.

The tent smells like forest and spilt whisky. The latter is so familiar from Greasy Ryan's it makes me feel oddly at home. "I keep thinking about the way they murdered Elizabeth," Freya says, a chill in her voice that has nothing to do with the weather. "And how we had to leave her body in the parking lot like she was a stranger. Do you think she has people here who will miss her?"

I tell Freya what Elizabeth said about choosing a secret life. "But maybe she had some U.N.A. friends." I only say it to soften the truth.

"If they were the only people she had it would've made breaking away from them even harder," Freya says. "Maybe if I could remember the wipe I would hate her for trying to make me into a blank slate. But I don't. She wanted to help us in the end. She could've been safely in Europe by now."

Some decisions you only get to make once. But I don't think Elizabeth would've taken hers back. "I can't hate her either," I admit. "But I can't forgive her for what she did to you." I glance down at my wet cast. It's looser than ever. No protection for a broken bone. My wrist whines at me; I know it needs a doctor but finding one will be the last thing on our list.

"Does it hurt?" Freya asks, concern in her eyes.

I smile. "Only when I move."

"Right." Freya smiles too. "So you just sit tight here while I go save the world."

Laughter races up my throat. For a second my body forgets to feel cold. Then a cloud passes over Freya's face. "Maybe it's better that I can't remember Latham changing in the ways you saw happen to Kinnari. But I wish I could remember other things. You do feel familiar, more familiar than you should considering the wipe. Maybe that means there's a deeper part of me they couldn't make forget."

"Maybe." My esophagus tightens. Freya must sense how much I want her to remember. Even without that, and even if we don't make it through this, I'd rather be with her at the end than anyone else. In a way nothing has changed.

There's a thread running between us that stretches and slackens but never breaks. I feel it tug as Freya pulls her feet back behind her and leans in close to me. Her head tilts, our lips lining up just right. As much as I want this, I make myself wait. She has to be the one to do it. I'm not the one without memories; I'm not the one who is new to this.

When it does come, her kiss is as soft as new skin. More like breath against my mouth than genuine pressure. Then Freya opens her lips and lets me in. Our tongues are sweet and slow against each other. The same old parts finding their way afresh. It feels like the very beginning of a long story. A beginning I already know; the rest of it is the mystery. Then Freya pulls away, her retreat as soft as what came before. "In case there isn't another chance," she murmurs, her cheeks rosy with the cold and the same determination in her face I've seen there a thousand other times.

This one, at least, she'll remember. What might be the last kiss.

"We should go," she says. "The woman who sleeps here is coming back. She'll be angry if she sees us."

We scramble out of the tent and back into the wet, a husky figure in a hooded yellow slicker lumbering through the forest towards us. "Stay away from what's not yours," she shouts hoarsely. The woman's still too far away for me to guess her age when Freya and I turn to break into a run. A hurled stone thumps onto the ground behind us. "Go back where you came from and don't come back!" she howls. "This forest is mine."

Freya and I stumble onto the nearest trail, glancing back over our shoulders to check if the woman's following us. She's not. "I guess we shouldn't have gone in," I say. "The tent is probably all she has."

Freya's frown sets into her cheeks. Her feet root to the soil underneath her feet, her toes muddy and her eyes looking beyond the forest at something I can't see. I stop next to her, watching her face. She presses her eyelids together and lifts her face to the sky. Her gift is magic, pure and simple. No less so than the chute that transports people through time.

It's finally stopped raining. Weak sunshine breaks through the clouds overhead. The forest scatters the faint yellow light, only the thinnest wafer of sunlight striking Freya's red hair as I stand waiting.

Freya blinks at me, her eyes darkly alert. "He's awake. On a paved pathway. There's water on one side of him. Much more than the lake we passed here. Mountains across the water and a long bridge behind him."

Vancouver's Stanley Park. "I think I know where he is, then." Everything she said fits. Lion's Gate Bridge behind him. Burrard Inlet, a sheltered coastal fjord of Georgia Strait, at his side. Considering where Isaac was picked up, Surrey made more sense, but we're in the wrong place. It will take well over thirty minutes to reach Stanley Park once we leave here. "We have to hurry."

We retrace our way through Green Timbers, Freya

describing the sense of purpose powering Minnow's steps. Wherever he's going now, it's important. He's finished waiting.

As we tear towards the road Freya flashes in and out of visions, seeing Minnow's steps almost as clearly as her own. People on bicycles wheel past him. People on foot too. Stanley Park's seawall promenade is one of the most picturesque walks in Vancouver. The second the rain stops people flock to it like ants to cracks in the pavement. With the Lions Gate Bridge at his back Isaac must be on his way out of the park. According to Freya he's stronger than before he slept but not yet his usual self.

The muck underfoot slows us down. It takes longer than it should for me and Freya to reach the street and longer than it should for a taxi to stop for us. The driver makes it up to us in speed when we tell him we're in a hurry. The cab hustles north over the Fraser River, races west along the Trans-Canada Highway, and then swings hurriedly through downtown Vancouver, Minnow keeping pace with us behind Freya's eyes.

It's possible we're not the only ones watching him. The U.N.A. might be trailing him too—waiting for him to lead them to his destination—and as the car enters the park and winds along the seawall, my tension level skyrockets. "Totem poles," Freya cries. "Like the one we saw in Seattle, but more of them. He can see them in the distance."

"They're in the park. We're almost there." I stare at the back of the driver's head and tell him to take us to the totem poles at Brockton Point. He pulls abruptly over to the curb at the crosswalk ahead. Freya jumps out of the car and sprints across the street, moving deeper into the park. I crumple a collection of bills into the driver's hand and stagger after her, opening my mouth to yell at her to wait and then clamping it shut again without spilling a word. *I can't give us away.*

Twenty-five to thirty feet in front of me, Freya's been stopped by a group of people gathered on the stony path. One of them has thrown his arms around her and I realize, with a start, that it's Scott. Dennis is standing next to him along with three other people I don't recognize—two women and one man. Freya's smack in the middle of the chattering group, overwhelmed and struggling to extricate herself. She wouldn't remember Dennis or Scott but they might be able to keep her safe anyway. I stream past them, Dennis shouting something at my back.

The sun's brighter than when we left Green Timbers and I squint at the sight of the totem poles as they come into view. Freya and I've come to visit them at the park several times. They look like visions from a dream. Vivid. Other-worldly. Mesmerizing.

A ditch separates the totem poles from the viewing area, lowering the temptation people may feel to touch or deface them. The magnetic pull towards them is undeniable. Who doesn't want to see the face of another world?

But today I barely look at the totem poles. My eyes flick to the tourists and Vancouverites surveying the native visions. Behind me, in the distance, lie snow-capped mountains across the water. Ahead of me, beyond the totem poles and the park, sprawls the city itself. Glass towers reflected in the clarity of Vancouver Harbour. This place is stunning any way you face.

But I don't notice that today either. I know the views from memory but it's Isaac that fills my eyes. His clothes are torn and blood-splattered but he's steady on his feet, holding his spine straight. Even blood-stained and in rags, he has the bold bearing of a leader.

A figure approaches him from the left. Isaac sees her and turns. My jaw drops in disbelief. Seneval. *Here.* He let me believe she was dead, pretended he thought I could've been her murderer. Instead she's standing in Stanley Park in 1986 with a knapsack resting on her back. *Still in allegiance with him.*

Seneval shrugs the knapsack off her shoulders to hand it to Minnow. I'm a second behind, paused by shock. Then I lurch to life, pebbles scattering under my feet as I run.

Neither of them has seen me yet and for a moment I have the upper hand. Cutting between Seneval and Isaac, I grab for the knapsack. The bag's not heavy but not empty either. Shoving Minnow to the ground, I wrestle it out of his grip. Hard earth wallops his head, making him groan. "Is this it?" I shout, spinning to face Seneval as I jog backwards, putting distance between the three of us. "How could you do this?"

The truth is so murky it's nearly impossible to stare in the eye. I thought I knew her. No matter how much Seneval admired Monroe, I was sure she'd have stood against his plan.

"Stop!" she commands. "Put it down." In the same moment that I see the gun in her hand, my mind ferrets out the truth. Her face and the timbre of her voice are *almost* Seneval's, but not quite. This girl's forehead is higher, her cheeks rounder. She's like an echo of Seneval instead of the real thing.

Seneval wouldn't point a gun at me or hand sixty percent of the population a death sentence. This isn't the girl who told me not to be a hero because she'd feel bad if something happened to me. This is a stranger, and she'll kill me if I don't comply.

It's too late to replay the scene and do things differently. There wouldn't have been enough time for Freya and I to do this right anyway. Not with what we've been through.

I hear the gun go off.

My left leg jerks out from under me.

I collapse, my right hand still gripping the knapsack and my crippled left wrist smashing on the gravel. Tears spring to my eyes. Pain empties my mind, everything disappearing except the idea that I can't let go of the bag. The woman with the eerie resemblance to Seneval strides closer, standing over me with the gun. "You don't understand what you're trying to get in the way of," she says adamantly. "Let it go and I'll let you live."

"Until the virus kills me," I rasp, pain chipping into my voice. "Things are already changing. You don't have to do this. It will be different this time."

"You can't promise that."

When it comes to the future, no one can make any promises. We all know that.

"*Seneval.*" The impulse to raise her name from the dead lies beyond rational thought. I don't know where I think it will get me.

The woman flinches. "You knew my sister?"

As soon as she says it, I realize I'd already guessed who she was. Who else but Seneval's sister would look and sound so much like her. "She was a friend," I spit out. "She told me about your parents going missing while salvaging and your time in the camps together." Explaining my admiration for her sister would only sound like a ploy. I can't think anyway. I'm barely holding on.

"If she truly was a friend you should understand," the woman says. "This is bigger than us."

The woman shifts her aim to behind me. I don't know what's happening around us. I can't see anything but her and Isaac, him laid out unconscious in my peripheral vision and Seneval's sister towered over by wooden carvings exploding with colour. "Stay back!" she yells at someone I can't see. "I'll shoot whoever I have to."

Her gun swings back to my face. I reach up for it with my good hand, ignoring the pain in my left leg as pulsing black spots begin to crowd out my vision. Somebody screams, a high-pitched noise like a squealing train. There are other noises too, indistinct and hazy. Onlookers reacting in ways my overworked senses don't have a chance to process.

Panic and agonizing hurt are all I can feel now, and neither of them matters. The only thing that counts is that she can't win.

The guns fires in both our hands. A white raven with red and blue wings breaks free from its crowning place atop one of the totem poles and soars into the sky. Even as I see it I know I must be hallucinating. It's my right shoulder the bullet hit this time and it feels like fine china shattering underneath a thin covering of skin. My ears are buzzing as the raven makes circles in the sky, leaving contrails in its wake like a jet plane.

This isn't death. The gunshots I've taken wouldn't achieve that right away, even without a functional Bio-net. But Seneval's sister will fire another bullet any second now. She'll have to, because I still won't let go. And when she does, the white raven will settle back on top of its totem pole and my mind will switch off for good. Or maybe it won't. Not even the future knows whether there's life after death.

Another flash of blue yanks my gaze down to earth again—a flurry of movement behind Seneval's sister. She keels face-down next to me, Freya standing in her former place with the gun in her hand. My eyes burn with wonder. I should've known she'd come in time. She always does.

Chest heaving, Freya stares at me, her eyes glinting in the sunlight and her mouth moving frantically. I don't know what she's saying; I can't hear over the buzzing. But I can still see, and there's only gravel where Isaac's body should be. I watch him launch himself at Freya, and I howl at the air, unable to hear myself do it. Freya spins to face him, training the gun at his head.

Meanwhile, Seneval's sister rolls over, pushing herself upwards. It happens slowly, yet in a heartbeat. Maybe she has another weapon with her and thinks she can help take down Freya...I don't know. The raven's still looping overhead, its wings casting monstrous, dancing shadows on the ground. The park is darker by the second. Like night falling in mid-afternoon.

But we're not there yet. Maybe everyone has his or her day, but ours isn't finished.

I thrust my back off the ground and lunge for the woman's knees, bringing her crashing down to the earth with me. Agony convulses through my body, midnight fast closing in. I can't hear the gunshot—I can't hear a thing except that unending buzz—but there must be one because Isaac drops into the gravel with a hole in his head.

It's the final thing I see before the raven's shadow blocks out the sun.

TWENTY-ONE: 1986

The first time I wake up I think I see the director. The one who questioned me at the house out in Surrey or Delta. She's wearing a long white coat and looking over a chart, so absorbed in it that she either doesn't know I can see her or doesn't care.

I don't know where I am. I'm not awake for long enough to figure it out.

The second time I open my eyes I'm in a hospital bed, a nurse fiddling with my IV and a doctor in scrubs standing over me. It's so quiet, I wonder if my ears haven't started working again. Then I begin hearing electronic whirring noises and the quiet tread of the nurse's shoes across the floor.

The third time I wake up, Freya's sitting in a chair beside my bed and Dennis is standing by the window, flipping through a magazine. Freya hops up when she sees my eyelashes flutter. At a glance I can see she's fine and a sense of peace ripples through me. "He's awake," she says, leaning carefully over me. My body feels like an action figure that's had its limbs pulled off and then jammed back into the wrong slots. I'm broken several times over and my brain attempts to register my condition—limbs propped up on pillows, lacerations, breakages, bandages, tubes—before giving up and realizing the physical damage doesn't matter now.

"What happened?" My vocal chords spit out the words like a rusty nail. "Where are they?"

Freya's eyes dart to Dennis at the window.

"I'll be outside with Scott if you need me," he tells her, his gaze shifting to me as he shuffles towards the door. "I'm sorry I didn't believe you before, Garren." There's so much regret in his face that I almost feel sorry for him. "I don't know what to say. We let you down."

As soon as the door has shut behind him, Freya says, "They're both riddled with guilt. I don't even know them—well, I don't *remember* that I know them—and they've been so nice. They want me to stay at their house until this is over." She might not remember them with her mind but she's drawn to them all over again. *The uncles she never had.* They were there when it counted after all.

I'm too tired to explain any of that or repeat my question; I just wait for Freya to explain what's going on. "Someone called for help," she says. "We could hear the sirens getting closer. But before the police or ambulance arrived the U.N.A. snatched Isaac and the woman with him. Them and the backpack."

But not us. Does that mean what I think it means? And are we safe from the virus?

"Scott said they must have been monitoring police radio," Freya continues.

"Did they talk to you?" I mumble.

"Not the U.N.A. personnel but the police did. They're going to want to speak to you too. Dennis and Scott had to help me with them. They told the police I'd been in the hospital with a concussion recently and was having a lot of trouble remembering regular things. Just before the police reached the totem poles, the three of us agreed you should say Isaac and the woman stole your backpack when we were walking in the park. You chased after them and the woman pulled a gun on you when you tried to take it back."

It sounds suspicious. What was in this backpack that they could want so badly that they'd pull a gun on me in the middle of a tourist-heavy section of Stanley Park? The cops might think I'm dealing drugs. They won't be able to prove it but if they start digging around in our identities things could get messy. We must be on the missing persons list on the other side of the country.

Nothing I can do about that. Nothing I can do about anything, really. I can't even move.

"Dennis and Scott?" I prompt, hoping Freya understands what I'm asking without me having to elaborate.

"I told them I was sorry I couldn't really explain things. They already seemed to understand that from whatever you said to them when I was taken. Some of their friends were visiting from out of town—the ones with them in the park—and Dennis and Scott kept them away from me so they wouldn't bother me with questions either." Freya looks at me like she can read my mind. "Don't worry. Everything's going to be all right."

"You saved my life again," I whisper, my eyes aching along with the rest of me.

"You saved everyone's lives, Garren." *No, we both did that,* only I'm too exhausted to say anything more. Freya's face dips in close to me, her blue eyes blurring. She presses the gentlest of kisses into my forehead. It's the only thing I can feel that doesn't hurt.

* * *

For a while I'm not sure when days begin and end. Sometime later the doctor itemizes my injuries, explaining I was lucky the bullet to my leg missed the femoral artery. The other bullet hit my clavicle and fragmented, shattering the bone. During surgery they had to leave some pieces of the bullet in the bone because it would've caused more damage to dig them out. My wrist was fractured in three places and had to be realigned in surgery. The bottom line is that I'm going to be in pain for a long time and the recovery process will be slow.

Then the police come, like Freya told me they would. I say the things I'm supposed to say and they stare at me warily, jot down my answers, tell me they'll be back another day, and then go.

I'm not surprised when the director returns. This time she's wearing cords and a plaid shirt, like a normal person, and she sits in the chair beside my bed, tugging it closer to me like a concerned relative. "Don't get up," she says with a sly smile.

I don't have the energy to be afraid of her for myself—too much has happened since I last saw her for that. "Did you get it all?" I ask. "Or is there more of the virus out there?"

"We got it. Thanks to you and Freya." Her brown eyes drill into me. "Both of you should really think about coming to work for us. Freya could be a particularly big help."

I grunt, my anger at the suggestion fermenting in the back of my throat. "You seem like you're doing pretty well on your own. I heard the news about President Nelson and the task force."

The director nods coolly. "It's a start. We've been buying up some crucial multinational corporations too. It's going to take more than the U.S. government to provoke the sea change we need. But you and Freya—we might not have found Monroe without you."

"You owe us. You need to leave Freya alone." My voice is as hot as an Australian bushfire but we both know I can't make good on any threats. "We still haven't told anyone," I add brusquely. "Our friends from the park don't know a thing. They think all this has some organized crime angle."

"Good. You might like to know I had your missing persons bulletins erased. Your Ontario past won't catch up with you. That would've been awkward for all of us. In fact, if you don't want to work for us I'm going to make a suggestion you would be wise to follow." The director sits forwards in her chair, her hands folded in her lap. "Go get lost in the world. Tuck yourself into some far-flung corner of the globe and let us forget about you and concentrate on our jobs."

This is everything I hoped the U.N.A. would say. *We've earned the right to be left alone.* But there's one small problem. "I'd love to.

But it looks like it could be awhile before I can go anywhere." I shift my head to indicate my left wrist and leg, each of them elevated on pillows, safely immobilized so I can't do any further damage to them. Even when the hospital lets me out there will be months of rehab therapy.

"We know that," the director says, "and we're not unsympathetic. But once you can go, you *must*. The two of you." The director's chair scrapes as she rises, pushing it back behind her. "Get well soon, Garren. And thank you. We're truly grateful to you and Freya. In fact, we've put together a little get well fund for you. It should arrive at your friends' house within the next few days."

"*Wait*," I tell her. The director humours me and stands by my bed as I ask, "How do you know it's really over? And even if it is, *this time*, how do you know more of them won't come through the chute and try again?"

I hate that the director reminds me of Bening, even remotely. But if this is the last time I'm going to see her—and I hope it is—I need reassurance.

The director hesitates, her eyes searching my face. Then she says, "Monroe wasn't quite dead when we took him. His mind broke when we tried to read him. The process finished him off. We had more luck mining Joelle." I didn't know Seneval's sister's name until now. *Joelle*. "It was Isaac who was supposed to be in possession of the virus. The rest of the group were meant to protect him, allowing him a chance to get to Sydney. They'd catch up with him there and he'd hand the virus off to several group members who would ready it for transmission in various countries. But our people in Lake Mackay put up a better fight than Monroe and his group counted on. In the heat of the moment he lost sight of his mission and tried to save his people. The virus ended up in Joelle's hands instead. They hastily arranged to communicate via a newspaper and when Monroe didn't show up quickly enough in Sydney, she kept running. Until she saw his ad. That was how she knew to meet him in the park. It wasn't the first day Monroe had run it, but it was the first day they both made it to the park."

"Why didn't she just release the virus herself?" I ask.

"Her chief job was to deliver it. When she left Lake Mackay she wouldn't have known there wouldn't be any survivors except her and Monroe. She thought she'd be making more deliveries. But I'm sure Joelle would have released the virus herself in the end. If you and Freya hadn't found her and Monroe when you did we'd have two sets of the virus to locate." As the director blinks, her gaze momentarily floating to the window, I notice her eyes are bloodshot. Probably from lack of sleep. "As for the chute, there are so many SecRos on guard at Lake Nipigon now that it would make your head spin. They'll be monitoring every journey back. Preventing any unauthorized ones. Nobody but our people will get through."

She smiles at me in a way I almost believe. "Try not to think about it anymore. Live your life."

Before I can ask whether Bening's okay or if Monroe's people left casualties on the Nipigon side of the chute too, the director turns on her heel, abruptly making for the door. I hear it click shut behind her, but it seems like a long time before I drift off to sleep again. I'm on a natural high. Things haven't turned out how Freya and I planned—there'll be no Puente Nuevo in our future and one of us has a defective memory while the other's body is in pieces—but Freya was right. Everything really is going to be okay.

TWENTY-TWO: AUGUST, 1987

have the same dream every couple of weeks. Freya and I are running through a strange city, a place I've never been. The streets are filled with orange smoke, buildings erupting in flames. The heat from the fires makes our faces sweat and when I wake up from the dream I'm soaked for real. But before I hit consciousness there's always more. Freya runs so quickly that she becomes a speck in front of me, and when I lose sight of her entirely I know she's gone for good. I call her name but no sound comes out of my mouth.

In real life I can't run like I used to. I have a slight limp, even more than a year after the shooting. I probably always will. My right arm is weak and I can only really lift it about halfway, but I'm working on that.

In the dreams, though, I can run like a racehorse, but it doesn't seem to matter. I can never catch up to Freya. It happens that same way tonight. She disappears off the face of the earth and I wake up in our bed in Cordoba in a pool of sweat, my T-shirt drenched. Sometimes after I've had the dream I go to the window and stare out at our street until I feel better. We live in the old part of town, full of narrow streets and stunning ancient buildings. It's a feast for the eyes and the sight roots me in time and place.

Argentina doesn't feel like home yet but it's beautiful and warm like the Mediterranean. When our Spanish is strong enough Freya and I are both planning to attend the National University. There's plenty of money for that. We could spend the next fifteen years sitting in cafés if we really wanted to.

But the dream...this time when I wake up from it I don't get out of bed. I lie next to Freya, watching her breathe like I did that morning in the car with Elizabeth behind the wheel. Freya's memories haven't returned. The series of hypnotherapists we tried didn't change that. By now I've gone into so many details about the lives we had before she was taken that I think Freya knows everything about us, even that I was pissed off with her for forgetting about the laundry and riding me about giving up cigarettes.

In the present I hear our mutt, Bruce, pad across the hardwood floor and settle himself down nearer to our bed. Freya snakes her hand across my chest as she snuggles into my arm. She does that in her sleep sometimes so I don't know if she's awake or not until she says, "I had an idea. About your dream."

"What kind of idea?" I ask.

"The next time, stop running after me." Her tangled hair falls across my good shoulder. "Just sit in the street and wait for me to come to you."

"You'll disappear. The same way you always do."

"I won't," Freya insists sleepily. "It's like with my visions. Whatever I see can be changed. The dream can be changed too. You just have to do something different. And even if that doesn't work, I'll still be here when you wake up."

"I know." I brush her hair back and bend over her to kiss the tip of her nose.

She lifts her face to kiss me firmly on the lips. Hers are so warm and ready they instantly make me crave more. "If you go back to sleep right now maybe you can slip back into the dream," she says.

"I'm humouring you," I tell her. "But if it doesn't work I have some other ideas about what we can do."

Freya smiles and then nips me playfully on the chin. "Just try it."

So I do. And before long I'm sprinting through that same strange city I must've seen two dozen times in my dreams. Freya's twenty paces ahead of me already. Fires rage all around us, the blazing temperature wetting our skin. With every step we take, the gap between us grows. I panic and run faster. I open my mouth to shout at her to wait for me, the same way I've done each time I've had this dream.

But this time is different. This time I remember what Freya said about stopping and I come to a halt in the middle of the road. The heat closes in, threatening to suffocate me. My body wants to break into a run again, to chase Freya down the street until she disappears into orange. I fight the urge and drop into the middle of the street. I sit and wait for her, like she told me to.

And just like she told me, she reappears in the street, her image growing larger as she approaches. Still, I refuse to move. Only when she's standing directly in front of me, reaching for ones of my hands, do I get to my feet again. "I thought you were right behind me," she says urgently. "Let's go!"

I laugh in my sleep, ready to wake myself up and tell Freya she was right. Ready for us to do something else until the sun comes up. Ready for the next seventy years or however long our bodies will give us. Ready to live my life.

ABOUT THE AUTHOR

C. K. Kelly Martin began writing her first novel in a flat in Dublin and finished it in a Greater Toronto Area suburb. By then she was thoroughly hooked on fiction about young people. Currently living in Southern Ontario with her husband, C. K. is the critically acclaimed author of *I Know It's Over, One Lonely Degree, The Lighter Side of Life and Death, My Beating Teenage Heart, Come See About Me,* and *Yesterday.* You can visit her website and blog at ckkellymartin.com.

Made in the USA
Charleston, SC
16 April 2014